Praise for
New York Times and USA Today Bestselling Author

Diane Capri

"Full of thrills and tension, but smart and human, too."
Lee Child, #1 World Wide Bestselling Author of Jack Reacher Thrillers

"[A] welcome surprise….[W]orks from the first page to 'The End'."
Larry King

"Swift pacing and ongoing suspense are always present…[L]ikable protagonist who uses her political connections for a good cause…Readers should eagerly anticipate the next [book]."
Top Pick, Romantic Times

"…offers tense legal drama with courtroom overtones, twisty plot, and loads of Florida atmosphere. Recommended."
Library Journal

"[A] fast-paced legal thriller…energetic prose…an appealing heroine…clever and capable supporting cast…[that will] keep readers waiting for the next [book]."
Publishers Weekly

"Expertise shines on every page."
Margaret Maron, Edgar, Anthony, Agatha and Macavity Award Winning MWA Past President

TEN TWO JACK

by DIANE CAPRI

Published by: AugustBooks
http://www.AugustBooks.com

ISBN: 978-1-942633-12-9

Original cover design by: Cory Clubb
Digital formatting by: Author E.M.S.

Ten Two Jack is a work of fiction. Names, characters, places, and incidents either are the product of the author's imagination or are used fictitiously, and any resemblance to actual persons, living or dead, business establishments, events, or locales is entirely coincidental.

Published in the United States of America.

Visit the author website:
http://www.DianeCapri.com

ALSO BY DIANE CAPRI

The Hunt for Jack Reacher Series:
(in publication order with Lee Child source books in parentheses)

Don't Know Jack (The Killing Floor)

Jack in a Box (*novella*)

Jack and Kill (*novella*)

Get Back Jack (Bad Luck & Trouble)

Jack in the Green (*novella*)

Jack and Joe (The Enemy)

Deep Cover Jack (Persuader)

Jack the Reaper (The Hard Way)

Black Jack (Running Blind/The Visitor)

Ten Two Jack (The Midnight Line)

The Jess Kimball Thrillers Series

Fatal Enemy (*novella*)

Fatal Distraction

Fatal Demand

Fatal Error

Fatal Fall

Fatal Edge

Fatal Game

Fatal Bond

Fatal Past (*novella*)

Fatal Dawn

CAST OF PRIMARY CHARACTERS

Kim L. Otto
Carlos M. Gaspar

Charles Cooper
Lamont Finlay
Kirk Noble
Rex Mackenzie
Tiffany Jane Mackenzie
Serena Rose Sanderson
Arthur Scorpio
Louis Thorn
Terrence Bramall
John Lawton

and
Jack Reacher

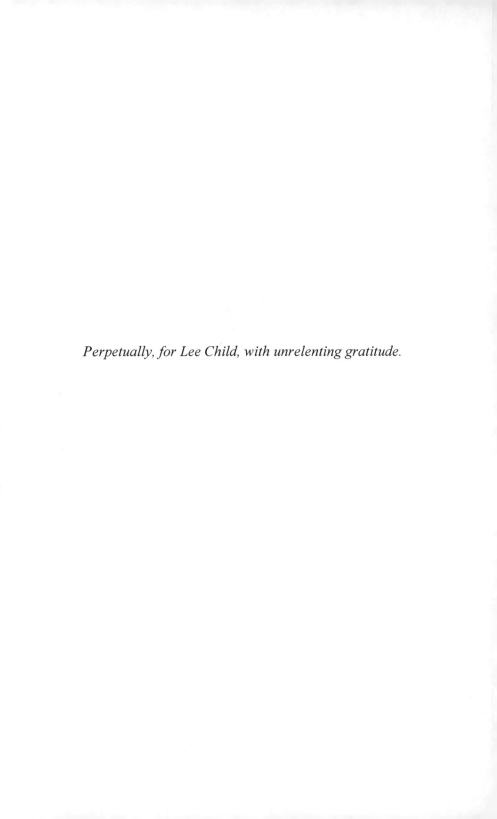

Perpetually, for Lee Child, with unrelenting gratitude.

TEN TWO
JACK

THE MIDNIGHT LINE

by Lee Child

2017

The West Point Superintendent, General Simpson, said, "You could put my mind at rest by letting me take your measure."

Reacher was quiet a beat. "I get uneasy," he said. "I can't stay in one place. I'm sure if you gave the VA enough time, they could come up with a name for it. Maybe I could get a check from the government."

"It's a medical condition?"

"Some would say."

"Does it bother you?"

"Turns out I don't want to stay in one place anyway."

"How frequently do you move around?"

"Constantly."

"Do you think that's a fitting way for a West Pointer to live?"

"I think it's perfectly fitting."

"In what sense?"

"We fought for freedom. This is what freedom looks like."

CHAPTER ONE

Thursday, February 10
4:20 p.m.
Lake Forest, Illinois

WHEN THE MANSION CAME into view, Arthur Scorpio's smoldering rage burst into white-hot flames, licking his damaged body as if he had burned at the stake. He rubbed his scarred scalp behind his right ear, once again feeling the heat from the tumble dryer as it had seared his flesh.

Jack Reacher had a lot to answer for. Scorpio would make him pay.

The driver, Thorn, rolled the rented SUV into the long driveway and stopped close to the front entrance of the grand old Tudor with ancient bricks, leaded windows and a spectacular view of Lake Michigan.

Much too big for one couple with no children, although the owner had lived here alone until he married.

Concealed by the thick snow blanket, none of the landscaping was visible now, and the dark clouds gave the entire place a Gothic feel. Which suited Scorpio's mood perfectly.

He had located the mansion easily enough, the internet being what it was. A month ago, only exterior satellite views, shot in the summer, had been posted.

A lush green lawn and a garden to rival an English palace surrounded the house and extended all the way to the street. The photos showed off the back of the house, which was equally grand.

He'd become obsessed by the house. During his time in the hospital and afterward, at the rehab center, he'd spent hours staring at the images. His product was stored in there. Those who helped Reacher to steal what was rightfully his, too. Jane and her sister Rose.

What kept him going, all those long days after he survived Reacher's effort to kill him, was planning to get his property back, leaving nothing but corpses behind.

When the mansion popped up on a real estate site about a week ago, his pulse quickened, and his eyes popped. Selling the house? Odd. Very odd. Why would they do that?

Scorpio would find Reacher again. He had scores to settle. But first things first. Because the mansion was for sale. When it sold, they'd all be in the wind, taking his product with them, no doubt. He had to act fast, even though he wasn't ready.

The first order of business became the twin sisters. The real estate agency had posted videos of the interior, the way they do these days. He'd studied every room carefully, repeatedly, until he was sure.

Rose had moved into one of the guest suites on the second floor a while back.

He only wanted what was rightfully his. He knew precisely where to look.

"Wait here," he said. "I'll call you if I need you."

"Ten-four, boss," Thorn replied, like some idiot who spent his days watching cop shows on television.

Scorpio plopped a hat on his scarred head. He unfolded his skinny length as he crawled out of the SUV, left hand resting uselessly in his pocket. His recovery from his last encounter with Reacher was not complete. Rehab was exhausting. Rage and determination, in equal parts, fueled him on that score, too.

He stumbled awkwardly up the steps to the massive dark wood door. He lifted and dropped the door knocker against the strike plate, twice. He stepped back and leaned on the head of his cane to wait.

The agent was expecting him.

An attractive, smiling woman with expensively messy blonde hair and perfect skin opened the door. If he'd never seen photos of the sisters, he might have mistaken her for one of the twins. The twin sisters were spectacular. This woman's facial features were pretty enough, but not spectacular.

She stepped aside to let him enter and started her prattling motor running.

"Mr. Scorpio, right? I'm Brooke Malone. Please come inside. It's unbelievably cold out there, isn't it? I hate February. It seems to go on forever. All that lake effect snow. And the wind! It can blow you right over sometimes..." She closed the door behind him and continued babbling like a running brook.

He tuned her out as if he'd flipped a switch in his head.

The foyer was enormous and tastefully appointed. Entire families lived in smaller spaces. A wide staircase wound up the right side of the room to a bridge on the second floor. The online videos showed two wings of the house with guest suites on each side of the center.

Rose's rooms were in the back of the house overlooking the lake and the lawn, according to the house plans on file with the Lake Forest property tax assessor.

Scorpio cleared his throat and pounded the metal tip of his cane on the marble floor.

Babbling Brooke's eyes widened, and her mouth briefly opened into a perfect "O" before she recovered. "Was there something, in particular, you wanted to see, Mr. Scorpio?"

He cleared his throat of the near-constant phlegm that settled there. His voice was raspy, and he struggled to produce enough volume to be heard. "I'd like to see the guest suites overlooking the lake. My daughter fell in love with the online videos of those corner rooms," he croaked.

Mentioning the fictitious daughter seemed to solve the woman's problem. Her frown smoothed instantly as if an airbrush had erased it. She glanced at his cane pointedly. "Would you prefer to use the elevator?" She turned to lead the way.

Bile rose in his throat. Elevators were for decrepit, weak-boned old women and broken men in wheelchairs with warm shawls covering their hunched shoulders. He glared a hole into the back of her perky sweater. Reacher would pay for reducing him to this.

Scorpio followed as she pointed out features of the house that didn't interest him in the slightest. He was exhausted and breathing heavily long before they reached the elevator door under the stairs.

Babbling Brooke's travelogue continued all the way to the second-floor suite, where she opened the double doors with a flourish, like a magician revealing the grand finale.

Scorpio hobbled into the suite, consisting of a generously sized sitting room, larger bedroom, and private bath.

"How many closets?" he asked, mainly for the brief respite in the constant babbling. "I can't abide clutter, and my daughter seems to have an endless supply of stuff."

"I know what you mean. All kids are like that these days, aren't they?" She nodded and smiled and continued talking as she pointed out all the features of the rooms, opening closets, doors, and drawers. She mentioned not a single thing that interested him.

Scorpio scanned for his property in every closet, cabinet, dresser, and bedside table she displayed. Rose lived here. Her coats and shoes and clothes were stored in the closets and dressers. Her toiletries filled the bathroom shelves.

He saw no room safe anywhere in the closets. He would have checked behind the artwork on the walls and knelt and searched under the bed. Two things stopped him. Babbling Brooke would have asked too many questions. And if he got down on all fours to search under the bed, he might need her help to get up again.

"These rooms are tidy. Is no one living in the suite now?" he asked, to confirm what he suspected already.

"I believe the owner's sister is living here. She's been visiting for a few months." She barely paused for breath before she continued babbling on topics that he tuned out.

She was wrong.

Maybe Rose used the Lake Forest house as her permanent address on her tax returns and her driver's license and what not. But Scorpio was a man who lived by his wits, and he would place a bet with every loan shark in Chicago that she had vacated the premises.

The bed didn't look as if anyone had slept in it for a while. He sniffed. No lingering female scents. No clothes in the laundry hamper or razor in the shower or hair strands in the sink. Unless an exceptionally thorough cleaning crew came in this very morning, there was no way Rose slept here last night or any night in the past week, at the very least.

She might have been gone even longer.

Scorpio sat in one of Rose's chairs to think. Could she be with Reacher? Were the two of them blowing through his product right now? And what about the sister? Jane Mackenzie? Where was she?

Suddenly, he noticed something he hadn't heard for the past hour.

Silence.

Brooke had stopped babbling. When he glanced toward her, she had cocked her head and was staring at him strangely.

He said, "I'm sorry. Did you ask me a question?"

She cleared her throat. "I have only one more appointment today. They're arriving any minute now, Mr. Scorpio. I don't mean to rush you. Please stay as long as you like. Wander around the house as you please. But I do need to greet them downstairs when they arrive."

"No problem." Scorpio hid a wry smile with a phlegmy cough behind his hand. "You go ahead. I'll be down in a few minutes."

She nodded, turned, and left the room. When he heard Brooke's spike heels clicking down the hardwood stairs, he satisfied his urge to look under the bed. He slipped off the chair and rolled his skinny body toward the bed, which was a lot easier than walking.

While he rolled along the carpet, he used his microbeam flashlight to look under the sofa, chairs, and tables. He found exactly what he'd expected to see. Nothing.

But under the bed, out of reach, he spied a foil pack the size of a fat playing card. The kind used by pharmaceutical manufacturers to keep twenty prescription fentanyl patches sterile and potent. He felt around behind him for his cane.

His position was awkward, and the cane wasn't meant for the job. Progress was slow. But he inched the foil pack toward him with every swipe of the cane until he could reach it with his fingertips.

Breathless with the exertion, he pulled the pack into his hand and then toward his body, holding it like a kid might hold a squirming frog.

He flopped onto his back to rest a minute while he let reality sink in. He held the empty foil pack above his face to examine it carefully. The blue logo. The silver foil embossed with the brand name. He'd seen them thousands of times before.

The truth hit him like a wrecking ball to the gut. Even though he'd suspected it all along, confirmation was another thing. His heart pounded hard and his face flushed. He drew a few ragged breaths, attempting to regain control of the rage.

He'd been right. He had the proof now. Rose had cost him hundreds of thousands of dollars. Along with Reacher. And Jane. They'd destroyed him and went on their way, assuming he was dead.

Laying on the floor wouldn't change anything. He shoved the foil pack in his pocket.

He struggled to his knees and then pushed his body against the bed, using the cane to force himself upright and regain his footing. Fueled by increasing rage, panting and sweating, he straightened his clothes and dusted the carpet lint from his black wool coat.

He heard Babbling Brooke headed this way. *What the hell?*

CHAPTER TWO

Thursday, February 10
5:20 p.m.
Lake Forest, Illinois

THE LAST THING SCORPIO needed was more interference from her. She'd want to know what he'd been doing up here all this time. He didn't have the energy to lie to her, even if he'd wanted to make an effort. Which he didn't.

Her heels tap, tap, tapped on the hardwood along the corridor, ever closer. She was alone. He knew because she wasn't talking. Had anyone been with her, she'd be running at the mouth, as usual.

He swiped his good hand across his face to remove the thin sheen of perspiration, and then straightened his hair while he leveled his breathing.

She strode into the room as if she owned the place and, without so much as a brief pause, offered him an explanation. As if he cared. "My appointment canceled, Mr. Scorpio. Too cold to bring the baby out, they said. So, it's just us for the rest of the day. Would you like to see the remaining guest suites, or would you rather move on to the rest of the house now?"

He gripped the head of the cane until his knuckles whitened. "Actually, I'd like to talk with the owners. When will they return?"

"The owners? You mean Mr. Rex Mackenzie? He's the sole owner of the house. He's married, of course, but his wife has no ownership interest. I can reach him by phone. Is there anything, in particular, you wanted to know?"

Without stopping for an answer or a single inhaled breath, she continued like a fire hose opened to full capacity. *God! The woman would never stop.*

Scorpio's rage had reached the boiling point. He'd developed a throbbing headache. The lights in the room pierced his skull like a cleaver. He couldn't summon the strength to scream at her to *Shut the hell up!*

She probably wouldn't have, anyway.

There was nothing in this room he wanted or needed now. Why was he wasting his time with Babbling Brooke?

Still leaning against the bed, he released the cane, slid his hand into the deep pocket of his coat, and pulled out a nine-millimeter pistol. He pointed the gun directly at her torso, center mass.

She took half a second to comprehend. When she did, her eyes widened, and her mouth circled, and she gasped. The silence that followed was the first momentary peace she'd offered since he arrived.

He pulled the trigger three times in quick succession, but the first shot was the one that did the job. The last two almost supplied full satisfaction.

She fell to the floor, eyes wide, mouth still open. Gravity pulled the blood from the exit wounds in her back and pooled it around her torso like a small lake.

He fired again, just for the pleasure of hearing the soft thump when the bullet went through and exited her body into the floor.

After that, for more practical reasons, he shot her in the face. The blood had already stopped pumping, but three shots at close range were sufficient to maul her features beyond recognition by her own mother.

He slipped the pistol into his pocket and plopped down into the upholstered chair next to the bed. Scorpio waited three full minutes. Plenty of time to compose himself.

He pulled his phone out and called Thorn.

"Yes, boss?"

"Come inside," Scorpio said. "Second floor, in the back."

"Roger that," he replied before he disconnected.

Scorpio listened for sirens but heard nothing. The mansion was a significant distance from other homes in the area. He thought it conceivable that no one would have reported the gunshots immediately.

Thorn appeared in the doorway. He barely gave the body a second glance.

"Check behind the artwork on the walls for a safe. Check everywhere else, too, just in case Mr. Mackenzie has one of those concealed storage spots," Scorpio said.

Thorn performed the task efficiently and returned empty handed. "Nothing."

"Check the other rooms on this floor," Scorpio said and glanced at the bedside clock.

Thorn performed as instructed. Same as always.

Scorpio heard his footfalls on the hardwood floors, receding and returning.

"No luck," he reported. "All the heat registers are just that. Nothing concealed in the plumbing or anywhere else."

"Any of the rooms look like someone's living up here?" Scorpio asked.

"No. The whole place looks like it's been sterilized or something," Thorn replied.

"Grab her phone from her pocket."

While Thorn bent to the task, Scorpio struggled to his feet. Thorn handed him the phone. "Take a look around downstairs. I'll meet you at the elevator on the first floor."

"Yes, boss," Thorn said on his way out.

Scorpio didn't expect him to find anything remotely useful. The house had been abandoned. It had that vacant feel. He knew that now.

He scrolled through the last dozen calls, looking for Rex Mackenzie's number. He memorized it. Then he checked the voicemail messages. Mackenzie had left two. Scorpio listened to both twice, to be sure he'd recognize the voice when he heard it again.

He scrolled through the contact list until he found Rex Mackenzie's office address and committed it to memory.

Finally, he removed the sim card from her phone. He'd explore the rest of its contents later. He tossed the phone next to her body and left the room.

He shuffled to the elevator and rode down two floors. When he reached the basement, he pushed the button to hold the door open and glanced around the cavernous, empty space. No boxes. Nothing stored here at all. Like it had been cleaned out before they put the house on the market.

"Crap!" He swiped a palm over his face and let the elevator door close again.

He rode up one floor to the massive foyer and stepped out. Thorn was waiting. "Well?"

Thorn shook his head. "Even the garage is empty. No vehicles in there. I found the wall safe in the master suite like you expected. It's empty. But there's a second safe, hidden behind a bookcase."

"Show me." Scorpio's intel had shown a wall safe in the master bedroom, but not big enough to contain full pallets or large, shrink-wrapped boxes.

The cleverly concealed safe was a surprise. Mackenzie must have added it later, knowing that most thieves would stop looking for a safe after they found the first one. Mackenzie was smarter than Scorpio had assumed.

"This way," Thorn replied, leading Scorpio to make his slow, labored progress toward the opposite side of the big foyer.

Like the rest of the mansion, the master suite felt abandoned and not simply unoccupied. At the door to the suite, Scorpio said, "Wait here. Tell me if anyone approaches."

Thorn turned his back to the room and filled the open doorway with his bulk, performing as expected.

When Scorpio reached the safe and opened it, like everything else in the house, the interior held nothing he sought. He flipped through a few papers and moved them aside. He didn't care about wills and trusts and real estate deeds. He closed and locked the safe's door.

He moved on to the second safe behind the bookcase. Inside, way in the back, was a nine-millimeter pistol, and a hinged jewelry box. Nothing else.

He leaned his left shoulder against the wall and reached into the safe with his right hand. He grabbed the pistol and dropped it into his pocket.

Then he pulled the jewelry box out of the depths. Probably contained baubles worth a few thousand, which was pocket change compared to the value of Scorpio's property. Still leaning against the wall, he tried to open it to check the contents, but the hinges were too tight. He slipped the box into his pocket, too. He'd open it later.

He closed and locked the safe and returned the bookcase to its proper position. He glanced around the suite one last time. The whole house had been scrubbed and staged for buyers. He considered looking under the furniture, but he didn't have the energy. He wasn't likely to find anything useful there.

"Let's go," he said when he'd finally made his way across the room to the exit.

Thorn walked ahead. He crossed to the front door, opened it for Scorpio to step through.

"Close the door." No reason to entice the curious to come inside.

Thorn pushed the door lock and closed it solidly. "I'll get the car."

He took the steps two at a time and hurried across the snowy driveway while Scorpio watched from the porch. A few minutes later, Scorpio was seated in the SUV, as they headed away from the house.

"Where to, boss?" Thorn asked. Scorpio gave him Mackenzie's office address from the woman's phone. Thorn entered the address into the navigation system.

CHAPTER THREE

Thursday, February 10
8:10 p.m.
Detroit, Michigan

FBI SPECIAL AGENT KIM Otto was alone at the underground
training range beneath the Detroit Field Office. The last of her
colleagues had completed the virtual simulation exercises and
left a while ago.

She should have been headed home, too. The temperatures
had been below zero for days, and the forecast called for wind
chill to hit negative double digits overnight.

"Welcome to February in Detroit," she said aloud.

She glanced at the digital clock mounted high on the
soundproofed concrete block wall, surprised to notice the time
was well past eight o'clock. She'd been practicing alone for
more than two hours. She'd achieved a perfect score on the
eight-stage FBI Qualification Course of Fire. Twice. She was
tired, but she couldn't allow fatigue to be an excuse to quit.
Active shooters in the field wouldn't walk away from close-

quarters combat because she was exhausted. She had to be ready for anything.

The world had changed. Suspects confronted agents at point-blank range these days. Seventy-five percent of shooting incidents involving FBI agents included suspects who were within a distance of three yards when shots were exchanged. Which meant the suspect was not likely to miss. The agent would be down before she had a chance to draw her weapon.

She squared her shoulders. She wouldn't quit yet.

Whenever she was asked about her ethnicity, she teased that she was tall, blonde, and one hundred percent stubborn on the inside, like her German-American father. Truth was, her body was petite to the point of absurdity for an adult woman, thanks to her Vietnamese-American mother. Not quite five feet tall, not quite one hundred pounds. Without her more essential qualifications, she'd likely have been rejected by the FBI because she didn't meet the heft requirements.

Hand-to-hand combat would too often be a losing game. She kept herself in physical condition at all times, but she was no match for an average-sized man determined to win. Sure, she could deploy self-defense techniques well enough. She simply didn't have the mass to subdue a charging meth-head, or even to lay out a mean drunk.

Fortunately, her work for the FBI didn't often require her to use brute force. Problem-solving and marksmanship were the skills she relied upon. She kept those skill sets in peak condition at all times, too. She had no choice.

She shrugged. Nothing she could do about her DNA, so she honed her marksmanship skills as if lives depended on them, which they too often did.

She loaded another fifteen-round magazine into her service

weapon and returned it to her holster. Although the gun's compact size meant some compromise, the Glock 19 Gen4 was an outstanding choice for a woman with small hands.

She pulled up another Q target reduced silhouette, started the eight-second timer, and cycled through stage two of the FBI standard qualifications again, ignoring her fatigued muscles.

Three yards from the target, she drew her weapon from the holster and fired three rounds using her dominant right hand. She transferred the gun to her weaker left hand and fired three more rounds well before the timer buzzed.

Her arms quivered as if the loaded thirty-ounce gun weighed thirty pounds instead. She reset the timer for three seconds, gritted her teeth, gripped with her left hand, and fired in sets of three rounds each until she emptied the magazine with time to spare.

She dropped the gun to her side, pulled off her ear protection, and checked the target. Agents were required to hit somewhere on the silhouette with eighty percent of the shots to pass the test. Ninety percent was required for an instructor's score. She'd hit fifteen of fifteen dead center, like always.

She nodded. She had won enough marksmanship awards and competitions against her colleagues to know that no one in the Detroit Field Office could shoot more accurately or faster than she did. Few agents anywhere could do better. She had to hope gun-wielding idiots performed a lot worse than trained agents, even as she knew the idiots sometimes got lucky.

She glanced at the clock again. Eight forty-five. Definitely time to pack it up and get home. At the front desk, she signed out.

"Hang on a second," the agent manning the desk said. "I've got a package for you."

"A package?" She cocked her head.

He returned with a padded envelope bearing a plain white label with her name on it. No other identifying marks. Not that she needed any. She knew where it came from and what was inside.

"Thanks," she said. She dropped the envelope into her coat pocket and headed for the exit leading to the bureau's secured parking garage.

The garage was enclosed and protected from the elements, but frigid cold nonetheless. She stuffed gloved hands into her pockets and pulled her hood closer around her face. The crisp air burned her lungs as she inhaled.

"I need to get assigned to Miami or Los Angeles or somewhere that isn't so damn cold," she said under her breath.

She hurried across the concrete floor to her SUV. In her peripheral vision she saw a man advancing from her right.

"Agent Otto?"

Every muscle in her body tensed. He was probably okay. Only authorized personnel should have been in the garage. But complacency was a luxury she could not afford.

She turned toward the voice, hoping he wouldn't prove to be a field test of her close-quarters combat training.

An average sized man bundled in an oversized parka approached. He threw his hood back to reveal a round, boyish face. Longish brown hair, sharp brown eyes. His nose and cheeks were dusted with freckles and reddened by the cold. She wondered how long he'd been waiting.

He held out a badge wallet, right arm extended. She recognized the worn gold shield with the eagle on it. He came close enough for her to examine the plastic card, like a driver's license, printed with the words *Department of Justice, Drug Enforcement Administration*. The photo was definitely the same guy, although he'd been a little younger and a little neater back then.

"I'm Kirk Noble, DEA Special Agent." His name sounded like one of the comic book characters her brothers would have loved when they were kids.

Kirk Noble, Boy Detective. She could imagine him in a boy scout uniform, holding a magnifying glass. The thought made her smile.

"How can I help you, Agent Noble?" She struggled to prevent her teeth from chattering. Her nose probably resembled a ripe tomato.

"I'm looking for information about a witness."

She cocked her head and narrowed her eyes. "Why didn't you call my office? I don't have an eidetic memory for every witness I've interviewed over the years. Access to my files would be a big help, don't you think?"

"Unfortunately not," He shrugged inside the bulky parka that made him look a lot bigger than he probably was. "Nothing on this witness in your computers. I already checked."

"What do you mean?" She frowned.

The FBI was a government agency operating in what critics called the surveillance state. Which meant the FBI was a data-collecting machine. Absolutely everything could be found in FBI computers these days, whether it should be there or not.

If she'd interviewed a witness, the data would be stored in FBI computers somewhere.

Unless someone made sure it wasn't there.

Only a few men on the planet had the power to make that so, and one of those men was her boss.

Which meant the Boss might be listening now. He usually was.

Noble cleared his throat. "For the past few months, you've been working a classified assignment. Off the books. If you help me, I can help you."

How did he know that?

Her assignment, running under the radar, should have been invisible to him and to everyone else. Strictly need-to-know.

Yet, he knew something. Enough to claim he had information to share. The Boss wouldn't have authorized that kind of leak. Where did Noble's intel come from?

The unpleasant sensation running along her spine confirmed her uneasy feeling. Her mother would say a cat had walked on her grave. The weight felt more like a giant tiger.

The Boy Detective said, "I need to find two women. It's important. A matter of life and death, in fact."

Otto relaxed a bit. The subject of her top-secret assignment was one man, not two women. "Why do you believe I can help you?"

"Because the witness I'm looking for is Jack Reacher."

Her mouth dried up.

CHAPTER FOUR

Thursday, February 10
8:30 p.m.
Chicago, Illinois

THORN PULLED UP IN front of T. Rex Cleaners, a small dry cleaner on the north side of the run-down old buildings along the decrepit Chicago street. The shop windows were covered with old posters promising cheap and fast service. The paper was yellowed and curling, suggesting they'd been in place a long time.

On the door, an old-fashioned sign that said, "Closed. Please come again," hung from a string. The flip side probably said, "Open."

The interior of the shop was dark. Scorpio saw no lights of any kind that might have suggested Rex Mackenzie or anyone else was inside.

Overall, Mackenzie's office was even less impressive than Scorpio's backroom headquarters at the laundromat in Rapid City, which was okay. A guy like Scorpio never wants to draw too much attention. He was barely surprised to see that Mackenzie might feel the same.

One big difference between the two was that Scorpio's laundromat had no customers to impress, and no need to impress any who showed up. Laundromats were self-serve anyway, and Scorpio's enterprise wasn't intended to produce a profit.

Mackenzie's operation was different. Or at least it should have been.

Dry cleaners required staff. Someone to take in the dirty items dropped off by customers and deliver the clean ones. Someone to collect the money, clean the laundry, press things, and so on. Dry cleaners kept regular hours, too. Usually.

Mackenzie's place was closed and dark tonight, which might have made sense. The posted business hours were seven in the morning until noon, three days a week. With hours like that, how prosperous could he possibly get? Not wealthy enough to own that Lake Forest mansion, Scorpio figured. The asking price for the house and grounds was over four million dollars.

Which meant Scorpio's suspicions were most likely true. No way Mackenzie made a legitimate fortune out of this decrepit place.

"Drive around the back. See if there's an alley entrance," Scorpio said.

"Ten-four, boss."

Thorn put the SUV in gear and drove around the block. On the second pass, he found the entrance to the alley, which had been blocked by another vehicle the first time. Scorpio peered through the SUV's foggy window. He pushed the button to lower the window and clean off the condensation.

"Pull in here. Check that back door. It looks like somebody applied a crowbar to it with a good amount of force. Stay alert," Scorpio said from habit more than concern.

Thorn was the size of a brick building. He rarely had occasion to prove it, but he could handle himself. His linebacker shoulders alone were intimidating enough. He had the bulk and fortitude to handle a thug like Reacher. Which was precisely why Scorpio had hired him.

Scorpio rolled down the window again. Thorn pulled his weapon and held it down to his side as he walked the few steps to the back door. Scorpio couldn't see past Thorn's broad back. He turned and nodded and pulled the open door wide. He turned sideways and stepped through the narrow doorway into the dark interior.

A few minutes later, Thorn reemerged and approached the SUV. "The place is a mess, looks like someone tossed it. If they found what they were looking for, they took it with them. There's nothing of value in there now."

Scorpio nodded. "I want to look around."

Thorn opened the back door of the vehicle and Scorpio struggled out. Using his cane, he walked the few feet to the back door. The vinyl letters on the door identifying T. Rex Cleaners had peeled, and a couple had fallen off long ago.

Scorpio went inside. "Flashlight."

"Right. Hang on." He heard Thorn rummaging in his pockets and shortly, a concentrated microbeam illuminated the interior. Thorn attempted to place the flashlight in Scorpio's hand. When that didn't work, he shone it in all directions while Scorpio held the cane.

They were standing in the back of the shop. Scorpio looked directly ahead through the windows adjacent to the front door, which led to the sidewalk. Streetlights projected weakly, providing enough visibility through the yellowed paper signs to see the customer counter parallel to the entrance.

Small items were strewn about. The cash register drawer was open and the machine lay on its side, empty of whatever it might have contained. Cleaned clothes should have hung on the automated rack to his right, but they had been knocked to the floor and trampled.

"Check out that counter. And the cash register," he said. "Sometimes they have hidden drawers or compartments."

"Ten-four, boss," Thorn replied, already moving as instructed.

On the opposite side was the shop's only interior wall, which was covered with flimsy brown wood paneling that might have been salvaged from grandma's basement decades before.

"Wait." Scorpio nodded left.

Thorn turned the knob and pushed the hollow paneled door inward. He shined the microbeam at the threshold and ducked his head to look inside.

When he moved, Scorpio saw dry-cleaning equipment filled most of the space. The rest was a row of shelves where chemicals and supplies were probably stored before they'd been knocked to the yellowing linoleum floor. Noxious fumes wafted toward him, irritating his eyes and burning his nose as he inhaled.

"I've seen enough." Scorpio backed away and Thorn closed the door against the chemical odors inside.

Scorpio leaned against the flimsy wall while Thorn took the flashlight and examined the front of the shop.

He blinked his eyes several times to reduce the irritation. When he opened them the fourth time, he caught a flash glinting off the floor behind an overturned trash can.

He used his cane to move the trash can aside. The reflection came from the foil backing on an empty blister pack. Scorpio recognized it, even in the semi-darkness. He leaned on his cane and stooped awkwardly to pick it up.

There was not enough light inside the shop to examine the blister pack, but Scorpio didn't need to study it. He knew what it was and where it came from. Grim satisfaction creased his brow. He was on the right track.

Thorn returned empty-handed, shaking his head.

"Didn't find anything?"

"Nothing useful to us. They weren't interested in cash, though. They left about three hundred bucks strewn all over the place," Thorn replied, handing Scorpio a creased twenty.

He put the bill into his pocket along with the empty blister pack, took one last look around and left the building. Thorn stayed to remove any fingerprints they might have left before he followed.

When they were seated in the SUV again, Thorn drove through the alley and turned north, away from the center of town.

Scorpio paid little attention to his surroundings. At this point, he knew three things for sure. Things he had not expected. He ticked them off in his mind.

The Lake Forest house was unoccupied. He sensed that wherever the sisters had gone, they wouldn't be back soon.

Rex Mackenzie's business, whatever it was, might have operated from the dry cleaner location, but his fortune wasn't made pressing wool suits.

And he'd underestimated his targets. By a wide margin.

Scorpio grimaced and patted his pockets to locate his phone. When he found it, in the same pocket was the hinged jewelry box he'd removed from Mackenzie's bedroom wall safe.

He found the contact he wanted, placed the call, and held the phone to his ear with his shoulder.

While he waited, he looked at the box carefully. Four inches wide, six inches long, and almost four inches deep.

He propped the box against his thigh. He used his good right hand to force the hasp open and pry the lid up, despite the sturdy spring that held it tightly closed. When the box opened, Scorpio's eyes widened right along with it.

The box was lined with purple satin and the interior was divided into three equal sections. The left section contained loose gemstones. Scorpio was no expert jeweler, but they appeared to be unset diamonds. Depending on the quality, he supposed they might have significant value.

The right section of the box also contained loose gemstones of various colors. Scorpio guessed they were emeralds, sapphires, and rubies, but they could have been more exotic stones for all he knew. Perhaps they were worth as much as the diamonds.

The center of the box held a high capacity data traveler flash drive with a zinc alloy metal casing. He recognized it immediately. Created for power users seeking to store massive amounts of data in a small form. He owned two smaller ones like this. Each one had set him back more than two grand.

Slowly, Scorpio closed the lid on the box and secured the latch. He disconnected the call and slipped the box into his pocket.

The contents of the flash drive could easily be worth more than the gemstones. Which proved one thing and raised several questions in his mind.

Scorpio figured the jewelry box proved Rex Mackenzie was bent. No way did he make enough money out of that shabby old dry cleaners to buy the contents of that box. Besides, this was Chicago. A guy like Mackenzie got a mansion in Lake Forest by being a certain kind of businessman.

Where did he get all those gemstones? What did he plan to do with them? Scorpio shook his head, thinking the situation through as best he could. His brain was sluggish. He couldn't come up with a plausible answer, so he moved on to the next question.

Why did Rex Mackenzie need so much portable data storage? Not for photos of his wife or home movies, for sure. The drive would probably hold more than six hundred thousand photographs and maybe a thousand high-definition movies. No casual photographer or film collector would need that much storage.

No, like the cleaners, the drive was probably used for criminal activities. Which is where his mind always went, even with people who'd never ripped him off before.

He grinned. Now he knew for sure that Rex Mackenzie, his wife, and her sister weren't law abiding citizens. Not even close.

He tapped his lips with his knuckle. Why so much data storage? Could be anything from virtual reality porn to global blackmail. Mackenzie had plenty of room on there for lots of both.

But then why did Mackenzie keep the flash drive in the bedroom safe?

The only rationale he could think of was that even ruthless thieves wouldn't expect to find it there. And only a knowledgeable person would assume the drive contained anything valuable, even if he found it.

He shook his head and a couple of sharp twinges pierced his temples. He closed his eyes a moment until the pain subsided.

For sure, Mackenzie was a more complicated man than Scorpio had expected.

Which meant he needed to see what was on that flash drive. As soon as possible.

CHAPTER FIVE

Thursday, February 10
9:35 p.m.
Detroit, Michigan

NOBLE HAD SETTLED INTO the small kitchen in her apartment, surrounded by the heavenly aroma of the fresh pizza they'd picked up on the way.

Otto could handle herself. She wasn't worried about being killed or maimed by a stranger she'd met in a parking garage and brought into her home. Although such behavior would have mortified her mother.

What she worried about was Noble. Where was he going with all his questions?

She watched as he swallowed pizza with a big swig from the brown Labatt longneck bottle. His second beer. Her first bottle remained almost full. She'd nibbled one square slice of pizza while he'd scarfed down six so far. Between swigs and swallows, he'd spent most of his conversation relating irrelevant background.

She'd let him talk, figuring he'd eventually get down to business. The Boss hadn't intervened yet, either. Which probably meant he was still waiting for a reason to shut Noble down.

"Like I said, I'm DEA. My area of expertise is heroin trafficking. Over the past several years, that's included the opioid epidemic. You know about that?" He arched his eyebrows as he licked the pizza sauce off his fingers.

She nodded. The more time she spent with him, the more he resembled the Boy Detective she'd first imagined. He was as irritating as any young boy could be, too.

"Every human in America is familiar with the opioid epidemic." She frowned. He'd been going on about heroin for an hour already. She was tired and cranky and she wanted him to get to the point. "You know I'm FBI, Detroit Field Office, and you're asking me if I'm aware of heroin and opioid trafficking? What do you think?"

He shrugged. "So, I can assume you know all the ins and outs? Like how prescription opioids are chemically the same as the street stuff? They can lead to serious addiction, and fatal overdoses, and all that?"

"Right." She gritted her teeth. He was trying to be helpful, not condescending. Heroin was not only his job, it was also his passion.

"A couple of years ago we thought we'd locked down every possible way that prescription opioids could be stolen and resold. At least, in mass quantities. We even knocked out the profiteering in naloxone," he said.

"The injectable antidote to an opioid overdose," Otto replied, hoping to avoid another half hour lecture on that topic.

"Basically, yeah. We went back to chasing the old-fashioned kind of heroin, the kind that gets smuggled into the country and sold in baggies and shot up at parties and in alleys and toilet stalls and stuff. The way we've been doing the job for a few decades." He offered a quizzical look while pointing at the last piece of pizza.

She nodded. He snagged it and took a big bite while she replied, "The prescription opioids are still out there on the street, though. Still being sold and traded. Still causing more deaths per capita than heart disease and cancer."

"Unfortunately, that's true. It's also why I hope we can help each other." He grinned like he'd just found a decoder ring in a box of Cracker Jack. He polished off the last of the pizza, dusted his hands together, pushed away from the table, and leaned back with his beer.

She glanced at the clock. "You said Reacher is a witness. Witness to what exactly?"

"I have no evidence to prove it," he cautioned.

She nodded. No surprise. One thing Reacher was very good at was operating outside the law without leaving an evidentiary trail. He'd been a military cop for thirteen years. He knew what to do and how to do it so that nothing could be proved against him. Which, she had to admit, worked to her advantage as well as his, more than once.

Reacher's natural ability to avoid consequences was only half of the story. Someone very high up the food chain had intentionally deleted all mention of Reacher from all government databases since he left the Army.

Anyone looking for Reacher had a long, slow road ahead. Otto could say that much for sure, based on hard experience.

Noble said, "Reacher showed up out west, at the tail end of a long-term sting operation a while back. I thought we were on the same team, so I didn't—"

"Wait. *What?*" Otto widened her eyes and sat a little straighter in her chair. "*On the same team?* You're saying Reacher is working undercover for the DEA?"

If that were true, a lot of Reacher's unexplained activities suddenly made perfect sense.

Like why he lived off the grid. Why there was no mention of him in FBI files. Why no one could ever find him. Why he'd seemed to be helping her lately. Why he'd saved her life, even.

And why the Boss had held the intel back, kept her working not only off the books but completely in the dark, too.

Reacher as an undercover operative.

Made perfect sense.

All the puzzle pieces could fit nicely into that picture. Her world would return to normal. She might relax, at least a little bit.

Maybe.

But Noble was already shaking his head before she had a chance to think the idea through. "Nothing like that."

The momentary hope died, and she slumped back in her chair. She was somewhat surprised at how reluctant she was to let go of the brief flicker.

"What then?" she asked.

Noble said, "He told me about his background. Thirteen years in the Army. Military police. Terminal at major. He was working with a retired FBI Agent from the Chicago Field Office, now a licensed private investigator. They were after a guy I'd been chasing down for opioid dealing."

Then she realized what Noble had said. She held her palm up. "Wait. Reacher *told you* this stuff? You talked to him? In person?"

Noble cocked his head as if he was perplexed by the question. "Yes. I said that, didn't I?"

CHAPTER SIX

Thursday, February 10
10:05 p.m.
Detroit, Michigan

"START AT THE BEGINNING," she said, perking up. She made no effort to record the conversation. She figured the Boss was already doing that.

Noble frowned. "Like I said, not much to tell. Met the guy and his friends once, that's all."

"His *friends*? He had people with him?" She stared. Reacher was a loner. He never stayed in one place long enough to connect to anyone.

"Yeah. Bramall, the private investigator, like I said. And a woman," Noble replied. He swigged the last of the beer. "Got another one of these?"

She waved him to the fridge. He stuck his head inside and rummaged around the empty condiment jars and moldy cheese until he found what he wanted.

"Give me the blow-by-blow on your Reacher interview," she said. "One word at a time."

"Not much to tell. I wouldn't call it an interview. More like a conversation. I went to take possession of a house we'd seized for illegal drug activities. Reacher was there." He closed the fridge and leaned against the counter. He twisted the cap off the last bottle.

"Reacher was living there? Out west?" Her mind was officially blown, and her patience had worn thin. She swiped fatigue from her eyes with her palm. "Explain this to me like I'm a five-year-old, Noble. What was Reacher doing in the house? Why did he have Bramall and the woman with him?"

"Okay. But can we find a more comfortable place to chat? No offense, but these chairs aren't big enough for my ten-year-old daughter." He tossed the beer cap into the trashcan beside the sink and nodded toward the sofa.

He must have noticed the astonished expression on her face because he smiled and winked and said, "I don't look old enough to have a ten-year-old, right? Everybody says that. She was born when I was six."

Otto grinned and shook her head as she led the way to more comfortable seating. The guy was personable, she'd give him that.

When they had resettled, Noble said, "I'm happy to answer all your questions about Reacher if you'll help me with the stuff I need. But we'll have time for that later."

Her nerves were immediately on edge again. Her work was confidential. Off the books. She couldn't tell him anything much. "Help you with what?"

"Following a lead." Noble reached into his pocket and pulled out a sealed plastic evidence bag. He tossed it to her.

She grabbed it in midair. Inside the bag was an empty blister pack. The kind that usually held prescription or over-the-counter medications.

This one was silver on the back. The front was embossed with a blue manufacturer's logo. The clear plastic bubbles were empty now, but they had held round tablets once.

Also in the evidence bag was an empty foil packet about the size of a deck of playing cards. Same blue logo.

"We found those in Chicago a few weeks ago. From the same manufacturer we were chasing when I met Reacher. We thought we'd stopped the traffickers at the source back then. Turns out we hadn't." He paused, swigged, took a big breath.

"What does that mean?" she asked.

"After a long hiatus, the case has somehow reactivated. The network we closed down found new connections," he replied.

"What are you doing about that?"

"We have a lead on the head of the distribution ring, but I'm stuck. I need more intel from the woman Reacher was traveling with to help us close the case."

Otto shrugged. She was FBI. She wasn't chasing drug dealers unless she was officially assigned to do it.

She tossed the evidence bag back to him. "Was she attractive?"

"What?" Noble asked. He slipped the evidence bag into his pocket.

"With Reacher, there's always a woman. Usually, she's law enforcement or military or both. Often, she's beautiful." Otto shook her head as if this was one of many mysteries she hadn't solved. "What it is about Reacher that's attractive to such women, anyway? You've met the guy. Can you clue me in?"

Noble laughed. "Sorry, but Reacher's not my type. Hate to crush your theory, but you're wrong about this woman, too."

Otto arched her eyebrows. "She wasn't beautiful?"

"Oh, yeah. Tiffany Jane Mackenzie was far beyond beautiful. She was one of the most stunning women I've ever seen in my life. She had the most amazing hair, too." Noble paused and grinned when Otto scowled fiercely. "But she wasn't a cop, and she wasn't military or even ex-military."

"That's a first." Otto's scowl deepened.

He shrugged. "If it's any consolation, Jane Mackenzie's sister was ex-military. By all accounts, she was stunningly beautiful, too. They're twins."

"Twins? Identical?"

"Apparently. I never met the sister." Noble's expression clouded. "I don't have all the details. All I know is that both women are missing, and I need to find them, so we can wrap up this new distribution ring."

"And you figure Reacher might know where they are?"

He nodded. "Or at least, know something that might help me locate one of them, and from there, maybe I can find a solid lead. Otherwise, I've hit the wall."

"What about the private investigator? Can't he help you?"

"I tried him before I came here. The sisters live in Chicagoland, too. Lake Forest. When I couldn't locate the sisters, I called him. No answer," Noble said quietly.

Otto cocked her head. "That's odd. You figure he's with the sisters? Or maybe he and Reacher are together again?"

"I don't know," he replied.

She asked, "What about the husbands?"

"Only one husband." Noble's voice went quieter still. He leaned in. "One sister is married. The other isn't."

She suspected what was coming next based on his demeanor, but she asked anyway. "And what does the husband say about all this?"

"When I find him, I'll ask. The husband is missing, too."

She plopped back onto the sofa and tucked her feet under her, shaking her head. "Seems unlikely to me. What reason would all three have to disappear like that?"

"Five."

"What?"

"All five have disappeared, counting the investigator. And Reacher." He paused. "And I don't know whether they're all together."

"Right." She uncoiled her coarse, black hair and ran both hands through to free it from the tight bun anchored at the base of her skull. "What have we got to work with?"

"I believe I know who made them disappear, and I think I know why," Noble replied. "And if I'm right, they're in big trouble."

Otto cocked her head. Noble was probably telling the truth as well as he knew it. But if the five were together, and he thought they were in big trouble, then he knew way less than she did about Reacher.

The guy was like Teflon. Nothing ever stuck to him. And in her experience, in every confrontation of any kind, Reacher was always the last man standing.

CHAPTER SEVEN

Thursday, February 10
11:35 p.m.
Detroit, Michigan

"YOU REALLY DON'T KNOW where to find Reacher?" Noble asked, his face the very image of sincere curiosity.

Otto shrugged and shook her head. "If I knew where he was, I wouldn't be sitting here talking to you."

"Where have you looked?"

She made a quick decision to confirm things he probably already knew or could find quickly. "Same places you have, I imagine. He has no fixed address, no cell phone, no registered vehicles."

"Family?"

"All deceased. One brother and both parents." She didn't mention the girl she believed to be Reacher's daughter. He had no reason to know the girl existed. No reason to send Noble off on a wild goose chase when Reacher was not likely to be found anywhere near the girl.

"Reacher's not working, I guess, or you'd have found employment records. What's he do for walking around money?" Noble asked.

"Probably not dealing drugs, if that's what you're thinking," Otto replied.

Noble shrugged. "I'm a DEA agent. What else would I think?"

"He's collecting a pension from the Army, which is automatically deposited into his bank account every month. He makes withdrawals from time to time, sporadically. Uses an ATM card. Rarely uses the same ATM twice. Not enough to support a normal person."

"So he's funding his lifestyle with ill-gotten gains? Some kind of ongoing criminal activity?" Noble considered a moment and then shook his head. "I've gotta say, he didn't seem the type to me. He seemed to be traveling whichever way the wind blows. Kinda tough to run a successful criminal enterprise with that kind of nomadic existence."

"He's had a lot of Army training. Honed his survival skills. He could live off practically nothing. Scavenge food and clothes from dumpsters. But none of that is very likely," she replied, shaking her head.

Noble seemed to consider things for a moment before he asked, "And there are no other withdrawals from his bank account by third parties, such as a mortgage payment or car payment, or a girlfriend?"

She shook her head. "He doesn't have a credit score or even a credit card. He doesn't donate blood or bone marrow and, so far as we know, nobody's received any of his organs."

"Good to know you've checked the organ banks." Noble laughed. "Trouble with the law?"

"Sure. But don't be so hopeful. Nothing we can anticipate or even trace," she replied. "He's been arrested a few times, but he's always released from jail by the time we find out about it."

"Driver's license?"

"Nope."

"Passport?"

She nodded. "Yeah. We've got standard traps running on all the airlines, trains, and border crossings."

Noble seemed to think about it for a while. He tapped his beer bottle with his forefinger. "I said I only met him once. Which is true. But I talked to him on the phone a couple of times."

"A pay phone? He likes pay phones." She didn't mention that Reacher also knew how to acquire and operate cell phones. He'd texted her a few times, and left voicemail messages, too.

He shook his head. "I called him. Or rather, I called the Chicago investigator's cell phone, and Reacher talked to me. I called the same number yesterday and again today and got voicemail. No call back yet."

Otto shrugged. "We're thinking of forming a club. Members will be everybody Reacher's left behind and never looked back."

"Which is why you were hoping he was working undercover for us or one of the other agencies after he left the Army, right? Because he's so far off the grid he's invisible?" Noble asked.

Otto nodded but said nothing.

Noble said, "It does sound like he's deep undercover for somebody, I agree. It's hard to live off the grid like that for fifteen years without support from somewhere."

Otto agreed. She still figured a private contractor was involved. But she wasn't about to say that to Noble. She broke eye contact for a few moments, considering how much intel she was willing to share.

Finally, she said, "He's only been off the grid for about twelve years, actually. Not the whole fifteen since he left the Army. Three years after, he inherited a house in upstate New York."

Noble's eyebrows arched and the freckles on his nose popped out. "Really? Inherited? So no loan application required, eh? No mortgage?"

"Right. He also owned a car back then, which he somehow paid cash for, so no loan docs there, either."

"He lived in the house alone?"

She shook her head. "For a brief time, he was involved in a steady romantic relationship. When that ended, he abandoned the house and disappeared again."

Noble cocked his head and seemed to be thinking things through. "So you and your partner, Gaspar is it?"

"Right."

"You've been interviewing Reacher's friends and colleagues, checking out places he might have lived? Scouring the databases. All the usual background investigation stuff?"

"Pretty much," she nodded.

"You've been on the trail more than, what? Twelve weeks? And you haven't seen the guy? Even once?" He raised his eyebrows all the way up his freckled forehead into his hairline.

Solid question. Otto broke eye contact again. Had she *seen* Reacher in person? Even once? Possibly.

Like Noble, she couldn't prove anything. But she believed Reacher had been there, in the background, several times.

She'd noticed shadows and odors. Things she couldn't explain. And she didn't believe in paranormal events, regardless of what her mother might say.

She took a deep breath. Once, Reacher had saved her life. She was sure he had.

Gaspar didn't believe that, though. He didn't have many warm fuzzies for Reacher.

But Otto believed she'd be dead now if Reacher hadn't fished her out of the Atlantic Ocean that day. Knew it the same way she knew Boy Howdy here, sitting across from her right now with his toothy smile and his freckled nose and his aw-shucks mannerisms, wasn't nearly as guileless as he pretended to be.

Her muscles had stiffened up. She straightened her back and stretched like a cat. She glanced at her watch. It was late. She needed to wrap this up and get some sleep.

"You already know that Gaspar and I have been assigned to the Special Personnel Task Force. We're working on a classified background check. I can't identify the target for you. We're never required to interview anyone in particular, but at some point, we'd like to talk to everyone who has knowledge, of course. All you need to know is that I'd like to interview Reacher. I think I have a pretty good feel for the guy at this point."

Otto climbed off the sofa. She collected her glass and walked it to the kitchen sink. When she turned, he was still seated across the open space, and she was within reach of her gun.

"But you aren't really looking for Reacher at all, are you?" She paused. "You're tracking those two sisters, and you think *they* might be with Reacher. You thought all of them might be here. With me. Didn't you? Which blows my mind, honestly."

"I told you I'd hit a wall." Noble nodded. "I'd heard through the grapevine that you were investigating Reacher. He could have been here in Detroit. At the very least, I figured you'd know where to find him by now. So I took a flyer and came here."

"You heard wrong." Her stomach did a few flips. Until now he hadn't suggested he'd learned the truth about her assignment. "We're not investigating Reacher. We're just doing the background check like I said."

He shrugged. "What's the difference?"

"You know the difference. We'd only be investigating Reacher if he was under suspicion of committing a federal crime," she said. "Until and unless he's suspected of a crime over which we have jurisdiction, investigating him would be illegal."

Noble grinned as if she'd admitted something. Which she hadn't.

The truth was that she and Gaspar were investigating Reacher. That was exactly what they'd been assigned to do. Yet, they had seen no proof that Reacher was engaged in terrorism, cybercrime, organized or violent crimes for which the FBI was responsible, either for preventing or solving.

The work was classified. Off the books. Nothing in the files.

She knew for sure the files didn't contain even a whiff of their actual assignment because she'd checked again today. Her cover story was the SPTF background check, and even that wasn't public knowledge.

Now Noble was saying he'd *heard* about an *investigation*. This loose talk was too serious to joke about.

"Come on, Otto. You've been on the job long enough to know how this goes. I asked around. People talk." He shrugged.

"What people?" she asked, but she knew he was right. All the agencies leaked like sieves. Everybody knew that. Why had she allowed herself to forget how much danger she was living with every day?

Noble stood and stretched and yawned. Mouth big and wide open like a fish. "Okay. Have it your way. You're not investigating Reacher. Anybody asks me, I'll tell them I got the straight scoop from the horse's mouth."

Otto nodded. "You do that."

Noble said, "Despite the great pizza and good beer, sounds like this was a wasted trip to Detroit for me."

"Yes," she replied.

"A promise is a promise, though," he said. "I don't have much to offer that you don't already know, but I'll answer all your questions in the morning. For your background check."

"Good." She agreed that he wasn't likely to know anything that would help her. He'd only met Reacher once. There were other people present. Not much he could have gleaned under the circumstances.

He nodded. "Who knows? Maybe you'll think of something I can use to help me find Reacher or the others by then. If not, I guess I'll move on."

"Works for me." She was tired, too. She craved sleep.

"Great." He nodded. "It's late and cold, and I don't have a hotel reservation. How about I spend the night in your guest room?"

The question jarred her. A few weeks ago, she'd been awakened in the middle of the night by an intruder. At the time, she'd suspected Reacher. Was Noble aware of that incident? Was that why he wanted to stay here tonight? Perhaps he believed Reacher would show up again.

If he did, she'd be prepared.

Otto shrugged. "Yeah, sure. This way."

She set Noble up in the guest room and left him there.

Then she moved into her bedroom with the envelope from the Boss, laptop, personal cell phone, a glass of red wine, and her gun.

She closed her bedroom door behind her and shot the deadbolt home, just in case Noble decided to misbehave. Although he didn't seem the type to sneak into her room at night for any reason. She sipped the wine and set the glass on the bedside table along with her gun and tossed everything else onto the bed.

In the bathroom, she washed her face and changed into comfortable yoga pants and sweatshirt. She returned to the bed and opened the Boss's envelope and dumped the contents onto the comforter.

As always, the envelope contained only one item. A burner cell phone, fired up and ready to go. She settled back against the pillows, sipped the wine, and waited. She wouldn't need to wait long.

The Boss was always aware of her every move unless she took steps to block electronic surveillance, which she had not done after her return from New York. Two reasons.

She might hear from Reacher again, for one thing. He'd contacted her several times recently. He might do it again if she gave him a chance.

And she'd discovered she liked the extra security the Boss's constant watching provided.

The Boss would know she was alone and available to talk.

CHAPTER EIGHT

Friday, February 11
12:55 a.m.
Chicago, Illinois

THEY'D STOPPED FOR A quick dinner before hitting the road again. Thick clouds blocked even the faint light of the crescent moon, but the city's ambient lights were as blinding as sunlight. Head injuries coupled with exhaustion made Scorpio's temples throb with every pulse beat. He closed his eyes and leaned his head back against the soft leather seat, but sleep was impossible.

Finally, Thorn accelerated the SUV onto the interstate's westbound ramp and merged into traffic. When the vehicle settled into a steady eighty miles an hour, he said, "Where to, boss?"

Scorpio glanced up to meet his gaze in the rearview. He jacked his body around in the back seat, trying without success to find any comfortable position. He'd spent a long, stressful, disastrous day on the road. He couldn't focus. His mind was too fuzzy. To solve his problems, he needed rest, a laptop, and privacy. In that order.

None of which would be easy to find in Chicagoland tonight.

The original plan had been simple enough. Only four parts to it. Get in, collect his property, kill the thieves, and get out. Afterward, he'd expected to sleep in his own bed back in Rapid City.

Nothing had unfolded properly. He'd arrived too late in the day. He had not found the thieves or his property. And he was forced to leave empty-handed.

Time to regroup. He pressed the fingers of his good right hand to his temple in a futile effort to massage the pain away.

"We'll be out of the metro area soon," Thorn said. "How about a mom-and-pop motel for a few hours' sleep?"

It was a reasonable question. After some rest, Scorpio's scrambled brain usually settled down. He'd be able to think straight. But sticking around so close to the city seemed foolhardy.

With Babbling Brooke dead and blood all over the floor at the Mackenzie mansion, he imagined Chicago PD's heat down his neck like dragon's breath.

How long would she remain undiscovered? If she had a family or an inquisitive boss, someone would have found her already, probably. Once they identified her, how long would it take to suspect he'd killed her?

He'd used a fake ID to make the appointment to view the mansion. But he had not been particularly careful about surveillance or leaving DNA at the crime scene. Unlike what they show on television, he knew processing a crime scene and analyzing forensic data did not happen instantly.

Still, Scorpio was no stranger to law enforcement. His DNA and other biometrics were available in several criminal databanks. Hell, basic facial recognition software would probably do it, if they had a clear image from a security camera at the house.

So the bad news was that he was a dog in the road. Only a matter of time before they found him and identified him as her killer.

Question was, how much time? Hard to say. A few hours to a few months.

Which meant he should have twenty-four to forty-eight hours of breathing room, for sure. Sleep was a smart first step.

Thing was, a few hours of sleep wouldn't solve the other two problems, both of which felt urgent for some reason. The flash drive he'd found in the back of Mackenzie's bedroom wall safe was the first big thing.

What was stored on that flash drive? To access it, he'd need a laptop. Which he normally carried with him everywhere he went. But nothing was proceeding normally in this operation.

Thorn had driven Scorpio's armored Lincoln sedan from Rapid City to Milwaukee. Even with the three a.m. departure, twelve hours of drive time and thirteen hours on the road was a long day. The time zone change meant they'd arrived in Milwaukee an hour later, too.

Thorn used a fake ID to rent the SUV at the airport rental counter and left the Lincoln in a remote off-site parking lot. Scorpio's belongings, including his laptop, were stored in the trunk of his sedan. Thorn's stuff was there, too.

"You okay to keep driving?" Scorpio asked.

"No problem. Roads are clear. No construction. So far, not much traffic. Take a nap. I'll stop for coffee soon, and we can make it back to Milwaukee in a couple of hours," Thorn replied, settling into his seat and setting the cruise control.

Scorpio leaned his head back and closed his eyes again. He would not sleep. He never slept in a moving vehicle of any kind.

He could barely hold onto a coherent thought, but he struggled to consider the remaining options.

Forty-eight hours wasn't much time. Now he had four targets instead of three, and all four were in the wind. Possibly, they were all together. More likely, they were not. Which meant he'd be forced to make choices between them.

He wanted Reacher. Wanted him bad. Wanted him with a rage that could never be quenched as long as the guy stayed vertical and above ground. His mental images of Reacher writhing in a pool of blood, in serious pain for a very long time before he gasped his last, wrenching breaths, had sustained him through months of recovery and rehabilitation. Nothing less than reducing Reacher to a sniveling, bloodied mass would satisfy him.

He had waited this long for satisfaction, and he could wait longer. He'd have to.

First things first. That was the rule. Everything else depended on the return of his product. He needed the drugs back from the sisters. Without the drugs, he had nothing to build his future upon. Which meant Mackenzie and the sisters were the first problem.

The empty drug packs had shown him the way. While it was possible that one of the three had received a legitimate prescription for opioids, that answer was unlikely. The serial numbers on the empty silver packs would prove his ownership if they matched his inventory list. Odds were heavily stacked in his favor on that score.

The list of his stolen inventory was saved on his laptop. When he picked up his laptop, he would check. He didn't have time to run down a bunch of blind alleys.

CHAPTER NINE

Friday, February 11
1:05 a.m.
Detroit, Michigan

SHE WAITED LONGER THAN she'd expected for the Boss's
call. She sipped more wine. Coupled with the day's physical and
mental exertion, the wine made her mellow and sleepy.

"Otto," she said when the call finally came, as she always did.

"How was your evening?" he asked.

The question surprised her. He didn't normally pretend to
care about her or her life. Nor did she normally feign interest in
his.

"As well as can be expected," she replied, wondering what
the hell he was up to.

"What is your assessment of your houseguest?"

She cocked her head and held on to her patience. "My
assessment? He's DEA. He knows Reacher. Claims to have
helpful data, which he's willing to share. What should my
assessment be?"

A quiet sigh traveled over the miles through to her earpiece. He didn't answer her questions. Instead, he pushed his own agenda. So predictable.

"You will find encrypted files available for download on the secure server. Your eyes only." He paused. "Which means don't share them with Noble."

Because he was the Boss, and orders were orders, regardless of how they were phrased, she was required to comply. But the orders were odd, so she asked, "What's in the files?"

"Everything I could dig up in the past few hours about Noble and his connection to Reacher." He paused. "We may find more."

"Noble coming here was a surprise to you?" She didn't believe that for a moment. Throughout this assignment, he'd been several steps ahead of her on every level. She'd felt constantly manipulated, intel parceled out as he saw fit, in ways that made no sense to her. Why should she believe this time was different?

"Until he approached you in the parking garage, I had no idea he existed. We might have begun this assignment with Noble instead of in Margrave, otherwise." He paused. "I'd have told you about Noble if I'd known. Trust me."

Trust him? After all he'd put her through? She almost spit red wine all over the bed. As it was, she swallowed and choked and coughed for what felt like a full minute.

When she got control of herself, she said, "Sorry."

He ignored her reaction and replied, "Noble could be a problem for us. Depending on what Reacher's involved in now."

"How so?"

"There's mounds of data on the case Noble was working on when he met Reacher. A lengthy, wide-ranging investigation into pharmaceutical opioid theft and trafficking. Noble's area was primarily Wyoming, Montana, and South Dakota."

"Reacher was out west when Noble ran into him, then? Which must mean this was a while ago," she mused.

He continued as if she hadn't spoken. "The investigation involved several teams of DEA agents and other agencies, as well as local law enforcement in multiple states."

She envisioned the government's well-deserved reputation for recording and reporting absolutely everything. The reports on such a long-term investigation could take months to read and digest. She groaned, feeling the weight of wading through reams of documents, most of which would be a waste of time.

As he so often did, the Boss seemed to read her mind. "Don't worry. Ninety-eight percent of the materials I've located so far have nothing to do with Reacher or Noble. We'll ignore them."

She glanced at the clock. Fatigue overwhelmed her. She'd pulled many an all-nighter in her life, but she never got that second wind people talked about.

Reluctantly, she set the wine glass on the bedside table.

She found her laptop and opened it up. "What's in the files you've sent me?"

"Distilled information on the two sisters and the husband. A brief summary of Noble's case."

She made the connection to his secure server and started the download. "What about the telephone calls Noble says he had with Reacher? Have you found those?"

"Still searching."

"And the investigator? The guy Noble says was with Reacher? Retired FBI. Shouldn't be too hard to find him."

"Terrence Bramall. He's a licensed private investigator in

Illinois. His office is in Chicago. Specializes in missing persons now. Noble is telling the truth. Bramall's out of pocket at the moment. We tried to reach him. No luck."

She said, "So you think Bramall and Reacher are together. And you're worried about it."

"I'm not worried," he replied.

"What, then? Why do we care about Noble or Bramall or the two sisters or any of this?"

"At the moment, I can't answer those questions," he said.

And wouldn't answer, even if he could, she figured.

She swiped a hand through her hair and shrugged. "Noble doesn't know where Reacher is. He met Reacher once. How much can he know? My plan was to interview him for our purposes in the morning, record what he says about everything that happened with Reacher, and send Noble on his way."

"Sorry, Otto, but that's not possible now. Your mission has changed. We're short on time. We need to find Reacher. Sooner is better." He sounded a little bit sorry, so maybe he was.

"Why? What are you not telling me?"

"Download the files. Read them. Then we'll talk." He paused again.

She heard someone walk into his room and deliver a brief, whispered report. When he came back on the line, he said, "Call Gaspar. Bring him up to speed. I'll send you more intel as I receive it. Forget that wine. Get some coffee. You're going to need it."

Before she could accuse him of spying on her again, he was gone. He'd disconnected the call.

She glanced at the laptop screen. The files were almost downloaded. She leaned back, closed her eyes, and sipped the wine while she waited.

A few minutes later, Noble knocked. "Otto? Are you still awake?"

"Just a second," she replied. She turned the laptop screen away from his view and placed her gun within easy reach. Then she climbed off the bed, unlocked and opened the bedroom door slightly. "What's up?"

Still dressed in his street clothes, he glanced into the room but made no move to enter. "I got a call. I've got to go."

"Go where?"

"Chicago. One of the missing sisters was murdered."

Otto widened her eyes. "Murdered?"

"I don't have much info yet." His expression was weary. Deep circles under his eyes belied his fitness to travel. Maybe he was a guy who slept on planes like Gaspar did and Otto could never do. "Body was found a couple of hours ago. A helo is due here shortly to take me to the airport."

"You're flying from Detroit Wayne to O'Hare?"

"Fastest, under the circumstances." He nodded and swiped a palm over his face. "It'll be tight. My flight departs in less than eighty minutes."

Few things were less appealing to Otto than flying in a helicopter. The whirlybirds were too unstable for her liking. Night flights in a helo were even worse. She took a deep breath and squared her shoulders. "I'll come with you to the airport. You can answer my questions about Reacher until your flight leaves. I'll get a taxi back here."

"Suit yourself," he shrugged.

"I'll change and meet you in my living room in two minutes." She closed and locked the door, which was more habit than any concern about him. She was careful, not paranoid.

The files had downloaded. She closed her laptop and stuffed

it into the case. She pulled travel clothes from her closet and headed to the bathroom to get dressed.

She placed her gun into its shoulder holster, slipped her phone into one pocket, and lifted the Boss's phone from the bed. A notification flashed on the screen, containing a flight number and the word "confirmed." No destination listed, but she figured he was sending her to Chicago with Noble.

After half a moment's consideration, she glanced toward the corner. Her rolling travel bag waited, always packed. She stacked the laptop case atop the travel bag and headed out.

Ten minutes later, Otto and Noble stood aside, while the helo landed on the roof. They dashed beneath the rotor wash and up the flight stairs. Noble closed the door and stowed her bags. They settled into their seats, fastened flight harnesses, and donned helmets. The pilot flashed a questioning thumbs up. Noble and Otto returned the gesture. Shortly afterward, they were airborne.

Even with the headsets, conversation inside the helo was difficult. She'd wait until they were on solid ground again to ask her questions. In the meantime, she pulled the Boss's phone from her pocket to check her Chicago flight details.

When the notification opened, allowing her to read the info, she raised her eyebrows. The Boss wasn't sending her to Chicago with Noble. Her flight was booked to St. Louis. Scheduled to depart in fifty minutes. At a departure gate half a mile from Noble's. She'd need to jog to her gate the moment the helo set down.

Whatever intel Noble might possess about Reacher, she couldn't discover it this trip. As it was, she'd be lucky not to miss her flight. Her stomach churned, and she reached into her pocket for an antacid, which she chewed slowly, wondering why the hell she was headed to St. Louis.

CHAPTER TEN

Friday, February 11
1:55 a.m.
Detroit, Michigan

AT THE AIRPORT, OTTO and Noble hurried through the special security checkpoint the Boss had arranged and parted on the other side for gates at opposite ends of the terminal. She dashed along the moving sidewalks and arrived breathless at her gate, flashed her boarding documents and her badge, and slipped into the jetway half a moment before the gate agent closed the door.

Her cell phone rang as she was rushing toward the plane. She reached into her pocket. Gaspar calling. The Boss must have contacted him. She skipped along to the jet's door and slipped inside. The flight attendant closed and snugged the door behind her.

All in one continuous motion, she flopped into seat 3C on the aisle, slipped her bag under the seat, snapped her seatbelt into place, and answered the phone on the tenth ring, breathing heavily. "Otto."

"Are you on board, Sunshine?" Gaspar said.

Trying to catch her breath, she replied, "Just barely. Where are you?"

He paused a moment too long. "Houston. And I can't get a flight out until tomorrow. I'm sorry that I won't be there to back you up."

"No problem." She heard something in his tone that she didn't like, but nothing she could do about it now. "Why are you in Houston?"

"Long story. I'll tell you when I see you. Meanwhile, I'm reading these files we got from the Boss. I'll do what work I can from here."

The flight attendant was demonstrating the safety features of the aircraft. As soon as she finished, she would be coming by to make sure seatbacks were up, tray tables were locked, carryon bags were stowed, and no one was talking on the phone.

"We'll be taking off shortly. I'll review the files during the flight, too. We can talk when I land. Anything, in particular, I should look for in this stuff?"

"The files on these subjects are almost as thin as Reacher's. I haven't had a chance to do much with what we have. All I know so far is that you're on your way to St. Louis to interview Bramall and investigate a storage unit. The Boss says something is going on there."

"A storage unit?" The flight attendant placed a hand on Otto's shoulder and gave her a pointed look along with a spinning index finger gesture to wrap up her call. "We're number one for takeoff. I've got to go."

"Okay. Call me when you land. I'll be done with these files and have some follow up intel by then."

"Will do," she said.

The flight attendant glared again as she hurried past on her way to the jump seat. Otto disconnected and dropped the phone into the seat back pocket. The engines revved up for takeoff. Otto closed her eyes and gripped the armrests as tightly as possible, praying for the best. Or at least not to explode on the tarmac, as the 727 raced forward and lifted off the runway.

She breathed easier after the jet was airborne. The actual flying was generally okay. After all, the number of bombs likely to make it onto the plane were limited, given modern security methods.

Once the autopilot was engaged, the plane would pretty much stay up without human intervention. It was the takeoffs and landings that worried her. At takeoff and landing, the potential for human error was enhanced beyond her maximum tolerance level.

Otto wasn't afraid of flying. Not at all. She simply knew too much about commercial air travel. She wasn't the least bit comfortable in a steel projectile filled with high octane, flammable jet fuel, and combustible materials, traveling 30,000 feet in the air at speeds faster than God ever intended humans to move.

Once the flight was airborne, she released her death grip on the armrests and opened her eyes. She ordered black coffee when the flight attendant asked. She lifted the lid on her laptop, opened the Boss's files, and began to read. She had ninety-seven minutes to absorb the contents, which shouldn't be difficult at all.

She finished the first read-through in no time. As Gaspar had said, the files were thin. There wasn't much to read.

The summary of the earlier investigation by the team Noble worked on was succinct and straightforward. DEA and other law enforcement agencies had been conducting similar investigations around the country at the same time. The opioid crisis, as it had been dubbed, was like a hydra with multiple heads and countless arms operating in hamlets and rugged locations, as well as urban areas. In short, the crisis seemed to permeate everywhere.

The resources consumed by those investigations had been substantial. So much so that agency budgets had been cut back in other areas, like organized crime, which was Otto's normal beat.

The massive effort had the opioid crisis on the run. Suicides and accidental overdoses had declined. The naloxone drug was something close to Kryptonite for opioids. Sort of like a defibrillator, it revived people so they could live long enough to get treatment. First responders carried naloxone everywhere. Countless lives had been saved. And the profiteering had been squelched.

As Noble had said, heroin addiction had returned to its roots. But due to the lack of law enforcement resources applied to other cases over those years, organized crime was stronger than it had been in decades. New gangs, organized mobs, and old mafia families thrived again in every city, town, and village.

Reacher's name, of course, was not included in any of the original opioid crisis files, according to the Boss. Which was probably why he had had no idea Reacher was within a thousand miles of that case before Noble approached her a few hours ago.

In addition to the concise summary of the old case, the Boss had sent files on three subjects.

The most interesting of these was Terrence "Terry" Bramall, retired FBI Special Agent from the Chicago Field Office. Now, a high-end, expensive licensed private investigator in Illinois, Bramall's file was straightforward. It contained a headshot from his FBI personnel file showing an ordinary man who might have been an actor in a television drama.

Bramall's life had been devoted to his job. He retired to care for his wife and was widowed when she died of cancer three years ago. He had no children. His personnel file was a textbook example of what every FBI agent's should be. Commendations, successful cases, medals and awards, a steady rise through the ranks, no blemishes at all, and retirement with a full pension. In short, nothing even remotely odd about this guy.

The other two files were labeled Tiffany Jane (Sanderson) Mackenzie and Serena Rose Sanderson. Twin sisters. Jane and Rose, as they were called. Otto stared at the photos. They were flat-out stunning. Not merely attractive, but the kind of surreal beauty Otto had rarely seen outside of supermodels and starlets.

They grew up in Wyoming, the files said, and parted ways when Rose attended West Point, like Reacher. After West Point, Rose was in the infantry. Iraq and Afghanistan. Bronze Star, Purple Heart. Which meant she'd been injured at some point, but her injuries were not detailed in the files. Terminal at major, like Reacher.

Sanderson was younger than Reacher, though. So they didn't attend West Point or serve in the Army at the same time. If Reacher knew her at all, the connection between them must have been something else.

The sister chose a more domestic path. Jane was a housewife. Junior League, charitable activities, tennis, and golf at the club. Old-fashioned pearls and twinset sweaters making a comeback among the preppy crowd. That sort. Met and married her husband, Theodore Rex Mackenzie, while Rose was deployed in Iraq.

The husband, called Rex, was a wealthy businessman in Chicago, and the couple lived in Lake Forest. Otto whistled when she saw Mackenzie's house. A mansion by any standard, it was currently on the market for almost five million dollars. Looked like sister Jane had hit the jackpot while Rose was off doing the grunt work serving her country and getting shot at for her trouble.

After Rose was injured, she was discharged, and then somehow fell off the radar. Otto's nerves began to twitch because Rose had disappeared. Just like Reacher.

Jane hired Bramall to find her sister. When he did, Rose moved in with Jane and her husband, because Rose had nowhere else to go. Her home had been the Army. When her career ended, she had to start over.

Rose was a bit older than Otto. Coping with a career change like that couldn't have been easy for her. It definitely wouldn't have been easy for Otto.

The sisters were emotionally close, probably. Looked like Jane rescued Rose from whatever issues she had after she was discharged. Since Noble had run across them during the DEA case, it was safe to assume Rose had some connection to illegal opioids.

Otto stretched and rubbed the back of her neck. The files suggested nothing but career success all around for Rose, and blissful domesticity for the Mackenzies.

She shook her head. Not likely.

Reacher was involved with this crowd somehow. Domesticity was the exact opposite of everything Jack Reacher embodied.

Which meant these files were the tip of the iceberg and only the pretty parts.

She rang for the flight attendant and requested more coffee. She was running on pure caffeine at this point, but she'd need to find a hotel room and get some sleep soon.

She turned her attention to the last file, which contained her orders. As Gaspar had said, she was on her way to a storage facility not far from the airport in St. Louis. She was to arrive and be in place before zero five hundred hours. The mission was to intercept Bramall.

And then what?

Her orders didn't say why Bramall was approaching the facility far from his home base in the wee hours of the morning.

Nor had the Boss explained who owned the storage unit, why she was being sent there, or what she was supposed to accomplish.

She shook her head. Par for the course. Could be he didn't know. More likely, he wanted her to figure it out. Which she would.

Otto's experience with everything involved in the Reacher case was that trouble lurked, crouched like a jungle predator ready to attack.

She spent the rest of the flight reviewing the materials again and programming travel routes into her phone, so she could hit the ground running. Drive time to the storage facility was estimated at twenty-three minutes.

The flight landed in St. Louis at Lambert International Airport on time and without incident. Otto was among the first to deplane. She pulled her rolling suitcase along the corridors of the deserted airport until she reached the rental lot where her vehicle stood ready.

A few minutes after that, she was on her way, still wondering what the hell she was doing here. Skies were dark, the air was cold, and an icy rain bounced off the windshield like a hail of bullets.

She connected her phone to the rental's speaker system and called Gaspar. He answered immediately, which was no surprise. The guy rarely slept. He was in pain most of the time, and he hadn't quite recovered from a recent gunshot wound. He never took anything stronger than Tylenol, though she often wondered how he managed. She worried about his liver, too. Tylenol toxicity was no joke.

"Tell me you've acquired more intel," she said. "The only things in those files that Noble hadn't already told me were pretty useless."

"Not much more, I'm afraid. The obvious connection between all the players is prescription opioids. But I've spent the past couple of hours on the phone with my contacts and your Boy Detective, who wasn't especially helpful."

"What did he tell you?"

"He was still traveling toward the Mackenzie mansion in Lake Forest, so he didn't have anything new. He said Reacher wasn't involved with the earlier opioid investigations case. Their paths crossed, but not because Reacher was a target of the investigation."

"You believe that?"

"I do, actually. Reacher wouldn't be the first soldier to find himself on the wrong side of drug addiction. It happens. But he's been out of the Army too long to have been caught in the opioid thing. Besides, if he had addiction issues, we'd have heard about it long before now."

"Makes sense," she said, nodding in the SUV alone in the dark, even if Gaspar couldn't see her.

"Noble said the two sisters might have been witnesses to the case against one of the low-level dealers out in Wyoming. He wasn't sure. But no one had interviewed them at the time because they didn't need to. DEA was able to make the case without them, and by the time Reacher and the sisters came across the radar, Noble and his team were winding things up."

"How about Bramall? Did Noble have anything more to add on that score?"

"He said he'd tried to call Bramall a couple more times but kept getting voicemail."

The icy rain had slicked the roads now. She kept her hands on the wheel and her eyes forward. She'd be arriving at her destination soon.

"One more thing. Could be nothing." He paused to be sure she didn't miss the punch line. "Rex Mackenzie had a mistress."

"With a wife as gorgeous as Jane? That's hard to believe."

"Some men are intimidated by wives like that," Gaspar said.

She replied snidely, "And some men have their head up their ass."

Gaspar chuckled. "Yeah, well, my bet? He's up to his eyeballs in some kind of mess. His mistress died of an opioid overdose a few weeks back."

"You don't say," she deadpanned.

"Be careful, Suzie Wong. A lot of this stuff doesn't add up yet. But none of this is good news."

"Don't I know it," she murmured as she slowed to turn.

CHAPTER ELEVEN

Friday, February 11
2:25 a.m.
Milwaukee, Wisconsin

THE AREA SURROUNDING GENERAL Mitchell
International Airport in Milwaukee looked like any other. Fast
food joints and cheap chain hotels and litter blown by gusty
winds against the fences. At this hour of the morning, traffic was
sparse. The airport remained open around the clock, but few
flights arrived or landed after midnight.

Thorn drove a couple of miles past the airport entrance and
turned west onto a service road. He pulled up next to the sedan in
a dark corner of the remote lot. He handed the keys to Scorpio.

"I'll return this vehicle to the car rental and catch a ride
back. Probably take me thirty minutes or so," Thorn said.

Scorpio struggled out of the back seat, his pockets laden with
everything he'd collected from Mackenzie. Once he was upright
on the pavement, he leaned his head into the cabin. "I have
plenty to do. Don't worry so much."

"Roger that," Thorn replied.

Scorpio closed the door and turned his back on further conversation. As Thorn pulled away, Scorpio made his way to the trunk of his sedan. He pushed the button on the key fob to unlock the trunk and all four doors. He retrieved the laptop and slung the cross-body strap over his head. He closed the trunk and shuffled slowly toward the passenger compartment. Every small exertion almost overcame him. By the time he was seated in the back seat, he was winded and perspiring heavily. He flopped his head on the seat back and closed his eyes to rest.

Exhaustion swallowed him whole and he dozed off. Thorn's voice from the front seat awakened him thirty minutes later.

Scorpio felt the engine idling. He cleared his throat, met Thorn's gaze in the rearview, and asked, "Sorry? I didn't hear you."

"No problem, boss. I asked where you'd like to go?" He paused, glanced at the instrument panel, and returned his gaze to the rearview. "It's zero-three-thirty-three hours here. Still time to find a bed for the night before we tackle twelve to fourteen hours back to Rapid City if you'd like."

Scorpio figured Thorn was merely offering him an opportunity to save face. It was the sort of thing a military officer like Thorn had been trained to do. Scorpio hated it, along with every other form of solicitous behavior foisted upon him these days. One more thing Reacher would pay for soon.

"You still okay to drive?"

"Yes, sir."

Scorpio considered his next move. He wanted to get home, but he had to admit he wasn't likely to find anything he was looking for there. There was no point in traveling 840 miles home only to turn around and come back.

"Let's get a few hours west of here before we stop. Somewhere in Iowa. Not a chain hotel." Putting a couple of state lines behind them made visceral sense. Scorpio lived by his wits and always had. Jurisdictional boundaries could only help him. Law enforcement agencies were loath to cooperate or even communicate with each other. He had exploited that weakness more than once to his great advantage. Deploying the tactic here felt like the right thing to do, too.

"You got it, boss. Copy that," Thorn replied. He pulled his seatbelt over his shoulder and clicked it into place. Scorpio felt the transmission slide into reverse. Thorn rolled the Lincoln back a few feet before he cut the wheel and engaged the transmission for a slow and easy forward takeoff.

Scorpio's patience snapped. "For cripes' sake, Thorn. I'm not about to fall into the footwell. Just drive the damn car."

"Ten-four, boss," Thorn said, but his heart was not in it. Scorpio could tell. The Lincoln accelerated slowly, made a smooth right turn onto the street, and rolled westward to the expressway entrance ramp.

Once they were underway, Scorpio extracted the laptop from its case and opened the clamshell. He fished around in his pocket for Mackenzie's flash drive and inserted it into the laptop's USB port.

In the plush silence of the Lincoln's passenger cabin, Scorpio heard the laptop's soft whir as it attempted to access the data on the flash drive. Half a moment later, a message popped up on the center of his screen. His nostrils flared. The drive was encrypted and required a specialized thirty-two-character password.

Sweat trickled down his temples and dropped from his jaw. His body was shaking and felt clammy inside his coat.

Before his injuries, Scorpio could easily have solved these problems. He'd had appropriate equipment back in his laundromat office. He also possessed the mental capacity to handle much more complicated data tasks. Not tonight. He needed rest.

He ejected the flash drive and replaced its cap. He closed the laptop and returned it to the case. And then he smiled slightly as understanding dawned. The flash drive needed sophisticated security to protect the contents. Because whatever was stored behind the encryption barriers was worth protecting. He was on the right track. He could feel it.

Scorpio spent about a nanosecond thinking about what to do next. He owned the kind of equipment he needed to breach the encryption on the flash drive. His stuff was all set up in an environment where he could get all the privacy in the world. He could take his time. Do it right.

He cleared his throat, which caused Thorn to meet his eyes in the rearview.

"Let's stop for coffee and a bathroom break and fill up the gas. After that, we'll head back to Rapid City," he said.

"Roger that, boss," Thorn replied. He used his turn indicator and took the first exit off the interstate.

CHAPTER TWELVE

Friday, February 11
4:05 a.m.
St. Louis, Missouri

OTTO PULLED INTO THE driveway at U Store Stuff and peered through the windshield. It was early, dark, and cold, but the icy rain had stopped. The place was deserted.

The business was contained in an enormous lot, surrounded by an eight-foot chain link fence topped with razor wire. The entrance was blocked by an equally enormous electronic gate. Surveillance cameras were mounted along the fence and on the buildings. Sometimes these places used mock cameras as a deterrent. They didn't actually record anything. Which meant it was impossible to know whether the area was monitored constantly by a remote team.

From her vantage point, more than two dozen parallel rows of rectangular yellow brick buildings with flat roofs were laid out inside the fence. Each building was divided into individual units, visually defined by gray roll-up garage doors. The building rows were separated by wide lanes of pavement roomy enough for moving vans and forklifts to maneuver while loading and unloading. The lot was large enough to add more buildings.

There was no guard shack. She eased her vehicle up to the keypad, lowered the window, and reached out to punch in the code the Boss had supplied. A green light flashed on the keypad, and the gate rolled silently from left to right, opening wide enough to admit an eighteen-wheeled car hauler.

She rolled the rental vehicle through the open gate. Once she was past the sensors, the gate reversed course and closed solidly behind her. Lights were posted randomly in the lot, casting too many concealing shadows. She swiveled her head in all directions but saw no headlights or taillights anywhere. She lowered the window and heard no growling engines in the clear-aired darkness.

The unit she wanted was D-6. She followed the signs until she located block D, two lanes east of the main entrance, and turned left, heading north. Number six was one unit south of the center of the building on the west side.

The D-6 garage door was closed. It was secured like many others, with a long-shackle, heavy steel padlock. There were no vehicles parked nearby. Row D and all ten of its units were quiet and undisturbed. As were the units in Row E, opposite.

She pulled to the north end of the building and parked out of sight. She squelched her headlights and hunkered down to wait.

Less than thirty minutes later, a dark sedan pulled up to the gate and punched a code. Otto's stomach clenched. She regulated her breathing while she watched the sedan enter the lot and drive straight to unit D-6.

He parked, left the engine running and headlights on, and got out of the car.

From this distance, she saw only a neat, compact man fitting retired FBI Special Agent Terrence Bramall's general size and shape. He approached the D-6 garage door and examined the padlock. He lifted it away from the hasp, hefted it in his cupped palm, and let it fall against the door with a loud clang.

He returned to his sedan and opened the trunk, pulled out long-handled bolt cutters, and approached the padlock again. He adjusted the blades. One swift, hard push of the handles was all it took. The blades cut through the steel shackle, and the lock fell heavily to the ground. He propped the bolt cutters against the exterior wall and bent to lift the steel door by the handle.

She heard the door creaking as it rolled up. Bramall disappeared inside. Definitely breaking and entering. No question.

She slipped her rental into drive and accelerated quickly toward the open door. She faced the door head-on and flipped the headlight switch to bright, flooding the scene with more blinding illumination.

He turned toward the lights and raised his forearm to block his eyes. Otto drew the Glock and stepped out of the vehicle, poised behind the door. She assumed a textbook shooter's stance. The rental's engine idled quietly.

"Show me your hands," she said, as she'd been trained to do.

He held both gloved hands up, palms out, squinting against the lights. So far, so good.

She asked, "Terry Bramall?"

"That's right. Who's asking?"

"Show me your ID." She didn't tell him to take it slow and easy because if he was Bramall, he'd know. If he wasn't Bramall, she had a whole new set of problems.

He held his right hand up, palm out, and reached across his chest with his left arm to enter his breast pocket. Slowly, he pulled out his ID, opened the wallet, and held it out.

She left the flimsy safety of the vehicle's door and kept her gun pointed center mass as she approached him. He made no false moves or threatening gestures.

From twenty feet away, she could see he held out his private investigator's license issued by the state of Illinois, but she couldn't read it. She hoped she wouldn't need to. She walked closer until she could see that the photo matched his face. Brown hair, neatly combed, a lean and ageless face, which she pegged somewhere between sixty and seventy years old, which was exactly right.

"Open your coat."

He used his right hand to do as she demanded. His pistol rested in its holster, snugged securely against his ribs.

"Keep your left hand extended and your right hand holding your lapel," she said as she approached. Still beyond his arm's reach, she stopped. Quickly, she glanced beyond him to his left side and then his right, confirmed no one was inside.

The headlights illuminated the contents of Unit D-6 well enough.

A wooden pallet held stacks of shrink-wrapped boxes. She recognized the pharmaceutical company logo from the evidence envelope Noble had shown her.

"I suspect we're on the same team here. I promise not to shoot you if you return the favor," Bramall said.

Holding her Glock in position with one hand, she displayed her badge wallet with the other. "FBI Special Agent Kim Otto."

"I figured. I recognized the moves. Retired from the bureau's Chicago field office myself a few years back. Can I put my hands down now?"

"Slowly." She nodded toward the boxes. "You're a long way from Chicago, Bramall. What's going on here?"

"You were watching. You saw me arrive and cut the lock off. Everything was exactly like this when I opened the garage door not twenty seconds before you pulled up." He gestured toward the boxes. "You know I don't own this stuff and can't tell you what's going on here. Otherwise, I'd have had a key to that lock, and I don't."

"All I know so far is that you broke in here. Breaking and entering is a crime, which you well know. Unless you own the place or have permission to enter from the owners. You tell me."

He smiled. And nodded his head a couple of times in approval. "You must be a good agent. Never jump to conclusions. Analyze the evidence. You had good training. And I really appreciate that you didn't shoot me. Where's your partner?"

She nodded in return. "You've been retired a while. There's been a lot of changes at the Bureau."

He arched his eyebrows. "Such as?"

She tapped the waterproof, night vision camera attached to her coat. "Field agents can be monitored twenty-four seven now. This body cam records everything that's happening. Full HD video at a 140-degree viewing angle. Transmits to the bureau in real time. Response times near airports are damn fast now, too. Which means you could harm me, but you wouldn't get away with it."

"In my day, agents worked in pairs. I didn't know about the body cams, but I figured they didn't send you to the middle of nowhere in the dead of night by yourself." He paused. "Regardless, you're in no danger from me."

She paused another half second and then lowered her gun.

She believed him. Simple as that. He put his ID back in his pocket and dropped his hands to his sides.

"What's going on here?" she said again.

He answered easily. "I'm looking for two missing women. My investigation started in Lake Forest, Illinois, and led me here. I haven't had a chance to check this place out yet."

"Who are the women?" she asked, which was a sort of test, too.

"A housewife from Lake Forest. Jane Mackenzie. And her sister, Rose Sanderson."

"Who hired you to find them?"

Bramall cocked his head. "Under different circumstances, I might protect my client's identity. In this case, it's no secret. Jane's husband, Rex Mackenzie hired me."

"When was that?"

"They've been gone about two weeks."

"*Two weeks?*" She arched her eyebrows. "It took you *two weeks* to trace a housewife and her sister from Lake Forest to St. Louis? Three hundred miles? You could drive that distance in half a day."

"Everything always sounds easier than it is," he said, with a defensive frown, followed by an all over shiver. "It's damn cold out here. You want to look around inside, or you want to keep insulting me for a while first?"

She grinned. Everything in the Boss's file on this guy suggested he was a straight shooter. He had retired honorably from the FBI with a full pension and a spotless record. His private investigator's license issued by the state of Illinois was squeaky clean. If he was dirty, she'd seen no evidence of it so far.

The only glitch was that Noble claimed Bramall was traveling with Reacher. She'd met several of Reacher's sidekicks by now. They were almost always involved with law enforcement in some capacity. They were rarely cooperative. Always skeptical and defensive whenever Reacher's name came up. So far, she hadn't met a single one who was willing to answer her questions. Even Noble, come to think of it, had ducked out before she could get any real answers.

Still, she kind of liked Bramall, and he looked harmless enough. So far, anyway.

"Let's see what we've got," she said. She returned her gun to its holster and reached into her pocket for her cell phone. The body cam would do the job for the Boss, but she liked to have personal copies of everything. Just in case.

She opened the video camera on her phone and turned it on. She established time, place, and date on the recording before she aimed the lens at herself and then at Bramall. Then she began a video record of the contents of Unit D-6 while they inspected.

The space was ten feet wide and ten feet deep. Smaller than a single car garage. Dozens of shrink-wrapped boxes were stacked along three walls, leaving the center open to walk around or to use a small forklift, maybe. Had the boxes been abutted to each other, she estimated they'd have created a thick block more than a yard wide, a yard deep, and a yard high.

"This stuff is pristine. Looks like all of these boxes came right off the loading dock at a pharmaceutical company. Like there's an inside man diverting the inventory," she said, partly for the video record. "I see tablets and patches. Mostly fentanyl. A half-dozen boxes of naloxone, which is the antidote. Just in case something goes wrong and somebody overdoses, I guess."

She ran the video until all boxes were captured before she turned to Bramall again. "Do you see anything else?"

Bramall shook his head and did not reply.

According to Noble, there was no way to get pharmaceutical grade opioids like this on the black market anymore. And yet, here they were.

Bramall had claimed not to know the drugs were here, but he didn't seem surprised, either. Which meant he wasn't quite the good guy she had believed.

CHAPTER THIRTEEN

Friday, February 11
5:10 a.m.
St. Louis, Missouri

OTTO STOMPED HER FEET to gin up some body heat, but she was losing the battle. February was no warmer in Missouri than most other places in the country north of the Mason-Dixon line.

Snidely, she said, "Is your client a doctor? Pharmacist? Pharmaceutical rep?"

Bramall grunted. "Not even close."

"But this is his storage unit, right?"

Bramall shrugged.

"Where'd he get all this stuff?"

Bramall said nothing.

She walked the video around the room making sure to capture barcodes and product numbers wherever possible. The process didn't take long. She snapped a few still shots in case she needed them for witnesses.

Which was when she noticed one row along the south wall of the unit where the boxes were not snugged close to the concrete block. A twelve-inch gap ran the length of the wall behind the boxes. She leaned closer and used the flashlight on her phone to peer into the space.

Recessed from the front edge of the stacks of fentanyl tablets and patches in white boxes, she saw two brown shoeboxes. She bent over to grab one of the shoeboxes, but they were out of her reach. She turned sideways and tried to slip her leg into the opening, but the gap was too narrow, even for her.

She took a few still photos of the shoeboxes in position and then turned to Bramall. "Hand me those bolt cutters. There's something back here."

Instead of handing them over, he said, "They're a bit heavy. Let me."

She moved aside and held the phone's flashlight to illuminate the crevice. He leaned forward holding the long-handled cutters in one hand. He extended his arm and used the closed blades awkwardly to drag the stacked shoeboxes toward him. After a slight struggle, the boxes emerged. Bramall stood aside.

Otto snapped a few more photos before she donned a pair of gloves from her pocket and bent to lift both shoeboxes from the floor. She set them on top of the stack of fentanyl.

The shoeboxes were wide, and the tops were attached on one side. Both boxes once contained women's running shoes, size 8. She set the phone to video and flipped the first box top open. The stench of new money wafted to her nose first, followed by the visual.

Inside the box was cash. Newer bills. Twenties, fifties, and hundreds. Banded together in bricks, maybe an inch thick, as if they'd come straight from the federal reserve. She glanced at Bramall, who was shaking his head.

She opened the bottom box. Also full of cash, as newly stinky as the first.

She turned the video off. "What do you make of all this?"

He shrugged. "Looks like a drug dealer's stash to me. Inventory and revenue, all in one tidy spot."

Otto nodded. She turned the video back on and emptied the contents of both shoeboxes, displaying the stacks of bills and then the empty boxes for the video. She figured each box contained about ten grand. Twenty grand altogether.

At the bottom of the second box was a flash drive. She moved it to the side.

She refilled the boxes and spent half a moment thinking about the flash drive. She should have returned it to the box along with everything else and waited for a warrant. Let the FBI tech team handle the evidence the drive surely contained.

There was a time, not so long ago, when she would have done precisely that. But those days felt like a different lifetime on another planet from the world her job had become.

She tilted the video's all-seeing lens toward the crevice and slipped the flash drive into her pocket. Then she settled the lids on the boxes and put them back where she'd found them.

Neither she nor Bramall spoke while the video was recording. Partly because the images were more likely to be usable as evidence without running commentary. Mainly because neither one wanted to be tied to the images. Not yet, anyway.

She hit the send button to transfer the video to the secure server, where she, Gaspar, and the Boss would have access to it.

Bramall was waiting with his hands in his pockets outside, near the front door. If he saw her take the flash drive, he gave no indication.

"What do you want to do now?" he asked.

She cocked her head. "Did you bring a new padlock to lock this stuff up again?"

He nodded and pulled a heavy-duty padlock from his coat pocket. He yanked the garage door down. He inserted the new padlock to the hasp, which was secured to the brick wall on the right side of the garage door. He shoved the shackle down firmly, and the lock closed with an unnaturally loud click.

Bramall removed an evidence bag from another pocket and bent to lift the lock he'd cut apart off the ground. He slid the destroyed lock into the bag and sealed it. He wrote his initials on the bag along with the date and time. Then he retrieved his bolt cutters and turned to Otto.

"There's an all-night pancake place about a mile up the road. How about I buy you a gallon of coffee, and we can talk?" he asked.

"I love coffee. Lead the way," she replied.

Before they'd moved more than a couple of steps, she heard the growl of a large engine. She glanced toward the gate at the entrance. A black heavy-duty, extended length SUV pulled up to the keypad.

The hair on the back of her neck stood up and her stomach flipped. It was well after five in the morning. Possibly, the driver was on legitimate business, but she doubted it.

A man's arm extended through the open window. He punched a few buttons.

The big gate started its slow roll to open.

There was a slight chance the driver of the Expedition XLT hadn't seen them. Very slight.

Bramall said, "Come on. Let's go."

"Cut the lights," she said, as they hustled to their vehicles. They extinguished their headlights and rolled as quietly as possible away from Unit D-6, to the spot behind the adjacent building where she'd waited for Bramall.

She heard the big entrance gate open and the black SUV's engine growled as it crossed into the lot. The gate closed solidly behind it.

She watched as the Expedition headed directly to Unit D-6 and pulled straight in toward the garage door, just as Bramall had done.

Two big men climbed out. They might have been talking to each other, but from this distance, she couldn't hear the conversation. She found the Boss's cell phone and pushed the call button.

When he answered, she whispered, "You got eyes on this?"

"Yes. Running the license plates on that SUV now." He paused. She heard him talking to someone else before he continued. "Lay low. Wait it out."

Her lip curled. No questions asked that the Boss didn't want answered.

He said, "Can you get out of there right now?"

She glanced toward Bramall. He was watching from his sedan slightly behind and to her right. "Without subduing those two guys first? Doubtful."

He sighed. "Wait until they leave, and then you and Bramall get out. We'll pick them up after. When they're on the street."

She kept her eyes on Unit D-6.

These guys knew what they were doing. One carried a shotgun. Two loud blasts with door breaching rounds, placed near the hasp's attachment to the brick wall, did the job. The hasp jumped away from its fasteners and hung limply, still attached to the door by the hasp's opposite side. Bramall's heavy-duty lock was still in place.

The guy dropped the shotgun, bent to the ground, pushed the door up, and opened it wide.

"They're in," she said to the Boss, although he probably had a better view of the action than she did, given all the cameras perched around.

Before she could say more, Bramall pulled his sedan forward and accelerated hard toward Unit D-6.

"Oh, crap!" Otto exclaimed under her breath.

CHAPTER FOURTEEN

Friday, February 11
5:35 a.m.
St. Louis, Missouri

BRAMALL SCREECHED TO A stop behind the black SUV, blocking any attempted getaway.

She disconnected the call, turned her engine off, activated the body cam, drew her Glock, and followed Bramall on foot. She smelled the earlier shotgun blasts on the breeze.

Weapon held ready, she rounded the corner and crossed to the building where Bramall had parked. She crouched low and moved silently along the brick wall toward the two vehicles.

She was three units away when two warning shots from a handgun rang out.

"Drop your weapons!" Bramall demanded as he rushed forward. Shouts carried clearly on the night air.

All three men were now inside Unit D-6, out of her visual range.

She heard male voices but not distinct words.

The only one she recognized was Bramall's. The other two were mid-range with Chicago accents. She crept closer.

One man yelled, "You's not FBI anymore, Bramall."

The other guy screamed, "What the hell do you think you're doing?"

Bramall shouted, "Get down on the ground with your hands behind your back."

"Yeah, sure. We'll just do that," the first one jeered. "Big Mike would be thrilled."

She heard another shot, followed by rounds from three weapons that ricocheted inside the brick walls of the storage unit. She flattened her back against the wall to avoid any stray shots that might exit toward her, alert for a good chance to lean in and aim in the right direction.

The shooting stopped as abruptly as it started. She felt engulfed by a cloud of ominous silence.

After a moment, she inched closer to the door and craned her neck around to get a quick look inside.

The two thugs lay on the ground, face up, glassy eyes open, but lifeless.

Bramall stood beyond the seeping pools of blood, hands at his sides. He was breathing hard.

"Were you hit?"

He patted himself down and shook his head. "Amazing, but no."

Otto nodded. The thugs were exceptionally bad marksmen. She kicked their pistols out of reach, just in case.

Bramall was a better shot than his file reflected, too. Both bodies sported multiple ragged red splotches on their torsos.

She took a deep breath and moved into the open maw of the unit, avoiding the pools of blood on the floor. "You okay?"

"Yeah," he replied, with a slight quiver in his voice. "Just peachy."

She walked over toward the bodies, checked pulses to be sure they were both dead, and kicked their weapons out of reach for extra insurance.

"What the hell was that all about, Bramall? Did they say *Big Mike*? You know him?"

"These two are—were—muscle for Mike Bavolsky. Wetwork, mostly," Bramall said, nodding. "Bavolsky's a two-bit Polish mobster. Took over from his old man about ten years ago. His territory's on the north side of Chicago. Runs drugs, protection rackets, money laundering, illegal gambling. You name it, that's Big Mike's business."

She cocked her head, trying to make sense of events. "You know Bavolsky and his goons from your FBI days, I take it?"

"I arrested these thugs a couple of times, back in the day. I recognized Jocy Two when they got out of that SUV. The other one is Little Hugh. Usual story. Scooped 'em up. They served some time. Got out and went back to work. Served some more." His breathing had slowed, almost to normal. "Both of them escaped a death sentence for two murders in Kentucky. Popped a bookie with sticky fingers. They beat it because Big Mike eliminated the witnesses against them. The cases fell apart. Illinois found something else to charge them with and, last I knew, both were still locked up at Statesville."

She tilted her head toward the two goons. "So you're figuring you did the world a favor here, getting rid of these guys."

"Damn straight. Nobody's gonna lose any sleep about it, either." Bramall jutted his chin in her direction. "But don't get on your moral high horse. They knew me. They came at me. I shot back. Total self-defense. No question."

"You didn't lure these thugs here so you could have your shootout, I suppose?"

"Now why didn't I think of that." He laid the sarcasm on as thick as peanut butter on bread.

She nodded. "Okay. How did they know you were here?"

"What makes you think they were here for me?" He scowled, still breathing hard. "You could just as easily have been the target as me."

She cocked her head and shot him a glare.

"Not to mention," he waved his palm toward the storage unit. "There's at least a couple million dollars' worth of drugs and cash in here, in case you've forgotten."

"Let's get back to that. Where'd this stuff come from? Who stashed the drugs and cash here?"

"Good questions," he replied as if he didn't know the answers. Maybe he didn't.

But she wasn't as willing to believe him as she was a half hour ago.

She nodded like she'd accepted his version of events, even though the entire situation was just a little too convenient for her taste.

She said, "You know how it works. The investigation will sort everything out. After they process the scene and so forth."

"Yeah. I'll make some calls. Get a team going." He holstered his pistol and found his phone.

She noticed his hands shaking a little. She checked her watch. It would be daylight soon. "Can we still close that door? Keep the curious eyes away until our guys get here?"

He walked toward the garage door. While his back was turned, she snapped a few photos of the two dead men, sent them to the Boss, and slipped her phone into her pocket.

"Come outside. I'll get the door over the hole, at least," he said.

She watched Bramall reach up to the rope pull and give it a good yank. The steel screeched and resisted, but miraculously, the wheels rolled along the overhead track all the way down to the pavement.

When the door was closed again, she photographed the damage, which was mostly to the brick wall.

Shooting a padlock open with a gun was a Hollywood myth. She'd seen the tests. Even ran a few herself. The two goons must have known that, too. Probably because they'd had similar experiences before.

Joey Two had aimed his shotgun carefully at the brick where the hasp was mounted and blown the hasp off the brick wall. The shots had damaged the bricks, as he'd intended. But the padlock itself was still intact, and its shackle remained secure on the opposite side of the hasp.

Bramall picked up a few big chunks of brick and shoved them into the damaged wall. He propped what was left of the hasp into place, like putting a broken pencil back together. The hasp wouldn't hold. But from a reasonable distance, a casual observer might not realize the hasp was barely hanging on and could be removed with a sharp tug.

The drugs and cash in Unit D-6 demanded better security until they could be collected by the DEA or the FBI or even local law enforcement.

Bramall turned, walked out of earshot, and talked quietly on the phone. While he was occupied with his call, the Boss's phone vibrated in her pocket with a new text message. The timing confirmed he still had eyes on the situation and help was coming.

She read her orders at a glance. "Get out. Now."

Bramall finished talking and returned. "I called in a couple of favors. They're on the way."

She nodded.

He used his boot to jam the door so that it couldn't be opened again without effort.

Bramall said, "I'll hang around here. Explain things."

She gave him a level stare. "Just how are you going to explain all those opioids in there? And the cash?"

He shrugged. "It'll be better for both of us if you're not here when they arrive. Maybe get some sleep. You look like you could use it. I'll call you in a few hours when I'm done. Buy you that coffee I promised. We can talk."

Otto cocked her head and stuffed her hands into her pockets. Damp cold had seeped into her very pores. She shuffled her feet to work up a bit more body heat and narrowed her gaze to think.

Could she trust Bramall? She still didn't know who leased this unit. Or who owned the drugs. Or where that money came from. Or a hundred other things that mattered.

But she was tired. She'd function better with sleep. The Boss was watching things. And there would be several hours of work to do here before Bramall would be free to talk anyway.

"Okay. Here's my number. Call me when you're done here. I'll find a hotel near the airport and get a few hours' sleep." She sent him a text from her cell phone, covered a yawn with her palm, and walked back to her rental.

Three yards away, she turned. "Where is your client, anyway?"

His eyebrows raised all the way to his hairline, and his eyes widened to the size of nickels. "Rex Mackenzie? Home asleep in his bed in Lake Forest, I assume. Where else would he be?"

"Check your voicemail. See if he's called. Because he's not home and we can't find him." She nodded toward the garage door but kept walking backward toward her vehicle. "Now I'm wondering about those thugs. If they weren't after you, did Big Mike send killers for Mackenzie?"

Bramall's eyes widened further, but he shrugged and said nothing.

CHAPTER FIFTEEN

Friday, February 11
8:45 a.m.
St. Louis, Missouri

SHE OPENED ONE EYE when the phone began vibrating on the bedside table, bouncing like a tap dancer. When she saw the caller-ID, she pulled the phone to her ear and closed both eyes again. She needed another few hours' sleep before she could hope to function.

She managed a garbled, "Otto."

"Good morning, Sunshine. Aren't you awake yet?" Gaspar asked.

She groaned.

He chuckled. "Okay. I'll talk first. I've seen the videos from your body cam at Unit D-6, and the footage you uploaded from your phone. Looks like Bramall is involved in this thing up to his neck. What's your take?" Gaspar asked.

She heard him sipping something. Sickeningly sweet coffee, most likely. He usually filled a smallish cup with half espresso, half milk, and enough sugar to rot every tooth in his head.

"Same as yours," she mumbled into the pillow.

"That's only the first thing. He arrived at that storage unit fully prepared to break in and leave without the owner's knowledge. Which means he probably knew what was inside."

"Or at least he suspected some kind of contraband," she said quietly, head still on the pillow, eyes still closed, drifting toward sleep. "He didn't seem shocked when he saw the stash. But he wasn't pleased, either."

Gaspar paused a moment, considering. "Okay. I can go with that. For now."

Someone rapped hard knuckles on her door.

"Room service," the guy said from the hallway.

She hadn't ordered room service. Her eyes popped open, and her heartbeat quickened.

"Don't panic," Gaspar said in her ear. "I ordered coffee and pastries for you. Rise and shine. We've got work to do."

The waiter knocked again, harder. She groaned, slid out of bed, and padded to the door to let him in with the tray.

While he set up, collected her signature, and left, Gaspar kept talking. "Unit D-6 was leased by T. Mackenzie."

"Who is T. Mackenzie?"

"I figure it could be Theodore Rex Mackenzie. Could be Tiffany Jane Mackenzie. Could be someone else entirely," he said.

Her sleep-fogged brain wasn't tracking well enough.

"The unit was leased about six months ago. Paid up for a full year at the time."

She gave in and poured black coffee into one of the cups. "And when did Mackenzie store the drugs and money in the storage unit?"

"Can't say. Because of the security setup at U Store Stuff, there's no entry or exit log. No way to monitor when items are stored or retrieved. Which they claim is a personal privacy issue, but it sounds like a haven for crooks and thieves to me."

The coffee was pretty good, actually. She ignored the pastries. Gaspar was the one who mainlined sugar every morning. Black coffee started her engines just fine.

"Everything out there is monitored. Cameras all over the place. A keypad code is required for entry to the lot. Some electronic record should exist," she said, feeling a bit more awake, pacing the room in an attempt to stay that way.

"The Boss is working on that. The entry codes could be tied to the units. Which could mean visitors in and out show up on a log somewhere."

"At least the honest visitors. Assuming there were any," she replied. The caffeine had kicked in. She wouldn't sleep now even if she went back to bed. "Any luck tracing the serial numbers and barcodes on those drugs?"

"That's where things start to get interesting," Gaspar said.

"How so?"

"Pharmaceuticals are regulated and monitored more closely than used plutonium, right?"

"Yeah, well, not that many people have used plutonium laying around."

He replied, "True. But every medicine chest in America probably has a few pain pills in it left over from a root canal or an appendectomy. Pills that can be stolen. It's all traceable. In theory, we can find out everything we need to know by looking at the package. Or, if there's no packaging, the actual pills are stamped with traceable numbers, too."

"Sounds like good news," she said, hopefully.

"Every grain of controlled substances contained in those pills and patches *should* be traceable, yes," Gaspar said.

"Let me guess. Although the drugs *should* be traceable, they're not because…" her voice trailed off.

"Exactly." His tone conveyed the approval that a professor might lavish upon a particularly apt pupil. "According to the databases, none of those pills or patches in Unit D-6 were ever actually manufactured at all."

She groaned but did not reply. Somehow, she wasn't surprised.

He finished the thought. "Which means we have no idea where they came from. Or when or how. Or who stored them in Unit D-6, for that matter."

She paused a few moments, struggling to get her brain in gear. "What about the cash? On each of the paper wraps around those bills, there were identification numbers. Have you been able to trace them?"

"Yes. They came from the Chicago Federal Reserve Bank, according to all the computers." Gaspar said. "Which at least ties everything to Chicagoland. It gives us a place to start looking for disappearing drugs."

Otto nodded and then replied, "It does. What about those two dead thugs?"

"Bramall knows better than to lie to a federal investigator," was his smug response.

She said, "He knows more than enough to be dangerous on a lot of levels, it seems to me."

"And don't you forget it, Suzie Wong."

She scowled. Gaspar couldn't see her, but he knew her well enough to guess her reaction. He moved on. "It's just like Bramall said. Those two were foot soldiers in Big Mike Bavolsky's mob.

He's a two-bit gangster compared to his father, but he's looking to
move up in the criminal world. He's at the center of a big multi-
agency investigation right now. Which means he's nervous, too."

"When he gets wind of what happened to his guys and who
killed them, Bramall's gonna be looking over his shoulder for
the rest of his life," she said.

She was ambivalent about Bramall. He'd been an FBI agent
once. And a damn good one. She didn't want to believe he'd
gone sideways. Not without a lot more evidence than they had
right now. But something wasn't kosher with the guy.

Otto finished the coffee and poured another cup. "Bramall's
not sitting around waiting for Big Mike to kill him, I hope."

"Interesting you should ask." He paused. "You're fully
awake now, right?"

She widened her eyes. "Why?"

"Because all that was background. This part is important."

She sat on the edge of the bed with her coffee. The sheets
were still warm, and she longed to climb back under the covers
and sleep a while longer. "I'm listening."

"The bodies were moved."

CHAPTER SIXTEEN

Friday, February 11
9:15 a.m.
St. Louis, Missouri

"THE THUGS?" OTTO SAT upright. "Moved? Where?"

"Good question."

She ran a palm across her face and scrunched her eyes closed to think. "Bramall moved two bodies and that SUV? By himself?"

"Dunno." He paused like he had more to say.

"What?"

"You're listening, right?"

"What?" she squawked, like an irritated parrot.

"When the locals arrived at the scene, Unit D-6 was empty. Completely empty. To be clear," he paused, "the drugs and the money are also gone."

"Where did they go?"

"Still working on that. The Boss's video missed it somehow. Looks like someone tampered with the cameras."

More sleep was now totally off the agenda. She took a deep breath and a swig of coffee and walked toward the bathroom to get dressed. "Where's Bramall?"

"His sedan is parked in a remote lot at the St. Louis airport. But he's nowhere to be found."

"So far," she said.

"He's in the wind. Along with his client. And the two sisters."

"So we're back to square one?" The news was simultaneously energizing and exasperating. She could feel his frustration through the phone, too, along with something else.

"You can't really think I missed it." He tisk, tisked.

"Missed what?"

"Give me some credit here," he mocked, sounding hurt, which was a total ploy.

She figured he meant the flash drive she'd lifted from the shoebox. But she wasn't about to admit to evidence tampering. Not on a monitored call. Nor was he likely to be more specific, and for the same reason.

Besides, she had nothing to tell him on that score anyway. She couldn't open the flash drive. She'd tried. The encryption was too sophisticated for her laptop. She could break into the files back at the Detroit Field Office. Which was where she was headed next.

She said, "Where are you?"

"Still in Houston."

"What are you doing there, again?" Something was up. She could feel it. Call it cop's intuition or whatever. But Gaspar hadn't been the same since he'd been shot in Palm Beach. He'd been on leave for too long, and then returned to light duty. He wasn't bouncing back.

She was worried about him this time. Really worried.

With the change in their assignment from intel gathering to an active manhunt, her concerns were even more justified.

He said, "How about you meet me here and I'll catch you up?"

She considered the suggestion for a nanosecond. Resources were available to her in Houston. Not to mention how much warmer its February weather was compared to Detroit. She'd been cold all the way to her bones lately and that junket to Palm Beach sunshine a few weeks ago was nothing but a distant memory.

In Houston, she could sit down with Gaspar and find out exactly what was going on with him.

She opened her laptop to search. "Next flight from St. Louis to Houston leaves in three hours. Around two hours flight time. An hour to circle and then on the tarmac waiting for a gate, if history is any teacher. I can be there by late afternoon, if we're not delayed."

"I'll text you the address. And I'll keep digging for info on all the parties involved in the case," he paused briefly. "Do we have any actual intel that Reacher is anywhere near this thing?"

She understood what he meant. She cocked her head to think about known facts. "Noble believes Reacher may know where the sisters are. Which suggests Reacher is keeping in touch with them, perhaps."

"Do you trust Noble?"

"No reason not to."

"So far. That you're aware of."

"Noble is DEA, and the guy knows way more about heroin than we do. He's credible enough that the Boss is worried about all this. Which is why we are where we are." She ran a hand through her hair. "I'd bet a beer that it's possible Reacher's around somewhere."

Gaspar's tone turned deadly serious. "But you haven't seen him, or heard from him, or even *smelled* him, right?"

"Right." She smiled. She believed she'd smelled Reacher in the past. Gaspar had never accepted her olfactory senses as accurate.

"And you would *tell* me if you had seen him or heard from him or *smelled* him, right?"

"Of course." She meant it. But his skepticism was justified. She'd held things back from him before. She'd probably do so again. He knew it. She knew he knew. Which changed nothing.

His voice was low, quiet, all trace of teasing gone. "You think he's mellowed somehow, Kim. But you're wrong."

He was still talking about Reacher. He could have been warning her about the Boss. She didn't argue, but she didn't agree, either.

He said, "We don't have enough intel and what we do know has more holes than Swiss cheese. We can't say who our friends are at the moment."

"Agreed." She didn't promise anything. Because she needed flexibility. She had no idea what might happen next.

She changed the subject. "The Boss knows more than he's telling us."

"So what else is new?"

"How did he know I'd find Bramall at the storage unit? Surveillance of some kind, right?"

"Likely. And not unusual. Bramall drove from Chicago in his personal sedan. He probably had a cell phone on him," Gaspar said.

She replied, "Which means the boss could trace him, sure. He'd know where Bramall came from. The direction he was traveling. But he couldn't predict Bramall's destination if he had nothing but tracking devices."

Gaspar sighed. "So his crystal ball is better than yours. Or he's a good guesser."

"I'm going with good guesser," she said, not kidding.

"Really? How unlike you."

She laughed. "Okay, how about educated guesser."

"Meaning what?"

"I think he was tracking Bramall initially. But then, once he saw the general direction Bramall was headed, made an educated guess about the destination."

"That storage unit is near a busy regional airport. There's a lot of other places in the general vicinity Bramall could have been headed." Gaspar gave the situation a couple of beats, "It's more likely the Boss has some inside intel he's not sharing."

"And what would that be?"

"He's been on this less than twenty-four hours. But he knew a few names and dates, and he had access to Noble's DEA investigation files."

"Right." She waited.

"My guess? He found something in Noble's files that connected the Chicago mobster, Big Mike Bavolsky, to Unit D-6. Bramall is based in Chicago. Mackenzie is based in Chicago. Lots of Chicago connections going on. The Boss probably made the relatively short leap from one to the other." His phone clicked to signal another call. "I've gotta go. We'll talk when you get here."

After he hung up, she sipped her coffee and thought about the sequence of events. The Boss had sent her to St. Louis within a few moments of when Noble was called to Lake Forest. The timing was suspect.

Which probably meant the Boss sent Noble in the opposite direction from the drugs and cash stored in Unit D-6.

The only reason the Boss would bother had to be Reacher.

Gaspar must have already come to the same conclusion, and he was clear-eyed about Reacher. As far as Gaspar was concerned, Reacher was a dangerous vigilante. Simple as that.

As it happened, Otto agreed.

But Reacher was more complicated. Dangerous vigilante wasn't the only way she'd describe him.

It was only the least terrifying.

CHAPTER SEVENTEEN

Friday, February 11
10:15 a.m.
St. Louis, Missouri

SHE'D NAPPED, SHOWERED, DRESSED, made a couple of
phone calls, used the TV checkout option, and was on her way
out the door of her room when her phone rang. She checked the
caller ID. "Otto here. What's up, Noble?"

"I promised you a call when I had something to report.
Which I'd hoped would happen before now. But we're still at the
crime scene in Lake Forest." He paused for a breath. "Things are
going a bit more slowly than I expected."

"What do you know?"

"Not much. Victim ID is proving problematic. The body
was found in the Mackenzie home. More specifically, in the
bedroom Rose Sanderson was using. Made sense to assume the
victim was Rose, although the sisters are twins so it could be
either one."

"Okay. And it's not Rose?"

"We still don't know. The body's been removed to the morgue from the Mackenzie home. DNA will take a while."

"Fingerprints are better, anyway. Identical twins will have identical DNA, but not identical fingerprints. Sanderson's in the databases for sure. All Army personnel are printed, and DNA swabbed these days."

"You'd think so," Noble sighed. "Problem is, the victim doesn't have any usable fingerprints. Which, as you know, is odd but not freakish. It happens."

"Did you check with the Army? If Rose had fingerprints, you know the victim's not likely to be her, right?"

"Unless her fingerprints were altered after her discharge, Rose's prints should be in the system. And we're still checking. It's not as easy to get data like that about an inactive soldier, believe it or not," he replied.

"Oh, I believe it. Remember me? I'm the one completing the background check on a guy who's fallen off the face of the earth." She paused. "What about Jane? Was she on the known traveler list? Or registered with the global reentry plan? She'd have had to leave fingerprints for that if nothing else."

"Working on it, Otto. These things don't happen as quickly as you see on TV, you know. Procedures need to be followed. The scene is taking a while to process. This is a monstrously big house," he replied.

"So you just called to tell me you have nothing to tell me?" she asked.

"Not exactly. This thing is getting more complicated. I'm not sure where it's going. But I need to find Reacher more urgently now. How about we work together on that?"

"I already have a partner."

"Not the way I've heard it," he said.

"What do you mean?"

"Scuttlebutt is that Gaspar's on his way out. He should have been out a few years ago when he was wounded on the job. But they made him a charity case and kept him on a desk because the bosses felt guilty."

Otto couldn't argue about Gaspar's history. Partly because she didn't know anything more. And, as he would have said, it was what it was. "What's your point?"

"Since he teamed up with you, he's been shot twice more. He's still not cleared for active duty. Nor will he be. And he's got a new baby to go with the crew he already had. A stay-at-home wife, too." Noble paused again and took a deep breath she could hear across the miles. "Come on, Otto. Use your head. Exactly how far up the priority list do you think finding Reacher is for a guy in Gaspar's situation?"

"Tread carefully there," she said quietly, but her nostrils flared, and her face warmed with anger. Gaspar had worked through the pain. He'd taken gunfire, some of which was meant for her. He was due some loyalty and respect. If the Boy Detective didn't understand that, she didn't give a damn about him and never would.

Noble said, "Okay. Look at it this way, then. Exactly how much help do you think Gaspar will be if you do find Reacher? Are you willing to take the weight for whatever happens because you can't rely on him?"

She put cold, hard steel in her voice when she replied, "What do you want, Noble? You're suggesting we can't rely on Gaspar, but we can all rely on you? Is that it?"

"Precisely."

"Go to hell." She hung up, breathing heavily. If he'd been standing in front of her, she'd have punched him hard in the gut.

Hard enough to double him and make him feel it next week. Gaspar was twice the man Kirk Noble would ever be. What a jackass.

She retrieved her bag and headed out. Within thirty minutes, she'd stashed her bags in the trunk of her rental car and was on the road. The short drive to U Store Stuff felt familiar on the third trip, although daylight revealed squalor the darkness had concealed. Dirty snow was piled on the shoulders of the divided highway, but the pavement was clear and dry.

The U Store Stuff lot had been dark and quiet last time, but now she noticed papers, empty cups, plastic lids, paper bags, and other trash collecting along the fence. A few vehicles were scattered among the buildings. Men and women dressed in winter coats and boots moved boxes and furniture and countless other items into individual storage units. A few units were being emptied, too.

She pulled into the drive at the end of a long line of vehicles. One by one, they advanced to the keypad, punched in their codes, and drove through the gate. A man stood by the gate passing out flyers and pointing toward the west end of the lot where a group had already gathered.

Otto's rental inched up each time a vehicle passed through the gate until she reached the keypad. She punched in the same code she'd used before and rolled up to the man with the flyers.

"We had five auctions today, but you've missed three already. The next auction is Unit JJ 23." He offered one of the flyers to her before he waved westward. "Follow the vehicles headed that way. Park as close as you can. The auctioneer will direct you."

She nodded and followed the traffic, but she left the line and turned into the alley between Buildings D and E. She approached

D-6, driving slowly. Crime scene techs would have been long gone by now. There hadn't been much to process since the bodies and the drugs were missing. A few bullets, a few more bullet holes. That was about it. Workers were already on the scene repairing the brick that had been damaged by the shotgun blasts.

A cleaning crew was inside the empty unit, scrubbing blood stains from the concrete with a power washer. Red-tinged water circled the floor and drained into a covered hole in the center. Unit D-6 would be ready for the next customer by Monday as if nothing had happened.

Otto drove the length of the alley and pulled around the building. She parked the rental and got out. Her footprints were visible in the snow, as were the tire tracks she and Bramall had left last night. She saw no huge boot prints large enough for Reacher. She looked to her left and then to her right. Storage buildings as far as she could see in both directions.

She'd spent a few minutes online this morning at the U Store Stuff website. This one was the company's largest location. The sitemap showed thirty-four buildings, each with at least five units, ranging in sizes from five-by-five to thirty-by-thirty, for a total of 264 units. Some were big enough to hold vehicles of all kinds, everything from motorcycles to RVs. A few could store the contents of an entire household.

When customers failed to pay the rent, their belongings were sold as is, where is, no questions, no exceptions. Auctions were held almost every day between nine and one, the website said. Buyers were told to bring cash. No checks. No credit. All items required to be removed the day of purchase. "Bring your truck," the website said. "Move it or lose it. No refunds."

The Boss's phone vibrated in her pocket.

CHAPTER EIGHTEEN

Friday, February 11
11:25 a.m.
St. Louis, Missouri

SHE WASTED NO TIME on greetings. "When you ordered me to leave the U Store Stuff lot this morning, I thought you had cops on the way. What did they do, take a vacation en route?"

"Bramall made a call. You were standing right there. What would you have had me do? Leave you to try to explain what the hell you were doing when the cruisers showed up?"

"So you didn't have ears on his call?"

"Not at the time. He was using a burner. It was a reasonable assumption that he'd called the locals to report two deaths and a drug trafficking ring, don't you think?"

She ran a hand over her smoothed hair. "Why did you stop watching him after you sent me out of here?"

"What makes you think I stopped?"

She held onto her patience, but barely. "Then you saw him move the bodies."

He grunted. "Bramall retired from the FBI. He didn't leave his training on the hat rack on the way out."

"Meaning what?"

"Meaning he knew where the cameras were located out there and how to avoid them."

"You blew it. You lost him."

"Not immediately." He blew out a long stream of exasperated air. "The phone call was to an accomplice. After you left, the accomplice didn't show up for six minutes."

"And then?"

"All we have on the video is an empty driveway, a closed garage door, and a few shadows. Exactly like the images we have from before you arrived."

"He looped the video feed," she said, wondering exactly how he managed to do that without the Boss noticing. Which didn't matter, really, except that she might want to try it herself sometime.

"He and his accomplice intended to clean out Unit D-6 and he didn't want to be recorded while they did it," the Boss sounded supremely annoyed, which was unusual, too.

"Bramall is one of us. Why would he want to do that?"

"Because he'd just killed two wise guys," he replied. "Mob bosses don't forgive. They exact an eye for an eye."

"They'd need to find out about it first. Who would have told Big Mike so quickly? Maybe he would have worried when his guys didn't show up back in Chicago, but even that would have taken a few hours."

"True."

"And the shooting was justified. Which means Bramall wouldn't have been arrested. He'd have been on his way pretty quickly." She paused. "So Bramall's actions after he killed those thugs can't be explained by Bavolsky. Or at least, Bavolsky's not all of it."

"There's a lot we don't know about Bramall. Maybe he needs money. Opioids with a street value of a few million dollars and a fair amount of illegally obtained cash provided further incentives," the Boss said.

"Which Bramall knew about before he got there. Or at least, he knew the contents of the storage unit were worth breaking and entering to get." Her thinking felt a little sluggish, but she was coming closer to figuring things out.

The Boss waited while she worked things through.

She said, "So his accomplice was nearby all along. When Bramall called, he arrived quickly. The two of them could have planned to move the drugs and the money, but the bodies were an added complication. They could have left them."

She heard a powerful SUV engine behind her and turned to see a line of vehicles moving toward her from the west end of the lot. The auction was over. They were headed to the next one. She moved aside as the line rolled past.

Each vehicle was large enough to haul cargo away. Most carried only one passenger, probably to help with the heavy lifting. None of the vehicles or passengers were familiar to her.

When the last truck rumbled away, she asked, "So Bramall and his associate put the two bodies into that black SUV they arrived in, probably. Those guys were pretty big. It would have been hard to move them any other way."

"Agreed."

"Bramall moved the drugs and the money out quickly, too. What vehicle did they use to do that?"

"Still checking."

She tried the theory. "Bramall drives his sedan out, and the accomplice drives the victims' SUV. When did the SUV leave the lot?"

He took a big, audible breath. "Operating theory is that the SUV is stored somewhere, with the bodies still inside. Probably in one of those garage-sized storage units out there at U Store Stuff."

"What's the basis for that theory?"

"Bramall had disappeared before the next legitimate customer arrived. Which was sixty-six minutes after you went to the hotel."

She nodded. She figured he could see her. He usually could. "What about the drugs and the cash?"

"It's doubtful the drugs were removed in Bramall's sedan. Not enough room in the trunk."

"The accomplice didn't bring a panel van or something with him?"

The boss paused for a long moment. "It's possible he arrived on foot."

Otto blinked. Every nerve ending in her body came alive. "Meaning he was already in the lot when I arrived."

"Probably."

Anxiety clamped her stomach. "He was there when Bramall broke into Unit D-6. He was there when Bramall killed those two guys."

The Boss didn't reply.

Anxiety grew to anger. "The whole time, he was there. That's what you're saying."

He breathed heavily and said nothing.

Understanding dawned.

"You think it was Reacher," she said flatly.

CHAPTER NINETEEN

Friday, February 11
12:25 p.m.
St. Louis, Missouri

"POSSIBLY," HE SAID, BUT his tone implied certainty.

"And that's why you wanted me to leave the scene before the locals arrived."

"Partially."

"I'm not clear on my mission here. Not twenty-four hours ago you ordered me to find Reacher."

He said nothing.

"So we're about to find him, and then you order me to stand down." Her nostrils flared, and she pressed her lips together to hold her temper in check.

He said nothing.

She closed her eyes, cocked her head, and thought things through. Steadily, she said, "I can think of a half-dozen reasons why you would do that, and none of them are worthy of the FBI."

"When we locate the bodies and the drugs, you'll be among the first to know." His tone was quiet and stern. "Meanwhile, your assignment remains. Find Reacher. I'll handle the rest."

She opened her mouth to argue, but he'd hung up. She threw the phone onto the seat with enough force to make it bounce. She could feel the steam coming from her ears.

He'd said the bodies were most likely stored right here. How could they find Jimmy Two, Little Hugh, and their Expedition, stashed inside one of these units?

Dead humans had no heat signature, which meant thermal imaging of all the big storage units wouldn't help. He probably couldn't get search warrants, even if he'd wanted to, which he didn't. The whole process would take too long and require him to be a lot more transparent with his evidence than he'd ever agree to. A cabinet X-ray system might work, but the tech on those things was iffy at best.

U Store Stuff had hundreds of units on this lot, but not all were large enough to conceal an SUV of that size. And they'd all be leased by someone with a lock and a right to privacy. She could wait until tonight and cut the locks off all of them to check and then replace the locks. Which wasn't feasible.

Okay. Step back. If she couldn't look inside the units, what was the next best thing?

First, she had to figure out which units had the potential to conceal the SUV and the dead bodies inside. Maybe the drugs were inside, too. And if Bramall was the one who stored them, he might come back tonight.

She'd looked at the website and the map of the units on the lot. But the sizes of the individual units were not listed. She could get a look inside one of them, though.

She jumped into her rental and followed the line of vehicles to the last auction of the day. She parked at the end of the building block because the alley between Buildings R and S was already full.

A dozen people left their vehicles and waited in the cold for the auction to begin. A security officer stood near the hasp on the garage door holding a pair of bolt cutters. The auctioneer stood in the center of the closed door, hands in his pockets, waiting for the crowd to settle into silence.

According to the sitemap on the website, some of the units at this end were larger than Building D. Although the garage doors were the same size, meaning the units were the same width, these were deeper, allowing for more property to be stored inside.

All the units were locked. A few of the units had two locks through their hasps instead of one, which probably meant the lessors were delinquent on the rent. The owner added the second lock to prevent the renter from moving his stuff out without paying.

Otto joined the group, standing near the back next to a sturdy woman wearing jeans, boots, and a sheepskin jacket.

"What's inside this one? Got any idea?" Otto asked her.

"Could be a car. Maybe a boat. I got a sweet pair of snowmobiles once. Hard to say." She shrugged. "No way to know until we open the door. Except they always save the big ones for last. The other units went cheap today."

"You buy here regularly?" Otto asked.

She shrugged again. "Sometimes. Depends. But it's pretty much the same crowd all the time, yeah."

"What do you do with the stuff you buy at these auctions?"

The woman stared at her as if she was a few cards short of a full deck. "Sell it. Make a profit. What else?"

Otto nodded. "Right."

The auctioneer declared, "Now this is some serious storage, folks. Unit R-4 is ten-by-thirty, a whopping three hundred square feet of space. Ideal for a five- to seven-bedroom house. This puppy can hold entertainment centers, beds, refrigerators, even your truck. Anything at all could be in here. Today's buyer with enough cash could get an amazing haul. So let's get started."

The auction only lasted fifteen minutes. Three principal bidders broke away from the pack and raised each other several times until two fell silent. A big, brusque man wearing a Stetson won the bid. The small crowd cheered.

He pulled a wad of cash from his pocket and approached the auctioneer. While the paperwork was signed, the crowd thinned, but several spectators stomped around in the cold waiting to see what was inside.

Otto had surreptitiously snapped a few photos of the crowd earlier. She shot a few more of those hanging around until the very end. The sturdy woman in the sheepskin jacket gave up and returned to her truck. The two competing bidders hung around to see what they missed, or maybe to make Stetson guy an offer if he didn't want the booty inside. Both men stuffed hands in pockets and turned up collars.

Finally, the man in the Stetson stuffed the folded paperwork into his pocket and nodded to the security officer. He used a key to remove the U Store Stuff lock and then raised the bolt cutters and snapped the shackle on the owner-supplied lock. Both pieces thudded to the ground while the crowd held its collective breath.

The guy in the Stetson raised the garage door while everyone else watched.

While he emptied the contents of the storage unit into his truck, Otto spent twenty minutes talking to the security guy. He was a rent-a-cop from a local company who knew less about the U Store Stuff facility than Otto did. She took a business card from him and headed toward her rental, empty-handed.

The Boss's phone vibrated. She lifted it from her pocket.

"Otto," she said, still walking.

No greeting, just brief orders. "Bramall's on his way to a private jet. Flight plan says Las Vegas. Air traffic is holding it on the ground. Get on the plane. I've texted you the location."

She'd have protested, but what was the point? "You got things on the ground here, then?"

"Nothing worth watching yet. Get going before Bramall escapes again," he replied before he hung up.

She looked at his text. Bramall's jet was close by. She shrugged and walked back to her rental. On the way, she texted Gaspar to say she'd arrive later than expected.

She found a new burner phone in her bag and fired it up. She sent a text to Lamont Finlay, the man she considered her best source of intel on all things Reacher. Especially things the Boss didn't want her to know.

Her message was only four words: "We need to talk."

CHAPTER TWENTY

Friday, February 11
1:15 p.m.
St. Louis, Missouri

THE PRIVATE JET WAS a Gullstream G-100 perched near the gate. The pilot and co-pilot were aboard. The jet stairs were down, waiting for passengers.

Otto hurried out onto the tarmac, covered the distance to the jet, and hopped up the stairs carrying her bags. She ducked her head through the door as she slipped into the unoccupied cabin. Her breathing returned to normal as soon as she confirmed that neither Bramall nor Reacher was aboard.

The interior of the luxury jet had been modified from an eight-passenger configuration to a roomier six-passenger layout complete with a service bar.

The seats were akin to captain's chairs in an SUV. Larger, higher backs, more room in the seat, more comfortable leather upholstery. The result was compact but high-end private travel most FBI agents could never hope to experience.

Retirement was much plusher for Bramall than Otto's government salary afforded. No matter how much they paid her, she wouldn't have flown in a small jet if a paying client held a gun to her head. Which was practically what the Boss had done. Meaning, she was actively employed, and she had no choice.

Might have been nice if he'd told her what the hell she was supposed to do after she boarded the flight, though.

She moved through to the tail section, stowed her bag, and hunkered down in a seat near the back of the plane to wait.

Even advocates for airplane safety admitted that small aircraft went down at a higher crash rate than commercial jets. An average of five small planes crashed every day in the United States, and a staggering ninety-seven percent of aviation fatalities happened on private planes. The potential for human error was undeniable.

She popped a couple of antacids into her mouth and chewed.

Ten minutes later, the copilot came into the cabin and stood by the open door. Two more passengers hurried across the pavement toward the jet's stairs.

The first to arrive was Rex Mackenzie. She recognized him from the file photos.

The co-pilot said, "Welcome aboard, Mr. Mackenzie."

Mackenzie nodded, raised his index finger to cross his lips, and pointed to his Bluetooth headset attached to his ear. He was on the phone.

He didn't even glance in her direction but took his seat, still on the phone.

Fast on his heels was Bramall. She ducked behind the seat. He didn't notice her as he hustled to get settled and fasten his seatbelt for takeoff.

She waited for the third shoe to drop. When no one else
entered the plane, Otto released the breath she'd been holding.
She hadn't expected Reacher to show up. Not really.

But the Boss had suggested Reacher was the one who had
helped Bramall move the bodies and the drugs from Unit D-6. If
true, where was he now? Las Vegas? Were they flying out to
meet him?

The co-pilot closed the door and returned to the cockpit. The
jet began to taxi toward the runway.

Mackenzie was still engaged in last minute communications
with someone he must have felt was more important.

She made a mental note to check his call records.

The jet taxied into position for takeoff.

The pilot's voice came through the speaker from the cockpit.
"We're number one for takeoff, Mr. Mackenzie. Looks like
we're battling a strong headwind all the way. Expect some
moderate chop."

Her stomach flipped over.

Moderate chop meant way too many bumps and jolts. It
caused variations in airspeed, but the plane remained in positive
control at all times.

Or so the pilots claimed.

They weren't likely to admit otherwise, were they?

She pulled her seat belt a bit tighter. Unsecured objects,
including humans, could be displaced in moderate chop.

From her position in the back and across the aisle, Otto had a
clear view of Mackenzie.

Her sight line to Bramall was blocked by his seat. Which
was fine. If she couldn't see him, he couldn't see her, either.

Once they were airborne, she'd have plenty of time to handle
them.

Mackenzie wrapped up the call and pulled the headset from his ear.

"No word from Jane or Rose?" Bramall asked.

Mackenzie shook his head. "Nothing. We're booked at the Bellagio. Jane likes to stay there."

She crouched low and moved to a closer seat where she could hear their conversation clearly but remain unseen. Acoustics inside the jet were superior. The cabin must have been customized to improve sounds and decrease white noise, or something.

Bramall nodded. "Tell me again why you think they're in Vegas?"

"Educated guess."

"Based on what?"

"I was out of town when Jane sent me that text two weeks ago. She said they wanted a winter break and they'd found a great deal on a last-minute tour to Thailand. To have a little fun," Mackenzie replied. "I didn't expect to hear from them while they were gone, but when I got back, they weren't home."

"You checked with the tour company?"

Mackenzie nodded. "They told me Jane and Rose were booked for the tour, but they didn't show up for departure."

"So you said," Bramall replied. The vibe Otto picked up was that he didn't believe the story. "I don't follow your logic. How does failure to travel to Thailand mean they're actually in Vegas?"

Mackenzie shrugged. "Rose has been through hell, and she's got more medical stuff on the horizon. They're both big gamblers. Poker mostly. And Jane loves to be pampered. Nice spas in Vegas, too."

Bramall cocked his head, eyebrows raised. "I'm not getting this."

"I told you I made an educated guess. I don't know where they are for sure," Mackenzie said. "You know Rose did five tours in Afghanistan and Iraq. She wanted to make a career in the Army, sure. But she loves the desert and hates snow. Probably because of all those years growing up in Wyoming or something. Jane's the same way."

"February in Chicago is damn cold," Bramall spoke slowly as if he was wrapping his head around the idea while ticking off the boxes.

Otto couldn't tell if he thought Mackenzie was being straight with this story or not, but she didn't trust the guy. When a man's wife goes missing, the husband is usually to blame.

Bramall said, "Vegas is warmer, no snow, world-class gambling, and the Bellagio is about as luxurious as it gets."

Mackenzie smiled. "Exactly."

"Makes sense," Bramall said as if it made no sense at all. "Did you check to see if they're registered?"

Mackenzie's eyes clouded. "They're not. At least, not under their own names."

Bramall turned his head and frowned. "Why wouldn't they use their own names?"

"Why would they not show up for a tour they'd paid for? Why leave while I was out of town? Why didn't they tell me where they were going? Why haven't they called? Why haven't they come home?" Mackenzie shook his head and shrugged. "If I knew the answers, I wouldn't need your services, now would I? You tell me."

Bramall must have been totally out of patience because he did exactly that. "Here's how I read things. You're punching way above your weight, Mackenzie."

"Yeah?" Mackenzie jutted his chin forward.

"Yeah. You're a small-time guy who owns a puny dry-cleaning storefront in a bad part of town where only the undertaker would need his suits cleaned."

Mackenzie's face reddened, and his nostrils flared.

Bramall kept pushing. "And a guy like you doesn't own a mansion in Lake Forest with a view of Lake Michigan and a wife as hot and accomplished as Jane. Not without a sizeable helping of graft and corruption."

Otto understood. She opened her jacket, clearing a path to her weapon. The last thing she needed was a brawl at thirty thousand feet in moderate chop.

She sympathized with Bramall, though. He'd spent years investigating guys exactly like Mackenzie. Her gut said this guy was bent. So twisted, he should've been listed in the phone book under corkscrews. The sort of man neither she nor Bramall would cross the street to save from a vicious beating because the odds were that he'd deserved it.

So why was Bramall working for Mackenzie?

Bramall had history with Jane and Rose. That had to be it. Or at least, part of it.

Maybe he'd figured to get more, better, faster intel from Mackenzie if the bastard was comfortable. The best way to achieve that was to make him believe Bramall was actually on his payroll, and make Mackenzie pay dearly for it.

Like a lot of cheaters, Mackenzie probably believed he controlled everyone he employed.

Bramall probably charged Mackenzie five times the going rate to make him feel totally in control.

Guys like Mackenzie were brutal and sly, too. He had his own agenda and the best way to uncover it was to make him want to tell.

Mackenzie said, "You've only been on the case for two days, Bramall. Jane and Rose have been missing for two weeks. You think you can judge me? Dream on."

"Well, let's just see." Bramall cocked his head to convey pure skepticism. Right out of the FBI's playbook. "Neither your wife nor her sister have used their cell phones for the past fifteen days."

"I told you that," Mackenzie sneered. "Some detective you are."

Bramall nodded. "We located the phones."

CHAPTER TWENTY-ONE

Friday, February 11
2:05 p.m.
In flight to Las Vegas

MACKENZIE'S EYES WIDENED. HIS mouth dried up. He coughed before he rasped, "Good work. You know where Jane and Rose are, then?"

"Unfortunately, we don't." Bramall frowned and shook his head.

Mackenzie relaxed slightly. "Why not?"

"It was a little complicated." Bramall cocked his head. "We found both phones in a locker at O'Hare. They were powered off and the batteries were removed, which is probably why your search failed to locate them. Our equipment is better."

"Apparently." Mackenzie scowled. His fist clenched and pounded the upholstered armrest in short, hard, muffled bursts.

He looked like a street fighter. No man liked being told he was inferior. In another time and place, he might have thrown a punch. Good to know.

What else set the guy off, Otto wondered?

"Seems odd, doesn't it? Why not destroy the phones?" Bramall mused.

As if the thought had just occurred to him, Mackenzie demanded to know, "Who stashed the phones there?"

"Funny you should ask. We pinged the phones first, which led us to the specific location at O'Hare. Then we addressed that precise issue. Who did place the phones inside those lockers?" Bramall reported, like to a boss. "We made the assumption that the phones were stored on the last day they were used. We started looking at the CCTV inside O'Hare. It's constant and reliable, but it took us a while to go through all the footage."

Mackenzie nodded with approval. "Makes sense. While Jane still had her phone, she'd have been using it. My wife lived like her phone was an extension of her arm."

Otto heard the past tense, and her heart skipped a beat. *Lived*. Not *lives*. As if Jane was dead and Mackenzie knew it.

The kind of slip-up that a seasoned investigator like Bramall wouldn't miss.

"Makes sense. But didn't happen." Bramall shook his head. "The phones were stored three days *after* they were last used."

Deep white lines etched Mackenzie's mouth and his nostrils flared. "Where was she for those three days, then? Was my wife having an affair?"

"We don't know. Not yet." Bramall narrowed his eyes.

At least two things were hinky about Mackenzie's response.

Again, the past tense. *Was* she having an affair, not *is* she currently involved with another man.

Perhaps he was less interested in finding his wife than confirming his alibi, assuming he had one.

If his wife was dead, Mackenzie had to know he was the most likely suspect. He could probably come up with another alibi if he needed one.

But for that, Mackenzie would need to know more details, and he hadn't even asked.

Which could mean that he already knew.

The second hinky thing? Mackenzie's comment assumed it was Jane who stored the phones in the locker. But he hadn't asked about that, either.

Bramall didn't enlighten him. "There were actually two lockers. The phones and the batteries were stored separately."

"I didn't even know Jane's phone had a removable battery," Mackenzie said. "Why'd she do that?"

Bramall shrugged. When no more questions followed, he said, "We found a few personal items in the lockers, too."

A thin film of perspiration showed on Mackenzie's upper lip. He released the buckle on his seat belt leaving him free to move about the cabin. Not moderate chop yet, but the plane bounced a bit and returned to level flight.

Otto ducked deep into the footwell behind the tall seats to avoid being seen.

Mackenzie stood, steadied himself and walked toward the galley where he grabbed a napkin and dabbed the sweat from his face. "I need a drink. How about you?"

What was Mackenzie so worried about all of a sudden?

Bramall said, "Whiskey would be great. Thanks."

The plane bounced like a drunken sailor in what the captain would probably call light chop. She wondered how they'd be able to keep anything down.

Her stomach was too queasy to consider it. Even if Mackenzie saw her and offered. Which he wouldn't.

When he returned to his seat with two half-filled crystal glasses, Mackenzie handed the whiskey to Bramall and sat.

She returned to her seat.

Mackenzie asked, "So what did you find in the lockers?"

"We couldn't just go at the lockers with a crow bar. We had to get a warrant to open them. I called in a couple of favors to make that happen." Bramall paused for a sip of his whiskey. "Which means the local agents took possession of the contents."

With each new piece of information Bramall doled out, Mackenzie seemed more agitated, although he tried to control it. He lifted his glass to his mouth and took a gulp of straight booze.

Otto figured Bramall getting a warrant would have been Mackenzie's last choice. But then, unlike Bramall, Mackenzie didn't have a State of Illinois private investigator's license and a pension from the FBI to protect, either. Far from it.

"Right," Mackenzie croaked and cleared his throat.

"The good news is that I was able to examine the items from the lockers before they took everything," Bramall said. "And I have photos."

Mackenzie blanched. Then he stammered.

Before he'd figured out which lie he planned to tell, Bramall snarled, "Cut the crap, Rex, and tell me what the hell's really going on here."

Bramall gave him a level stare.

Mackenzie's blue eyes welled with tears, which was nothing but more bullshit.

Mackenzie was no emotional wreck over his missing wife. Not even close. He came across as a psychopath.

Otto wondered whether Mackenzie knew Bramall had killed Joey Two and Little Hugh not twelve hours ago. If he didn't start helping Bramall find Jane and Rose, he should be worrying about Bramall making him a dead psychopath pretty soon.

Bramall pulled out his cell phone and pressed to call.

"Hang up the phone," Mackenzie demanded. His face turned bright red. A fierce frown distorted his features.

Bramall shrugged. If they hadn't been flying at thirty-thousand feet in moderate chop, Mackenzie might have lunged at him. His rage was impotent inside the cabin. For the moment.

"Terry Bramall here. You guys making any progress on those items we removed from the lockers at O'Hare? Uh huh...okay..." Bramall waited a couple of seconds, listening. "Got it. I'll be landing as planned....Yeah, two agents at the gate plus you and me should do the job....Rex Mackenzie is with me. The husband....Yep....Thanks."

Otto figured the call was a hoax. It wasn't likely that Bramall would stick his neck out with law enforcement, given the two missing bodies back at U Store Stuff, along with the missing drugs and cash.

Bramall disconnected the call and dropped the phone into his pocket. Simultaneously, he pulled a pistol from his holster with his right hand and pointed it directly at his seatmate. "Sit back and relax or I'll cuff you. Which will be damned uncomfortable."

"You can't shoot a gun in an airplane," Mackenzie sputtered.

"Of course I can. You watch too many movies." Bramall's stare was no-nonsense. "I've had a lot of training, Rex. I know exactly where and how I can shoot. Trust me."

Mackenzie seemed shocked. "What the hell are you doing?"

"Sit back. I won't tell you again," Bramall growled, pointing the gun directly toward Mackenzie.

CHAPTER TWENTY-TWO

Friday, February 11
2:36 p.m.

AT THAT MOMENT, THE plane seemed to revolt. Her seatbelt pulled against her body as the cabin pitched and rolled. Bramall's whiskey glass went flying to the floor. Whiskey splashed everywhere.

Bramall held the gun steady, ignoring the chop. "You didn't even ask me who put the phones in those lockers. Why not, Rex? I'll tell you why. Because it was you."

Otto felt a little green around the gills as she listened carefully.

"Jane and Rose have been gone for longer than you said, haven't they?" Bramall demanded. "You found the phones. You held onto them for a while before you stashed them. You made phone calls to set up your alibi."

Mackenzie sputtered. "I did not!"

Bramall kept the pressure on. "But you screwed up, Rex. You made two calls to U Store Stuff using Jane's phone. You thought no one would find out? You must believe we're idiots."

Mackenzie's eyes had widened, and beads of sweat dotted his forehead. "Okay. Okay. Look, I did put the phones in the lockers."

"No shit," Bramall deadpanned.

"But I didn't kill Jane or Rose. I swear."

Finally, he'd said something Bramall must have wanted to believe.

"Prove it," he growled again.

Mackenzie flopped back in his seat, sweaty face and all. He raised his drink with a shaky hand. The plane hit another spot of turbulence, and the booze splashed on his shirt.

He put the glass into his left hand and swiped the liquid away with his right, smearing the stain.

"Okay, okay, okay." He snarled like a cornered animal. "Your precious Rose? She never loved Jane at all. It was all an act."

"Is that so?"

"Believe it." He jutted his chin forward. "She was jealous of Jane since they were kids. When she moved in with us, the old jealousy returned. With a vengeance."

Bramall eyed him coldly. "What are you saying, Rex?"

"You know she was addicted, right? Rose was high all the time. She said a lot of crazy crap." Mackenzie shook his head. "Said she'd sacrificed everything. She wanted her reward. She wanted Jane's life. She wanted our house, everything Jane had. Even me."

"Nope. Not buying that, either." Bramall shook his head. "Try again. I know what kind of woman Rose is. She wouldn't bother with a two-bit creep like you."

"You should believe me, Bramall. Because you're right. Jane is dead." Mackenzie's voice quivered, and tears rolled down his handsome cheeks. "Rose killed her."

"What a crock," Bramall said angrily. "That is complete crap and we both know it. Tell me where Jane and Rose went and why you're after them, or I swear I'll shoot you."

Just as he uttered the words, the jet plummeted, losing airspeed.

Otto gasped as she was lifted from her seat and held in midair by her seatbelt.

Bramall heard. He twisted his torso around to look over the side of the big seat. When he saw her, he scowled. "What the hell are you doing back there?"

Before she could reply, the jet was tossed violently into the air, and side to side by extreme turbulence. The kind that could cause structural damage. The kind pilots never chose to fly through.

Otto held on even tighter as the wild ride continued.

Bramall's face had turned green. He searched frantically for an airsickness bag. With the next plunge and bounce, he stuck his mouth over the bag and retched.

The sour stench reached Otto's nose, and she very nearly joined him. She pressed her lips together and concentrated on calming her churning stomach.

The copilot's calm voice traveled over the intercom speaker. "Mr. Mackenzie, you and your guests must remain seated with your seatbelts securely fastened. A line of unanticipated thunderstorms is heading our way, larger and faster than we expected. We don't have enough fuel to divert around them. We're landing to wait it out. You're in for a bumpy ride, but we'll be on the ground shortly."

Bramall's scowl deepened. He wiped his mouth with the back of his hand.

The next bout of turbulence was worse than the last. Otto grabbed both armrests and clenched her teeth to keep her stomach from revolting.

Mackenzie smirked. "I gather you're not a fan of roller coasters."

When neither she nor Bramall replied, he asked, "Just who the hell are you, anyway?"

She took a deep breath and replied steadily, "FBI Special Agent Kim Otto. I'd show you my badge, but I can't reach it right at the moment."

Mackenzie's eyes widened. His nostrils flared. Angrily, he turned to Bramall. "FBI? You led the FBI straight to me? What the hell is wrong with you?"

She made a quick assessment. Bramall was retching into the bag. Mackenzie was still belted in his seat. He couldn't reach her. But he did the next best thing.

He threw the lead crystal glass straight at her.

She ducked, and the plane bounced, and the glass plummeted to the floor.

The bottom edge of the glass struck the seat bolts at precisely the wrong angle.

The glass shattered into sharp-edged projectiles.

One sliced her left wrist. Blood seeped onto her skin.

Another shard nicked her ear. She applied pressure immediately.

Several shards shot back across the aisle toward Mackenzie. He turned his face away too late.

A line of blood traveled down his cheek.

Another, deeper gash on his chin bloomed like fast action photography.

A third sliced the top of his wrist.

Her cuts were superficial. Her blood coagulated quickly. Mackenzie's bled longer, spilling onto his shirt and his jacket. He wiped the blood away, even as anger still spewed from his face.

She freed her gun from its holster and aimed it directly at him.

"Yeah, yeah. I guess you know how to shoot a gun on a plane, too. Same kind of FBI bullshit." He sneered.

"You bet. I can shoot you in the head and not kill you, too," she replied calmly. "Of course, with the turbulence, I might accidentally hit your spinal cord, paralyzing you for the rest of your life."

She kept her aim steady, even as her stomach threatened to revolt at any moment.

He narrowed his eyes and smirked. "Do it right, little girl. Because if we hit another bit of turbulence at precisely the wrong time for your shot, we're all going down."

Otto was not afraid of flying. Not at all. Fear of flying was irrational.

She'd learned about planes and aeronautical engineering at her father's knee. Flying was a science, he'd taught her. Planes were properly engineered machines. Properly maintained, planes performed as they were intended.

Planes were not the problem.

What caused crashes and explosions and death were humans, through ignorance or active malfeasance.

Unfortunately, passenger planes were touched thousands of times by human hands, both competent and incompetent. Any one of those humans could simply have had a bad day. No malfeasance required.

No, she wasn't afraid of flying. Otto was aware and alert to the potential for human interference. Big difference.

Which was how she knew that four things might happen when a human shoots a gun on a plane. Three of those possibilities, under the wrong conditions, could create disaster. The fourth was relatively harmless.

Most people didn't know that. She hoped Mackenzie was one of the ignorant ones.

What she wanted to do right now was keep him under control until the jet landed. She had his attention. She needed to keep it.

She said, "You're right, Mackenzie. If I fire this gun and blow out a window, we're in trouble."

He smirked and held her gaze.

"I'm generally familiar with the engineering specs on this Gulfstream 100, but sure, I could hit wiring hidden in the walls or the floor. Lots of electrical stuff in there. All the high-end customization probably added several more wires and other things that aren't on the publicly available specs." She grinned as if she found the idea humorous instead of likely. "That would definitely mean lights out, I guess."

Mackenzie's smirk faltered, but his gaze did not. Nor did hers.

The plane bounced and swayed and bucked a few times. She compensated, holding a steady aim at his chest until the jet leveled out again.

"The big problem is the turbulence, as you said. Can't control Mother Nature. If I shoot at the wrong time, and she gives us another hard slam right at the wrong moment? Well, the bullet could hit a fuel tank. Big explosion. Everybody dies." She paused and cocked her head as if she was thinking about the possibilities. "But it would be fast. You'd never feel a thing, probably."

His lips were firmly pressed into a steady line. He did not reply. Like he was staring into the eyes of a cobra, mesmerized, his gaze never faltered.

Nor did hers.

"As Dirty Harry famously asked once upon a time, how about it, Rex? Are you feeling lucky?"

His face twitched. She watched him struggle. He wanted to be a tough guy. But he wasn't ready to die yet. And he didn't trust her. Which was smart.

Finally, he shook his head slowly just as the jet leveled out at a lower altitude. She felt the landing gear lock into place.

She glanced out the window. The storm had gathered intensity. Avoiding wind shear under these conditions could be a challenge. But this pilot seemed to have everything under control. She sent him a quick prayer.

Mackenzie broke eye contact and settled back into his seat. Otto returned her gun to its holster and grabbed the armrests again. They'd be landing shortly.

CHAPTER TWENTY-THREE

Friday, February 11
3:15 p.m.
Jasper, Kansas

WHEN THE PLANE'S WHEELS touched down on the runway, the nauseating pitching, rolling, bouncing, and swaying finally stopped. Icy rain slashed the windows, beating loudly on the fuselage. Strong winds buffeted the Gulfstream on the ground as it taxied to the gate.

The jet finally came to a halt. Otto pried her stiff hands from the armrests and flexed her fingers to get the blood flow circulating.

"We're sorry folks. Those storms came up a lot faster than we thought. According to the radar, they'll pass through in less than an hour." The co-pilot came into the cabin, visibly shaken. He swiped a hand through his hair as he glanced around, checking for damage, probably. "We'll clean up in here, refuel, and check out the plane. Why don't you go inside the terminal and walk around a little? Come back in about half an hour. We'll take off again in sixty minutes or so."

Bramall said, "I'll need my bag."

Mackenzie smirked.

Otto followed Bramall to the back of the plane to collect her bags. Her stomach was still roiling.

The co-pilot lowered the jet stairs and handed them each an umbrella. Otto went first, juggling the umbrella, her bags, and the flimsy handrail on the stairs. The wind pushed her back while the rain pelted her skin. She dared not hurry lest she fall flat on her face. Or her ass.

At the bottom of the stairs, she set the rolling bag on the icy concrete and slid it toward the door to the terminal. By the time she got inside, she was cold, wet, thoroughly miserable, and seriously wondering why she hadn't flown straight to Houston as she'd originally planned.

The terminal was practically deserted. A regional airport in the middle of the day in the middle of nowhere, Kansas, was not a busy place. She looked around. Surely, there was a coffee shop of some kind.

Bramall slipped inside behind her. Without a word, he spied the men's room and headed off in that direction. On the way past a trash can, he spiked the air sickness bag, which was filled to capacity.

Mackenzie came inside. His face had tiny dots of coagulated blood where the crystal shards had pierced his skin. His shirt was bloodstained.

Otto turned to face him, teeth chattering. "I'd tell you not to go anywhere, but where would you go in this weather?"

He smirked. "I've got a jet waiting to fly me out of here in less than an hour. What about you? You're not going to stow away twice."

The guy was a piece of work. She wished she could arrest

him. Nothing would make her happier than to see him behind bars. She'd talk to Bramall about his plans for Mackenzie before they reboarded the jet. If Bramall didn't have an arrest already set up, like he'd said, she'd make a call to the Boss and get Mackenzie handled.

She cocked her head and gave him a level stare. "Don't you wonder why I got on that plane?"

Mackenzie frowned. "What do you mean?"

"Bramall didn't mention that he'd shot and killed two of Big Mike Bavolsky's men? Couple of thugs looking for you. They tried to kill him. Self-defense, he says." She paused. "Jimmy Two and Little Hugh."

Mackenzie blanched.

"You knew those guys, didn't you? Business partners of yours, I'm guessing." She paused. "What'd you do? Steal money from the mob? You got a death wish or something?"

He shook his head slowly, but his worried eyes conveyed the truth.

She said, "It's not likely that Big Mike is feeling warm fuzzies for you right about now, is it?"

His voice was husky when he asked, "What's your point?"

"My point is that you're better off with me than without me. So cool your jets and find us a place to get coffee. I'll be back." When he did not reply, she shrugged. "Or don't. It's your funeral."

She turned and went to freshen up, pulling her bag behind her.

At the entrance to the women's restroom, maintenance had placed a yellow plastic bi-fold sign with a big "Do Not Enter" sign plastered across it. Closed for cleaning. She groaned.

She looked for another restroom nearby. The companion restroom was unoccupied. With so few people in the terminal, no one was likely to need it immediately. She ducked inside.

The room was a large, utilitarian space decorated entirely in stainless steel, like a prison. The tile floor had a drain in the center. A stainless steel changing table was bolted to the wall. No baby would be happy to spend time lying on that cold surface.

The lock was broken. She'd need to be quick.

She flushed the toilet. She ran warm water over her hands to loosen her tight muscles and splashed a few handfuls over her face. With her eyes closed, she reached for a paper towel.

The door opened and closed, and the room went black.

Before she could draw her gun or escape, a man moved in fast and hard. He pushed her against the wall, lifting her off the floor, arms and legs pinned, one big hand squeezing her neck.

She tried to turn her head to the side, but his hold was too strong. She opened her mouth to scream and nothing came out. He had closed off her windpipe.

She bucked and squirmed, and he shoved harder.

He squeezed harder.

One after another she attempted the best self-defense techniques in her arsenal, to no avail. He was taller, wider, stronger, heavier.

He had every advantage.

He was in total control.

The best she could hope for was that he wouldn't kill her just because he could.

Bramall might intervene, get this guy off her if she could hang on until he arrived.

Which was her last thought before she blacked out.

CHAPTER TWENTY-FOUR

Friday, February 11
4:45 p.m.
Rapid City, South Dakota

SCORPIO FIGURED WHATEVER WAS on Mackenzie's flash drive could be turned into cash pretty fast. He knew the dark web well. Before Reacher, he'd sold the majority of his products there using Tor clients and I2P services.

He was willing to expand his product lines. As it was, his business was highly specialized. Pharmaceuticals only. Single sourced from a top-notch manufacturer. He had an inside man to keep an eye on things, but he handled most of the fulfillment himself. Safer that way. The fewer fingers in the pie, the better.

He was tired but glad to be home. He settled behind his desk and awakened multiple screens to check the status of his business. He'd been away for less than thirty-six hours, but a lot could happen in that short time. He clacked the keys quickly, moving from one computer to the next, reviewing each segment briefly.

When he'd satisfied himself that all was well, he found Mackenzie's two-terabyte flash drive and inserted it into a buffered reader on a computer segmented from the rest of his network.

His pulse quickened as the volume successfully mounted inside the sandboxed environment. A dozen directories with hashed and unreadable names were listed, along with the text file. He opened it to see a warning from BlackTech, makers of one of the most secure encryption algorithms on the planet.

Each algorithm BlackTech created had a unique aspect, the bespoke elements that were specifically designed for the user. Far more secure than a salted hash, it was like salting the entire algorithm with the user's life.

He wondered again why Mackenzie needed such high-level security. What could he possibly have stored on the flash drive to justify this kind of protection? Several options came to mind, and none of them were legitimate business enterprises.

Whether he was a genius or an idiot, Mackenzie was playing with fire here. The kind of people who used systems like these were, well, men like Scorpio. Drug dealers, data thieves, corporate spies engaged in lucrative intellectual property espionage and the like.

Scorpio's view of Mackenzie, before he found the flash drive in Mackenzie's bedroom wall safe, was far from any of those types of criminal enterprises. Perhaps he'd be forced to change his opinions.

But first, Scorpio had to look at the contents of that flash drive. He tried to puzzle through the steps.

His doctors had told him that some memories were still there in his brain and others were gone. He had to discover what knowledge remained and relearn the rest. The mere mention of his brain damage fueled his constant rage, which he directed solely at Reacher, where it belonged.

But Reacher wasn't here. First things first.

He slowly worked through the steps that once were second nature to him.

He'd need to find out the password and locate Mackenzie's private key file to decrypt the remainder of the file structure.

A private key file combined with a password would be used to generate a hashed token. That token would be used to unlock the encrypted section of the drive.

The plan sounded like gibberish and on the screen, it looked like a bunch of chimps had been pounding the keyboard for a couple of hours. But it was really multi-level security guaranteed to be hacker proof. Or so BlackTech claimed, to justify their ridiculously high prices.

Scorpio leaned back in his chair to think, which was harder to do since Reacher had tossed him into that tumble dryer. His brain worked poorly, especially when he was tired. But he had no time to rest. He needed to know what was on Mackenzie's flash drive before he lost his chance.

BlackTech created encryption security for governments to protect weapons, strategies, and covert operations. They designed encryption for high-tech industries to secure and prevent industrial espionage. In short, BlackTech was the best security money could buy.

No real hacker would fail to recognize the BlackTech logo. Script kiddies would give up the moment they saw it. Clever breachers might try to trick Mackenzie into coughing up the password using social hacking techniques. Which could work, sure. If you had the time to burn. Because Mackenzie wasn't the sharpest knife in the drawer.

Scorpio tapped the rim of his coffee cup. He was fully familiar with BlackTech because he'd used it for his business, too. He remembered exactly what the salesman said when he pitched the expensive product. BlackTech's advanced encryption algorithms would take a thousand of the world's most powerful computers until the heat-death of the universe to crack.

Could have been hyperbole, Scorpio supposed. But the point was made. BlackTech was unhackable.

Except for one thing.

The weakness in BlackTech's system was the end user. The user controlled the passcodes. No security in the world would protect anything if the user's loose lips could not be sealed.

A guy like Mackenzie was not a sophisticated computer user. Scorpio would bet Mackenzie had bought way more tech security than he understood. He'd have found the password process overwhelming and too difficult to remember.

Which meant he would have recorded it somewhere. A place where he could easily retrieve it when he needed it.

Scorpio leaned back in his chair and closed his eyes to think. Where would Mackenzie have written down that passcode?

He could have done something as stupid as writing it on a piece of paper and stuffing it into his wallet. Idiotic. But effective. Unless the wallet was lost or stolen.

He might have sent it to himself in an email. People did dumb crap like that every day. Searching Mackenzie's email would take a while, but not forever.

Scorpio thought about the Lake Forest mansion Mackenzie owned. The dry cleaner business in that dilapidated neighborhood. The jewelry box containing all those loose diamonds and emeralds. The amazingly gorgeous wife with the equally gorgeous twin sister.

No, a guy like that wouldn't carry around a passcode in his wallet where his wife might find it. And he wouldn't send it to himself in an email he'd have to search for several minutes every time.

Mackenzie must have been somewhat tech savvy. After all, he owned the flash drive. He kept it in a safe in his home, not his business. He must have had a computer he could use to access the contents of the drive.

Scorpio thought about the master bedroom in Mackenzie's mansion. He hadn't found a laptop there, or anywhere in the house or his destroyed dry cleaner.

Scorpio had located Mackenzie's identity on the dark web before the trip to Lake Forest. He pulled up those files now. He scanned through until he found Mackenzie's personal banking records. He scrolled through pages of transactions looking for patterns.

Which was when he noticed the monthly payments to DiamondSecure, a backup service. The payments were withdrawn automatically, the tenth of each month, going back several years. Would Mackenzie have been dumb enough to store his BlackTech passcode at DiamondSecure? Worth a look.

Scorpio turned to another computer and pulled up a web browser on the Clear Internet. The one most people used. He found DiamondSecure on the first try and attempted to log into Mackenzie's account.

He grinned when he made it past the first login prompts. *Mackenzie was such an idiot.*

And then the two-factor identification notice popped onto the screen. DiamondSecure had sent a code to Mackenzie's phone.

Scorpio moved back to the other computer and rapidly scanned Mackenzie's bank records seeking his phone provider.

When he found it, a feeling of relief filtered through him. It was one he already had hooks into. A few keystrokes later and he'd located the text. He memorized the code and then deleted the text. Mackenzie might have seen the notification. If he had, then Scorpio would have a whole new set of problems. But he couldn't think about that now.

He returned to the DiamondSecure screen and entered the code.

"Open sesame!" he said, flicking the five fingers of his right hand for emphasis, as the service opened to a dashboard listing all Mackenzie's files. A quick scan was all it took to locate the private key file. Scorpio resisted the urge to fist pump the air with his one good arm.

Now all he needed was the passcode to open the key file and generate the token to decrypt the flash drive.

Where would that dolt have saved the key file passcode? It wasn't stored with the files at DiamondSecure.

He looked through the materials he'd gathered on Mackenzie, seeking inspiration. He scrolled through bank records, tax returns, even emails for a while until he got bored.

Which was when he saw Mackenzie's phone texts were filled with reminders. Could he have texted the passcode to himself? Seriously? The guy was a walking grenade with the pin already pulled.

It didn't take long to scroll through.

"Bingo!" Scorpio shouted into his empty office. There it was. Right there.

He used the passcode to open the key file and generate the token. He moved to the first computer and used the token to enter the flash drive.

"Yes!" This time, he fist-pumped the air.

He walked around the room to stretch. He pulled a cold
bottle of water from the office fridge and struggled to open the
twist top, snuggling the bottle close to his body with his useless
left arm and twisting with his right hand. Water spurted from the
bottle, soaking his shirt, but he didn't care.

He took a long swig of the icy drink. He'd done it. He'd
beaten BlackTech's security.

"Dayum!"

He swigged the water again and swished it around in his
mouth before he swallowed it. His throat was always dry these
days. Something about the nerve damage, they said. He finished
the bottle and tossed it across the room into the trash can, hitting
the opening on the first try.

"You're on a roll, Scorpio," he said aloud, with a smile.
"Let's see what kind of national treasures Mackenzie has stored
on here, shall we?"

He returned to his seat, pulled up the contents of the flash
drive, and opened the first file.

All the color drained from his face.

CHAPTER TWENTY-FIVE

Friday, February 11
5:25 p.m.
Rapid City, South Dakota

AT HIS AGE, AFTER all the things he'd done, Scorpio would have said new and delightful life experiences were over. But the thrill of finding the flash drive, knowing how it would change his life, was one such surprise.

"Excellent," he muttered under his breath.

Extreme porn had significant retail value on the dark web, and Mackenzie's films were a treasure trove of potential cash. Scorpio was beyond pleased.

The drive contained video files numbered one through nine-hundred-eighty-six. Which left some storage room for more films in the future. All the files were dated in European-style, months first followed by day and year.

The production company was identified with a logo that looked like an old-fashioned dancing couple dressed in costumes. The logo reminded him of Slavic folk dancers of some kind. German or Polish or Czech, perhaps. The logo would be traceable, so he'd change it.

Each video film had a cutesy title, too, which made them seem tamer than they were. Just in case the FBI or Interpol came sniffing around. Things like *Frank and Joe Do Paris* seemed harmless enough.

He watched enough of the first file to be sure he had a marketable commodity. Then he opened another at random. *Marianne and the Teacher's Pet* was dated last summer.

He watched the opening credits, a few minutes of the beginning, skipped through to the middle for several minutes, and then to the end. Where the murder happened. His stomach churned. Disgusting.

He opened two more files and did the same quick perusal. Both ended with the death of at least one partner. Perfect. Snuff films were usually fake. But even if these deaths were not real, they looked real enough. The prices on these babies would shoot through the roof.

He'd check one more.

Film number four-hundred-seventeen. *The Senator, The Waitress, and Her Friends.*

The opening credits were followed by establishment shots of national landmarks. The Washington Monument, the National Mall, the Capitol Building. Briefly, the White House flashed across the screen.

The soundtrack continued through the next scene.

The camera panned across the entrance to a famous hotel. He'd seen it countless times on the news, usually when a politician stood in front of reporters to pontificate. Next, the iconic lobby with portraits found on US dollars, before the scene entered the stately restaurant.

A middle-aged couple was seated near the center of the room at a table for two. A champagne bucket stood beside the table, and two champagne flutes bubbled in the candlelight. They clinked glasses and sipped. Gold wedding bands glinted when they raised glasses to their lips.

Scorpio didn't recognize the actress, but the actor looked familiar. He was dressed in a suit and tie, like an undertaker or TV evangelist. His dark hair was gray at the temples. He seemed distracted. His gaze traveled the room.

A willowy blonde waitress dressed in a tuxedo approached the table. She talked to the woman before she turned to the man. He gazed at the waitress with a lustful expression. His date threw the glass of champagne in the man's face and marched from the dining room. The man grinned.

The next scene was a tastefully choreographed orgy. The man and the waitress having sex in a hotel room with another couple.

Unlike a lot of smut, this film felt very real, and he felt like a voyeur. Scorpio was impressed. Mackenzie had acquired top-notch porn, for sure.

Which was when Scorpio recognized one of the actors. The man from the dining room scene. The resemblance was uncanny.

He skipped all the way to the end of the film to confirm that the woman died in the throes of sex at the moment the senator climaxed with his hands around her throat. A moment later, the second couple's encounter ended the same way. Two dead women.

After a few frames, the men got dressed and left the room. The women continued to play dead. They lay with bulging eyes and open mouths as if they remained shocked.

The camera lingered a few more moments. The women never blinked. Their chests did not rise and fall as they breathed.

The end credits began to roll. When the credits finished, the women had not moved.

Most people in good health could hold their breath for two minutes. Scorpio had been a swimmer in high school. Some of the divers on the team could hold their breath longer. Those two women looked like dead fashion models, not trained athletes.

Scorpio rewound the film to the climax. From that point until the last credits rolled off the screen, eight minutes of elapsed time showed on the counter. Eight minutes was much too long for them to play dead. The video might have been skillfully edited, he supposed. Perhaps.

He stopped the video and turned to another computer. He typed Senator Ronald Brennan's name into the search engine. Within half a second, images of Senator Brennan filled the screen.

Several photos showed the senator's immensely wealthy wife by his side at fundraisers and events. Stephanie Brennan was a brunette, older than her husband by at least a decade. In every photo, she wore enough jewelry to buy a small kingdom. She was strikingly pretty. With all that money, she could buy beauty easily enough.

But she was most definitely not the same woman. Not the one the senator had been clinking glasses with at dinner. Not either of the women in the orgy.

Which was especially good for Stephanie Brennan, since both of those women looked very dead.

"Well, well, well. Not fiction after all. Actual sex. A sitting senator. Two dead women. Nicely done, Mackenzie." Scorpio flopped back into his chair and closed his eyes to think. He had a gold mine here. Not only could he sell the raunchier porn on the dark web, he could also blackmail the senator's very wealthy wife, too. Surely she wouldn't want her husband to go to prison for murder. And sordid murders would feed the media for months.

He nodded, pleased. Mackenzie was a lot smarter than Scorpio had given him credit for.

But what about the other films? Had he missed something here? Maybe Mackenzie just got lucky when he came across an actual video of Senator Brennan that he could make more than one fortune selling. Scorpio shook his head. Didn't seem likely.

He went back to the list of films and read through the titles again. He grinned. Just as he'd hoped. Several of the titles could have been subtitled "famous person behaving badly." *Celebrity in the Rough, The Congressman's Pages, Everybody's Boy Scout*, and so on.

Scorpio pulled a bottle of beer from his fridge, held it steady in the crook of his left arm, and twisted off the top with his right hand. He took a long swig.

It would take hours to watch all the films to be able to identify the best blackmail victims and cull the ones he'd sell on the dark web to audiences likely to pay big money for the kink. The work would prove well worth the time.

But he didn't need to sort them all now. Mackenzie had enough here to fund Scorpio's retirement for a good, long while. As long as Mackenzie was still alive, he'd be making more films, too.

He chose three of the snuff films to start his new store, copied everything on the flash drive over to his secure storage in the cloud for safekeeping, and closed up his computers for the last time.

One final task was to find Mackenzie. He found the dark web site he was looking for in half a second and typed

Mackenzie's cell phone number into the search box. Account holder information came back promptly. Along with a list of phones on the same account. Also listed were incoming and outgoing calls for all the phone numbers.

A few more keystrokes and he found what he wanted. He sent those files to the cloud, too.

He activated the malware he'd installed long ago, in preparation for the day when he had to shut down. He waited while it scrubbed every last bit and byte of incriminating evidence that might be hiding there. In his line of work, knowing when to cut and run was an essential life skill. Now was the time.

Babbling Brooke would be identified soon if she wasn't already. Chicago PD would be hot on his ass. Time to get moving. Mexico was nice this time of year. Guadalajara was one of the most cosmopolitan cities in the world. Good doctors there, too, who could fix him up. With the kind of money he'd make on the porn films, he could live like a king there.

He called Thorn. "I'm ready to go."

He splashed accelerant around the room, making sure to douse everything thoroughly. He lit two votive candles and tossed them into the fumes. Like many laundromats, flammable chemicals and electrical wires were plentiful enough to enhance the fire well beyond the point of no return.

By the time his office was ablaze, Thorn was waiting with the sedan in the alley. Scorpio took one last look and nodded his satisfaction. Everything in the place would be destroyed before the fire could possibly be extinguished.

On the short drive to his home where he would set another fire, Scorpio imagined ways to maximize Mackenzie's inventory to its full potential. Several ideas sprang immediately to mind.

The nicest part of the dark web porn business was that he could do it from anywhere. All he needed was an internet connection. Simple enough.

But first things first. His drugs. They weren't stashed in the Lake Forest mansion. Now that he'd seen the contents of the flash drive, he'd figured Mackenzie was to blame. He knew where Mackenzie had stashed his property. He'd fly to St. Louis. Collect what was rightfully his from the U Store Stuff facilities. Deal with Mackenzie. Move on from there.

CHAPTER TWENTY-SIX

Friday, February 11
7:15 p.m.
Houston, Texas

HOURS LATER THAN EXPECTED, and much the worse for wear, Otto finally landed at George Bush Intercontinental Airport and grabbed a taxi to the address Gaspar had given her this morning. At least she'd left the snow and frigid cold behind her in St. Louis.

When she had regained consciousness on the floor of the companion restroom in the airport bathroom, dazed, with a bruised throat and a pounding headache, Bramall and Mackenzie and the Gulfstream 100 were gone. So were the storms.

She'd replayed the attack in her head several times but couldn't positively identify her attacker. Logically, it was Mackenzie or Bramall. Both were bigger and stronger than her. Either could have exploited the advantage of surprise.

176 | DIANE CAPRI

Between the two, she'd bet on Mackenzie. But it could have been Bramall, too. An unknown third option was remotely possible.

She'd discussed everything with Gaspar. He'd said, "I'd put money on Mackenzie. But from all we know, Bramall's got plenty at stake here, too. Could go either way."

She called the Boss and reported what happened. He'd promised to find Mackenzie and Bramall. Meanwhile, he'd sent her to Houston.

She hadn't heard from Finlay yet, which was unusual. She'd come to rely on his responsiveness to her requests. He could be tied up in some high-level meetings. Or, with luck, he'd tracked down everything she already knew and would have good intel when he called back. Meanwhile, the new burner phone remained silent.

Her personal phone rang. The Boy Detective calling. She picked up. "Otto."

Noble said, "Hang on a minute."

Her voice sounded hoarse to her ears. She sipped warm water from the bottle she'd bought at the airport and swallowed more aspirin to help with the swelling. She'd put up a good fight. She could tell by her sore muscles. Her body ached all over as if she'd gone a few rounds with a heavyweight.

She watched the passing scenery and resisted the urge to fidget while she waited for Noble to finish his conversation. She heard movements and others talking in the background while her taxi made slow progress through Houston's late Friday night traffic.

"Have you found Reacher yet?" Noble asked when he returned.

She shot back, "Still no ID on the body in the mansion?"

"Not definitively. We've added a third option, though." He paused, but she refused to ask what the new option was. She had no interest in power games tonight. "Seems the real estate agent is missing. Her husband called in late last night when she didn't come home. She had spent the day yesterday at an open house at the Mackenzie place."

Otto took a quick sip. "So you think the dead woman is not one of the sisters but the real estate agent?"

"Could be. It could also be the wife or the sister. All three women are about the same size. All have a lot of blonde hair. All had a reason to be in that room." He gave a weary sigh.

Otto cocked her head to think. Her brain seemed a little weak, too. The taxi moved half a block at a time and progress was slow. "Sounds a little too clever, doesn't it?"

"How so?"

"What are the odds? A dead woman can't be identified when her body is discovered in the house of a man who is missing and running from the mob?"

"Could be a message to the husband, sure." He didn't act surprised to hear that Mackenzie was involved with organized crime. Which meant he already knew about Rex Mackenzie and made her wonder what else he'd been holding back. "Could be a plan by the two sisters, a Thelma and Louise scenario."

She scrunched her face like she'd just sucked on a lemon. "A what?"

"You know. Two women kill the husband and the real estate agent, steal the money, and run."

"You're talking about a movie?" She closed her eyes and leaned her head back against the seat, resisting the urge to groan. "Thelma and Louise didn't kill their husbands. They started out on a road trip. Bad stuff happened along the way."

"Same thing, in the end." He put a smile in his voice. "Everybody ends up dead except the sexy lawman."

"You think that's what's going on here?" Otto shook her head. "Sounds pretty far-fetched to me."

Noble replied, "Could be anything. Guessing is a waste of time."

"Is Reacher involved in any of your potential scenarios?"

Noble paused as if he was seriously thinking about the question. Maybe he was. "I want to say there's no reason to believe he is. But the truth is, there's no reason to believe he's not involved, either. We just don't know enough yet."

"What *do* you know?"

"The working hypothesis is that the murder could have been an afterthought. Things are missing from the house. We found a ransacked safe in the bedroom."

She arched her eyebrows. "What did they take?"

"We don't know. Point is, we're not sure whether this was a sophisticated robbery gone bad."

She thought a moment, glanced toward the taxi driver and lowered her voice. "Did you find any evidence of the contraband you were looking for anywhere in the house?"

"No. But we heard from Chicago PD that there was also a break-in at Mackenzie's dry cleaner."

She shook her head. "Man, Mackenzie has really pissed somebody off."

"Looks like it. The good news is that the mansion has reasonably good surveillance equipment, including cameras." He was stalling. Talking, but not offering anything of importance. "For the dry cleaner, we're relying on nearby video cams, but they're grainy. Bad angles."

She watched the traffic, which didn't seem to be thinning at all, and realized neither she nor Noble was getting anywhere. "Again, what *do* you know?"

"On the video, we've got the same two guys arriving and departing at the mansion and the dry cleaner. We don't know who they are, but we know neither is Mackenzie or Bramall, for sure."

Could have been Jimmy Two and Little Hugh, she figured. The timing was right. "How'd they get there, do the deeds, and get away without getting caught? Chicago has decent law enforcement. Response times can't be that bad."

"Nobody called anything in. Nothing to respond to," he replied. "They're driving a private vehicle. Big SUV. Maybe stolen. Caught a partial license plate on one of the cameras. Not Illinois. Could be Wisconsin. They're running that down now."

"Need any help?"

"From the FBI, you mean? Thanks, but we're okay. I'll let you know when we figure it out."

"So your plan is to hang around in Chicago until…"

"Until I get some answers or a better lead, yeah. I'm meeting the local DEA guys in an hour." He paused and then echoed her question. "Your plan is to keep looking for Reacher until…"

"Until I find him or get different orders."

"Guess we understand each other, then," he said.

"Guess we do. Stay in touch," she replied and disconnected the call. She checked the Boss's phone, but he hadn't called again. Which could have meant that he hadn't found Bramall and Mackenzie.

She returned both phones to her pocket. The third phone, Finlay's burner, had reconnected and received a delayed text message. He'd sent the message an hour ago. It said, "Call after nine tonight."

The taxi fought the traffic a while longer and finally stopped five miles from downtown Houston. She paid the driver and got out in front of a low-rise brick structure that had been built in the nineteenth century and housed only one tenant.

She followed the sidewalk up to the front door of the offices of Scarlett Investigations.

CHAPTER TWENTY-SEVEN

Friday, February 11
7:35 p.m.
Houston, Texas

A RECEPTIONIST LED HER to a conference room where
Gaspar was seated at a computer desk. Multiple screens were
mounted on the walls. The equipment seemed as sophisticated as
anything she'd have found in the FBI's Detroit field office.

She stowed her travel bag and her laptop case in the corner
of the room and took the seat next to Gaspar at the desk. He
closed the files he'd been working on. An image of Houston at
night moved about the screen.

Briefly, she wondered what he'd been doing and why he
didn't want her to see it. None of her business, of course.

"Let me get started on the flash drive." He held his palm out.

"The encryption programs I have on my laptop wouldn't
open this," she said as she retrieved it from her pocket.

He looked at the drive briefly before he slipped it into the
slot on the computer in front of him. "We could get lucky.

Depends on how sophisticated these folks are. Did you get any kind of feel for that?"

"Nothing is ever what we think it is. But Bramall says Jane Mackenzie is a housewife, and her husband owns a dry cleaner. I figure he's stalling."

"Why?" Gaspar asked, preoccupied with the keyboard.

"Judging from the house they live in, Mackenzie is bringing home the bacon. Which means he's more successful than your average dry cleaner. I don't know much about the wife yet. But the sister, Rose Sanderson, was a major in the Army. West Point grad. So she's no dummy," Otto replied.

She glanced around the tastefully decorated room. Everything she recognized was high-end. Nothing like her office back in Detroit or Gaspar's office in Miami.

Scarlett Investigations, whatever its business, seemed prosperous enough. What she didn't understand was Gaspar's relationship to the place. He'd been unwilling to talk to her about it so far.

Gaspar turned to the computer and, after a few keystrokes, said, "We may be in luck. The encryption software is proprietary, but I'm familiar with it. I've done some work with the company before. They're based here in Houston."

He reached across to a phone on the desk. He punched a couple of buttons. "Any chance you could come into the conference room? Yeah, thanks." He turned his attention back to the keyboard.

Otto spied a refrigerator across the room. "Anything nonalcoholic to drink in there?"

"Yeah, sure. Help yourself."

She snagged cold water in two glass bottles, returned to the desk, and offered one to him. "Anything earth-shattering in there?"

"Don't know yet. But given how hard someone is trying to keep it secure, I'd bet it's earth-shattering to the owner. I need some passcodes to get in there, though." He screwed the cap off his water. "Data security is a pain in the neck. Everything can be hacked, so people think security systems are an unnecessary hassle."

"Which they are," she nodded.

He frowned. "Point is, people can't be bothered to use the systems effectively. For passcodes, they choose things like the dog's name or their birthplace. Nonsense like that."

"Yeah, and since we don't know who that flash drive belongs to, the easy stuff like that is a little tough to guess." She took a long, slow sip of cool water to bathe her throat.

He nodded. "Well, normal people also reuse the same passcodes in a variety of places, so they don't forget them."

She raised her hand. "Guilty as charged. All my passcodes are phrases like *I love chocolate martinis with coffee* or *Chico is a pain the ass when he's tired.*"

"Smart. That kind of nonsense is harder for a hacker to break." He frowned.

She grinned. "Sometimes I'll add an exclamation point or a hashtag, just to make it interesting."

"Another thing people do is store more complicated passwords inside a file tree, kind of like putting your cash in the freezer at home instead of in the vault at the bank. They think hackers won't look there. Which is stupid." Gaspar continued to scroll through the files, shaking his head. "But I'm not seeing anything like that, unfortunately."

Otto warned, "That software probably has a limit on the number of times you can try before we get locked out."

The door opened, and a slender, exceptionally attractive woman with long, curly black hair entered the room. Her high heels tapped a staccato beat across the floor as she approached. She extended her right hand to shake.

"Carlos told me you were coming. It's a pleasure to meet you. I'm Kathryn Scarlett. Call me Katie."

"Kim Otto. It's a pleasure to meet you, too," she replied, looking up past bright teeth and full lips to her alert green eyes. Mid-thirties, Otto guessed. A little young for Reacher. And not his type, anyway. Which meant Gaspar wasn't here to interview her for their assignment. Why was he here?

Scarlett turned her attention to Gaspar. "How can I help?"

Gaspar replied, "We have a flash drive to open. It's encrypted by BlackTech. I've worked with them in Miami. They're headquartered here. Do you know anybody over there who can help us get past the security passcodes quickly?"

Scarlett nodded. "BlackTech's a client. The CEO is Larry Black. He's a friend. Let me make a call."

She scrolled through her list of contacts on her cell phone until she found the one she wanted. She placed the call. The phone must have rung a few times, judging from the wait, but it was eventually picked up.

"Larry, it's Katie Scarlett. I need some help with one of your systems." She put a lot of warmth in that greeting. She smiled at Otto and held up two crossed fingers on her left hand as if she was either lying or hoping.

Scarlett nodded while he talked. "You know I would never ask if it wasn't important."

She listened a bit longer, and then replied, "Exigent circumstances....Yes, life and death....Unfortunately, we don't have time for a warrant...."

More waiting and then her smile broadened, and she nodded. "That's really helpful. I'm handing the phone to Carlos. He's sitting at the keyboard. Can you talk him through it directly?"

She nodded again. "Thank you, Larry. Say hello to Elaine for me. And I owe you one."

Scarlett handed her phone to Gaspar.

"Tell me what I need to do," he said.

Larry must have offered a list of instructions because Gaspar's fingers flew over the keys. Every couple of seconds he said things like "Uh-huh...right...got it...yeah...okay..."

At one point, Gaspar read a long list of digits and characters aloud. After that, he paused until he received a much shorter list of digits and characters back, which he typed and then clicked.

A big grin lit up his face.

He said, "We're in. Thank you, Larry."

He disconnected the call and handed the phone to Scarlett

"Do you need anything else from me?" Scarlett asked.

"I think we're good here for now, thanks," Gaspar replied.

Scarlett smiled at Otto and left the room.

Otto sipped the cold water and asked the question much more casually than she felt. "Who is she, anyway?"

"We'll get into that," he replied, not taking his eyes from the screen. "This stuff on the flash drive looks like two sets of accounting records. I'm guessing one set is legit, and the other is not."

Gaspar continued flipping through the files. Otto leaned forward as he pointed out lists of customers, inventory, receivables, payables, and so on. More data attached to all of it, covering years, not weeks. Standard business stuff.

She was a trained forensic accountant, but her expertise was not necessary here. The duplicity was blatant.

Identical spreadsheets. One set contained very modest revenue numbers, while the other showed a wealthier enterprise. The sort of thing she'd seen from a guy hiding assets, or stealing, or cheating the IRS.

Gaspar was right. Someone was cooking the books.

"Two sets of bank documents, too. One set domestic, the other for offshore accounts. Big money. Lots and lots of zeros on here." He pointed to the lists.

Otto read the names on the bank accounts. Polka Brothers Limited. Bramall said Big Mike Bavolsky was the head of a Polish mafia in Chicago. She'd found the flash drive in Unit D-6 in a shoebox filled with cash, along with a stash of illegal drugs.

It wasn't a huge leap to connect "T. Mackenzie" to Bavolsky and drug trafficking, which usually involved other related crimes. Made sense.

But how did Bramall and Reacher fit into this puzzle?

And what about the two sisters?

"Let's close this up. We need to talk, and it's late. I'll buy you dinner," she said.

Gaspar's reply was a bit testy. "Your wish is my command, Suzy Wong. I know a place for great sushi."

CHAPTER TWENTY-EIGHT

Friday, February 11
8:15 p.m.
Houston, Texas

GASPAR ORDERED A CAR. It arrived a few minutes later, and they slipped inside. He gave the driver the address and Otto didn't ask any questions.

The car deposited them in front of an old gas station converted to an upscale eatery. Mouthwatering aromas spilled onto the sidewalk when the door opened. The flashing red sign featured an old-fashioned tow truck and the words "Jack's Blue Tractor."

She tossed a quizzical look Gaspar's way and he replied, "Trust me. You're gonna love it."

He pulled the door open and she walked inside. The interior décor was pure country. Tables were slabs of weathered barn wood and the chairs were aluminum tractor seats with sturdy peg legs. The hostess was dressed in boots, pricey torn jeans, and a plaid shirt.

"Welcome to Jack's Blue Tractor, y'all," she said with a drawl. "Two for supper?"

She led them to a table in the back and left menus attached to smaller barn wood slabs, promising the server would be with them in just a minute. Otto glanced at the menu, which listed items numbered with radio codes a wrecker might have responded to back when this place was an operating service station.

Otto grinned. "Only in Texas would you find good sushi in a place like this."

"Wait 'til you try it before you mock it," Gaspar replied.

They placed their orders and he leaned back in his tractor seat, extending his bad leg. She noticed the wince, and ignored it because that's what he expected. He'd never explained what happened to his leg. She knew the injury happened on the job, but nothing more. He'd made it clear that he didn't plan to explain further. She respected his wishes and in return, he refrained from crossing her boundaries, too.

Even in the dim candlelight, she noticed how tired he looked. Dark circles under his eyes and deep crevices in his face. He lived with constant pain, and it was taking its toll.

She'd seen him a few days ago in New York before he was released to return to work. Since he was back on the job, she'd expected more improvement. His health was a constant worry to them both.

"Okay. You've stalled long enough. What's going on?" she asked.

Gaspar took a deep breath before he replied, "Things have changed, Kim. We started out doing a background check, and now we're involved in a manhunt."

"Mission creep." She grinned. "Keeps us law enforcement types in business."

"Marie put her foot down." He shook his head and cleared his throat, and the words tumbled out as if he might change his mind unless he said them quickly. "I've got a tribe of kids. Bills. I'm done."

She said nothing because her heart seemed to stop beating. She relied on Gaspar every day. And they'd become good friends. She didn't want to lose him.

He lowered his voice, "And let's face it. I can't pull my weight anymore. It's time for me to move on."

She widened her eyes. "You mean after we find Reacher?"

"Can't do it." He shook his head. "I'll stick around until the Boss gets you another partner. He's got someone in mind. Won't take long."

He'd laid this off on his wife because Otto wouldn't argue with Marie. But Marie would never have interfered with her husband's career choices. She was a wiser woman than that. Gaspar had made up his own mind, as he always did.

Otto might have tried to argue with him, but she knew he was right. He'd been struggling to do the job from the beginning. He swallowed Tylenol like candy. He could barely walk. He'd gone above and beyond the call of duty too many times. He owed her nothing. She couldn't ask him to give up the rest of his life to stay on as her partner.

"If you're sure that's what you want," she replied, blinking glassy tears away before he noticed. She felt more emotional about losing him than she'd expected. They'd been through a lot together. More than that, Gaspar understood her in a way no partner had ever done before. He was irreplaceable, really.

He looked down while the server placed their meals on the table. When she left again, Gaspar said, "You're going to love this. Best sushi in Houston."

"Like you would know," she teased to cover her feelings and let him off the hook. "Tried all the sushi in Houston, have you?"

"A fair amount of it, actually." He looked down at the food to avoid her eyes. "I've, uh, been working here off and on with Scarlett for a few weeks now."

She stared at him. "A few *weeks*?"

"Since before we partnered up."

"A few *weeks*? Try a few months instead."

He nodded, still not meeting her gaze. "I've been putting off telling you until we finished our assignment, but with the changes...I just felt like it was time."

"You never thought to mention this to me before?" Her heart pounded against her sternum as if she'd been sprinting. "You didn't trust me?"

He squirmed. "It's not that. The Boss asked me not to tell you."

"Why?" She widened her eyes.

"Hell if I know. Why does he do anything?" He shrugged. "When we started out, the assignment seemed straightforward enough. I thought it would be fairly short. He told me not to mention my impending change in status, and I didn't question him. I never do. I was in the Army. A superior officer gives me an order, and I salute, you know?"

He paused until she nodded. He said, "As we kept going, things...morphed."

She stared across the table, straight into his eyes, unflinching.

He shrugged again. His all-purpose gesture for everything. "There was never a good time to bring it up. I didn't want to let you down. I tried to tell you in New York last month, but..."

He picked up his fork and dug into his food, shoveling it in, just like he always did. Nothing wrong with his appetite. The guy could eat his weight in sushi.

The thought made her grin.

Gaspar wasn't asking her permission. Hell, he wasn't even asking her opinion. He'd made up his mind. All she could do was support his decision and move on. They'd still be friends. But it wouldn't be the same. She knew it. He knew it.

Life goes on.

She took a deep breath and picked up her chopsticks. One of many things she'd learned from her mother was how to eat with chopsticks. Another thing was to recognize that when there's only one choice, it's the right choice.

All she could do was support his decision. She owed him that and so much more. "Just tell me my new partner is not Kirk Noble, Boy Detective," she said, scowling.

Gaspar laughed. "You don't like him?"

"He's annoying as hell."

"He's also DEA. The Boss isn't likely to reach outside the bureau. I'd say you're safe there," Gaspar replied.

"Okay, then," she said as if the matter were settled. She took another bite of the Dynamite Roll. "This sushi is really great."

"Told you so, Suzy Wong. You never listen to me," he teased with a grin.

She threw her chopsticks at him.

He ducked, just in time.

She swallowed her food and then returned to business, which was safer ground. "Tell me something useful for a change, Cheech. I've filled you in on everything I've learned. What intel did you find on the twin sisters that I don't already know?"

He smiled. "I started with the same files you have. Did some digging. Found some phone records, which led me to a witness."

She cocked her head. "You found a witness who knows where Jane and Rose are?"

"Not quite. I'll explain everything." He paused. "We need to go through the rest of the stuff on that flash drive, too, but you're dead on your feet. I made hotel reservations. Let's get some sleep. We have an appointment with the witness in San Antonio in the morning. We can talk on the way there."

CHAPTER TWENTY-NINE

Friday, February 11
10:15 p.m.
Houston, Texas

OTTO LEFT GASPAR AT the elevator and settled into her hotel
room. She hadn't mentioned her plan. He wouldn't have
approved, and she didn't feel like arguing about it.

She used the dedicated burner phone to place the call.

Lamont Finlay, Ph.D., was Special Assistant to the
President. His current position gave him power and resources
that no one else had. He operated out of the spotlight, without
oversight of any kind. Which made him flexible in ways that had
proved valuable.

Simply put, when Reacher's brother was murdered, he and
Finlay had partnered in a vendetta of violent and illegal vigilante
justice.

Reacher moved on.

When the dust eventually settled, Finlay not only escaped
unscathed, he was catapulted to a bigger, better career. Which

Otto figured he could keep only as long as his past deeds with Reacher stayed buried.

Finlay picked up on the fourth ring. "I see you made it to Houston."

"Eventually. After a couple of detours." She rubbed the bruises on her neck.

"Your assignment has changed and your partner is retiring. A bunch of folks are missing and you believe Reacher is involved. Cooper is obfuscating. That about it?" he said.

"Pretty close," she replied.

"What did I leave out?"

"If I knew that, I wouldn't be asking."

He chuckled. He had a damn sexy voice for such an imposing man. "When I got your text, I checked around. There's no record of Reacher being involved with Rex Mackenzie, his wife or her sister. There's also no record of any partnership, dubious or otherwise, connecting Bramall and Reacher."

"Same old same old," she said wearily. "Yet both Cooper and Noble insist that Reacher and Bramall worked together before and are working together again. What's your explanation for that?"

"Black holes? Alternate universe?" When she didn't laugh, Finlay chuckled anyway. His tone became serious. "A few weeks ago, someone put a flag on Reacher's bank account. The one that receives his military pension."

"What kind of flag?" She widened her eyes. "Do we know who it was?"

"The message was a military police radio code. *Ten Two,* which means wrecker requested."

"What kind of nonsense is that?" Members of Reacher's 110th Special Investigative Unit had used radio codes to contact him through his bank in the past. It was not a precise method of communication. She knew of two cases where it had worked, and no idea how many times it had failed.

"Hard to say. There was a phone number attached, which is where things get interesting," Finlay said.

"Why?"

"The number is a disposable cell phone. It's been active awhile and used quite a bit, so we have data on it, but no contacts from Reacher." He paused and cleared his throat. "Thing is, it's data your partner already collected."

"Meaning?"

"You're on your way to meet the guy tomorrow. General Sean Simpson."

"So Simpson went out of his way to try to contact Reacher, but he's had no nibbles on his bait yet, is that what you're saying?"

"That's how it looks." He paused. "But that's not the only interesting thing. Simpson's been chatting with your missing soldier, Sanderson. They've had several conversations back and forth over the past few months. Long chats, too, according to the phone records. I don't have the actual conversations yet, but we're working on it."

"You think he's having an affair with her?"

"Possibly. I've seen photos of her. She's freakishly hot. He wouldn't be the first man to be interested. Which brings me to another point."

"What's that?"

"Her last known lover, also a soldier, died of a drug overdose. Opioids, apparently." Another deep chuckle floated across the miles. "This woman is a Delilah for sure. Seems like no man can resist her. And there's two of them, don't forget. Her sister is every bit as beautiful."

She cocked her head. "You think Reacher was bewitched by her? Mackenzie, Bramall, even the General? All victims of Delilah's charms?"

"Stranger things have happened, Otto. Men are easily beguiled," he replied. "Trust me. Women have more power than they may assume."

"Okay. Thanks. Anything else?"

"Looks like Reacher and the general had a few conversations a while back, too. Reacher called West Point. They talked."

"About what?"

"Still checking. All I have right now is a list of calls and the duration of each. No contents yet." He paused. "Stay tuned."

Suddenly, the world crashed around her and she felt exhausted. Her eyelids drooped, and she forced them open. She paced the room to stay awake, but it wasn't working.

She said, "Cooper says Reacher was in St. Louis last night. Can you check that out?"

"Yeah. And I'm looking at Mackenzie and Bavolsky. I'll call you when I have anything definitive," he said before he hung up.

She flopped onto the bed, made a mental note to update Gaspar in the morning, and fell asleep.

CHAPTER THIRTY

Friday, February 11
11:20 p.m.
St. Louis, Missouri

SCORPIO OWNED HALF A dozen counterfeit passports from six different countries, but private jet travel inside the United States solved those problems. No passports required. Jets were faster than driving. They also avoided all the security screening issues for commercial flights.

He nodded, pleased with his decision. A private jet was the best option. He'd instructed Thorn to make it so.

He would not be returning to Rapid City. Nothing left to go back to now. Both his home and his laundromat had burned to cinders.

His physical possessions filled a single duffel bag, which Thorn had tossed into the plane before departure. Everything else he would ever need when he settled in Mexico was stored in the cloud. Gotta love technology. He grinned.

Scorpio had napped the entire four-hour travel time to St.

Louis. Along with the adrenaline flooding his system, the nap had energized him. He awakened refreshed and ready to finish the Mackenzie business tonight. His nerves were abuzz with anticipation.

They deplaned at the private airport, a short distance from U Store Stuff. Scorpio washed his face in the airport's executive lounge while Thorn collected the rental vehicle.

Scorpio approached the information desk, which was occupied by a middle-aged black man dressed in a business suit. "May I help you, sir?"

"I'm Arthur Scorpio. Do you have a package for me?" he asked. He'd called in a favor from a local contact to get what he needed. He'd never met the guy. Which was precisely the way he wanted to keep it.

"Let me check." The man pushed away from the desk and into a room behind him. He returned with a small padded envelope. "Here you are, Mr. Scorpio."

"Thanks." Scorpio took the envelope, felt the keys inside, and nodded. He walked as well as he could toward the valet exit where Thorn was waiting with the engine running.

Storage units in places like U Store Stuff were notorious havens for criminal enterprises of all kinds. Anonymous, secure, and protected by the Fourth Amendment of the United States Constitution. All of which meant that the contents remained private and the owners protected from prying eyes and prosecution. Much more reliable than storing product in somebody's basement, even if that meant the product was less accessible.

When his business was going strong, before Reacher screwed things up, Scorpio had rented several similar units in locations closer to Rapid City. Which was how he knew U Store

Stuff was a perfect place for Mackenzie to hide Scorpio's drugs.

And St. Louis was close enough to Mackenzie's Chicago base that a low-level crook could easily have driven there in a rented truck, unloaded, and high-tailed it back in a rented truck without losing much sleep.

Almost anything could be inside those storage units, limited only by one's imagination. Storage was private, solid, and cheap. Freezers containing dead bodies, stolen goods, drugs, cash, and more. All sorts of contraband could be stashed and reclaimed at any time.

Scorpio could have opened units all night long, and the odds were better than gambling in Vegas. He'd probably have found drugs of all kinds. But he was only interested in reclaiming property that belonged to him. He knew precisely where to look.

He had investigated the U Store Stuff facility website, which boasted security as well as twenty-four-hour accessibility. Both of which suited his needs perfectly.

The lot was surrounded by an eight-foot chain-link fence. Only a single electronic gate permitted one to enter or exit. Using a unique, personal security code to gain entry to the lot, one's possessions were available at all hours, every day of the year, U Store Stuff boasted.

Scorpio smiled and shook his head. So often, people overlooked the obvious. The huge lot allowed for business expansion, sure. It also left enough room for a small helicopter to land in the undeveloped corner. Thieves could bypass the electronic security completely in other ways, too.

Not that he'd need a helicopter or planned to break in by cutting the fence. Scorpio's forte was technology and familiarity with the dark web, where everything was available to seekers with the skills to hunt.

He began with a customer list for every leased unit on the U Store Stuff lot. Less than an hour of computer time, coupled with clever and knowledgeable searching, yielded three security codes, each of which would open the gate.

He shook his head. People would never learn. Which was the good news.

A few minutes later, Thorn pulled the SUV into the driveway. He stopped at the keypad and punched in the first code. Worked like a charm. The big gate rolled open and Thorn drove through.

Scorpio wagged his head. Laws and security systems work against law-abiding citizens. Criminals don't care. They are never stopped by such measures. When would people figure that out?

Mackenzie rented two units here, Scorpio had learned. Unit D-6 was leased to T. Mackenzie and rent was paid automatically by a monthly credit card charge. Unit K-7 had been paid in cash upfront for an entire year.

Scorpio figured the cash payment was more likely to yield results, but he was prepared to check both, just in case. A guy like Mackenzie was dumb enough to store all sorts of things. After all, he'd found loose gemstones, a pistol, and that flash drive in Mackenzie's bedroom safe, which a sharp teenager could have opened in a couple of seconds.

Unit D-6 was closest to the entrance. Thorn drove directly to it.

Scorpio frowned the moment he saw it. What the hell?

The door was open. Orange traffic cones were placed across the entrance. The concrete floor was wet. Large fans were set up to blow the water into a drain in the center of the floor and dry out the concrete before the overnight temperatures caused the water to freeze.

Another orange cone was placed in front of the exterior brick wall. A shiny new hasp was anchored in place by fresh mortar. Another fan was aimed at the new brick. Mortar could freeze, too, and the ice crystals would weaken the bond. The repairs had been done by a competent crew.

Scorpio shook his head and gripped the handle of his cane, thinking things through. Whatever had been stored in D-6 had been removed. Damage had been caused in the process. The damage was recently repaired. By tomorrow, D-6 would be ready for new tenants.

Not ideal at all.

"Park in the next lane and come back here. Check inside. See if you can determine what happened," he told Thorn.

"Ten-four, boss," Thorn replied. He parked the SUV, left the engine running, and trotted back. He was gone for ten minutes.

When he returned, he said, "Looks like a gunfight. Concrete block walls have been patched in several places. Ricochet damage from bullets, if I had to guess."

"What about the water on the floor?" Scorpio asked.

"Power washer did a good job of removing whatever it was. The floor's pretty clean. Around the drain were some dark spots that could have been blood caught in the crevices."

Scorpio nodded and took a deep breath. He didn't care that some fool was probably killed inside. He only wanted what he'd come to collect. "Let's try Unit K-7, four buildings east."

Thorn pulled through the lane and turned right on the other side. He turned right again into the lane between units labeled J and K.

Unit K-7 was almost in the center of the long brick building. From the exterior, this unit looked the same as D-6, but the sitemap had listed the dimensions as ten-by-twenty.

Thorn pulled the SUV straight into the driveway, headlights shining on the gray garage door.

Scorpio handed him the envelope with the keys inside.

Thorn slipped the transmission into park and climbed out of the SUV.

He used the headlights to illuminate the padlock, which was shackled to the hasp attaching the brick wall to the door on the right side. He poured the keys out of the envelope into his palm. He tried the first key, which didn't fit into the lock.

The second key slid in, turned, and the shackle released from the body of the lock as if it had been lubricated. He lifted the shackle from the hasp and dropped the lock with the key into his oversized pocket. Then he opened the garage door. It was well lubricated and rolled up without so much as a squeaky wheel.

When the door opened, Scorpio stared at the front grille of a black, late model Expedition XLT. The familiar Ford logo perched smack in the middle of it.

The SUV was enormous. More than seventeen feet long, seven feet wide with the mirrors, and six feet high, it pretty well filled Unit K-7. A big man like Thorn couldn't walk around it unless he turned sideways to do so.

Scorpio cocked his head as if a different viewing angle would solve the puzzle.

None of the personal data he had located on Mackenzie reflected ownership of the big SUV.

It had no license plate on the front, which was required in Illinois and Missouri.

That could mean this SUV was a rental from one of the nineteen states that required only a rear plate. Or the plates could have been removed to slow identification.

Scorpio could run the plate through the dark web databases if Thorn could get the number off the back.

Thorn went inside Unit K-7 to check out the vehicle. He turned sideways, leading with his right shoulder, and tried lifting the door handles. The vehicle was locked.

He used a microbeam flashlight to look through the tinted windows. He pulled out his camera and snapped the vehicle identification number through the windshield. Then he snapped a few photos through the side cargo windows.

By the time he'd closed and locked the garage door and returned to the driver's seat, Scorpio had his laptop set up and connected to the dark web using an encrypted hot spot.

"There's two dead bodies inside. I don't recognize them. Given the situation, I'd guess they're not exactly model citizens." Thorn passed his phone to Scorpio who flipped through the photos quickly.

"Anything else in the vehicle?" Scorpio already had the VIN entered on his screen and pushed the button to search.

"Not that I could see."

The Expedition was registered to a woman in Kentucky. With the VIN, Scorpio quickly located the key fob code to unlock the doors. He copied the code to an app in Thorn's phone and handed it back to him.

"Search the SUV quickly," he said. "If you find anything that belongs to me, grab it. Leave everything else in place."

"Ten-four, boss," Thorn replied as he left the warm SUV and retraced his steps to open Unit K-7 again.

While Thorn handled the SUV, Scorpio ran the corpse photos through facial recognition. It didn't take long to identify both from media accounts of several arrests.

"Joey Two" Rosinsky and "Little Hugh" Nowinsky. Killers in the Big Mike Bavolsky "Polish mafia" gang. Based in Chicago, but operating in Illinois, Indiana, and Missouri.

He found lots of data on Bavolsky. He was no choirboy, but he had a pretty daughter and a very hot wife. The girl was maybe sixteen or so. She'd been cursed with her father's stocky Slavic genes.

But the mother. *Wow!* A blonde, lanky beauty. Pretty enough to have been a model or an actress. Chained to Bavolsky.

Scorpio shook his head. She was spectacularly gorgeous, but she was no brain trust, for sure.

As he ran down Bavolsky's list of crimes, Scorpio saw Bavolsky was big league for a small-time guy like Mackenzie. If he'd killed two of Bavolsky's men and lived to tell about it, Mackenzie was a much bigger problem than Scorpio had anticipated. Good to know.

Thorn locked up Unit K-7 and returned. "Nothing in the Expedition belonging to you."

He handed his phone to Scorpio, who reviewed the photos.

Scorpio wiped the app and the code from the phone and tossed it into the front seat.

"Thought these might come in handy." Thorn tossed a shotgun and a box of breaching shells into the passenger seat. "Now what?"

Scorpio clenched his teeth and kept his hands working the keyboard. He ran through the client list for U Store Stuff again. He'd found a third possible storage unit. This one, Unit GG-4, was leased and paid for by S. R. Sanderson. Rose Sanderson. Jane Mackenzie's twin sister.

Could be nothing. But he'd come too far to leave without checking.

Scorpio said, "Let's try one more. Head back toward the gate and keep traveling west. We want Unit GG-4 this time."

"Ten-four, boss," Thorn replied. He backed away from Unit K-7's garage door and rolled to the end of the lane. He turned west, keeping the buildings between his vehicle and the highway.

CHAPTER THIRTY-ONE

Saturday, February 12
12:20 a.m.
St. Louis, Missouri

UNIT GG-4 WAS THE same size as Unit D-6, ten feet by ten feet. Thorn pulled the bolt cutters from the back of the SUV and snapped the shackle from the lock.

Stacked inside were boxes of fentanyl patches and tablets. Scorpio recognized them immediately, even from his position in the back seat of the SUV and from a distance. The packaging and logo were unmistakable.

Were these his drugs? Thieves had stolen a lot more. But that was a while ago. This might be all they had left.

No way to tell until he compared the serial numbers on the boxes to his missing inventory. Nor did it really matter. He'd take them regardless of who owned them. Spoils of war. Compensation. Finders keepers. Whatever.

A big grin split his face, and he said, "Yeah, baby!"

He crawled out of the back seat and walked into Unit GG-4 to get a closer look. The white boxes were stacked on a pallet in the center of the floor.

"Can you fit this into our small SUV?" he asked.

"It'll be tight, but we might make it if we lose some of the boxes and you sit in the front seat," Thorn replied.

He returned to the SUV to rearrange the cargo area. The only available light was the SUV's headlights, so he left the engine running. He began removing the opioids from storage.

Scorpio couldn't help with the work. The drugs were lightweight, but he could only use one hand, and he needed that one to hold the cane. Instead, he stood guard.

He didn't expect tenants or visitors to arrive at this time of night, but he leaned his left shoulder against a block wall and kept his right hand on the gun in his pocket.

He was cold, even inside Unit GG-4 where the wind couldn't blow straight through his clothes. But the process went quickly. No vehicles approached.

Once Thorn had stacked all the intact boxes he could fit into the cargo hold, he opened the remaining ones. He stuffed individual blister packs and sealed patches into nooks, crannies, and crevices. When he finished, the small SUV was packed completely full, but not one single pill was left in Unit GG-4.

"That's the last of it," Thorn said, as he closed the hatch and the back doors.

Scorpio took one final glance around. Only the wood pallets that had lifted the pharmaceutical boxes off the dirty concrete floor remained.

He returned to the SUV and climbed into the front seat.

Thorn closed the garage door and propped the lock onto the hasp as best he could. The ruse would fool no one upon close inspection, but they would be long gone before anyone bothered to look.

Thorn took his seat behind the wheel and headed toward the exit. After an interminable wait, the sensor at the gate registered the vehicle ready to exit. It began the long, slow opening pull.

The SUV rolled through the gate to the end of the driveway and stopped at the road.

Thorn asked, "Where to now, boss?"

Two hours ago, the question would have annoyed Scorpio no end. The question would have been stupid. Now it wasn't.

"You mean are we going to drive all the way to Mexico with an SUV full of opioids?" Scorpio said thoughtfully. "Just run these puppies directly across the border ourselves?"

The sheer boldness of the idea appealed, although the risk was great. Besides, he had unfinished business to conclude with Mackenzie and those two sisters. Not to mention Reacher

And he had to find them all first.

Reluctantly, he shook his head. "Head south. Be extremely cautious. We don't want to get pulled over for any reason. Let's see how far we can travel before daylight."

"Ten-four, boss." He pulled onto the road. A couple of miles later, he said, "What are we going to do with all this product?"

Scorpio's instincts said to get as far away from St. Louis as possible while he still could.

He pulled out his phone and began searching for truck rental locations a few hours south. He had never taken possession of his drugs before. In the past, his role had been management, not shipping and delivery. This was an unfamiliar challenge.

He'd already planned to leave the country. But taking the drugs into Mexico might prove difficult. Besides, his customers were located inside the US. The wiser thing was to find a place to store the product in the US. A place where he could reach it fast when he needed to.

Another storage facility was the best option for his purposes. Somewhere close to the border.

He checked Chicago area news. Nothing so far about Babbling Brooke's murder. It was smarter to assume that Chicago PD had managed to tie that to him because if they hadn't yet, they would. Yep, the sooner he left the country, the better. Leaving his drugs here was the smart move.

A vague plan was taking shape in his head.

He pulled up a map on his phone and clicked a couple of searches. He figured sixteen hours of drive time, give or take, without breaks. At least thirteen hours almost due south to San Antonio. After that, another three to Laredo, and into Mexico.

He found a good entry point for crossing over. One of his passports should get him past border security on the other side. He had counterfeit passports for Thorn, too. Mexico welcomed tourists from Luxembourg or Switzerland or Ireland. He wasn't worried.

Thorn navigated to I-44 west and entered the flow of late night traffic. As long as he kept his speed at the posted limits, continuing in the SUV for a few hundred miles before daylight should be safe enough.

After daylight, a panel van or small truck would be better. If nothing else, it would keep curious types from looking in the windows when they stopped for food and gas.

Scorpio found a truck rental that commenced hours of operation before sunrise. They'd reach it before the SUV ran out of gas. He read the address aloud, and Thorn punched it into the GPS system.

Now all he needed was a storage facility near Laredo. And then transportation into Mexico. With luck, they'd be across the border tonight.

"What do you know about Mexico City?" Scorpio asked.

"Warmer than Rapid City," Thorn grinned. Scorpio did not. Thorn cleared his throat and said, "I know that Guadalajara is a lot nicer. Why?"

Scorpio raised his eyebrows. He'd never been to Mexico City or Guadalajara. "Nicer in what way?"

"Newer, cleaner, more upscale. Luxury cars. It's a world-class city. Great restaurants," Thorn replied.

"Yeah?" Scorpio asked. The idea was appealing. He was scheduled for more therapy and a couple of surgeries before he'd be able to ambulate without the cane. "How about medical?"

"Excellent doctors. You'd get a lot better medical stuff in Guadalajara, for sure. Woman I know drove down there. Got a facelift and a boob job and a few tucks. Cost a fraction of what she'd have paid in Beverly Hills. I'm telling you, she came out looking amazing," Thorn replied with a low whistle, shaking his head.

"That so?"

"Damn straight." Thorn glanced across the console and nodded. "Man, you could live like a king there on relatively little money, too. Big house. Servants. The whole *Lifestyle of the Rich and Famous* thing. Absolutely."

Scorpio said nothing. But he searched websites referencing Guadalajara on his phone and flipped through the pages. After watching a few videos posted by tourists and journalists, he'd made up his mind.

He said, "Guadalajara it is. Make it so."

"Ten-four, boss," Thorn replied with a grin.

CHAPTER THIRTY-TWO

Saturday, February 12
7:15 a.m.
Houston, Texas

OTTO OVERSLEPT. WHEN GASPAR banged on her door, she opened one eye to look at the bedside clock.

"Crap!" she jumped up and ran to the door. "I'll meet you at the gate."

"They won't hold the plane, so don't miss it," he replied, already heading toward the elevator.

She jumped into a quick shower, dressed, and dashed out the door with her hair still damp. She made it to the gate and down the jetway, mere moments before the flight attendant closed the door.

Gaspar was already sleeping in seat 1A when she hurried past him. The guy could sleep anywhere. Two rows back, she stowed her bags, slid into her seat on the aisle, and fastened her seatbelt just as the plane was pushing back.

Houston to San Antonio flight time was fifty-eight minutes to cover the one hundred ninety miles. A quick up and down,

214 | Diane Capri

which meant Otto only had time for one puny cup of coffee before they were on the ground again.

Gaspar waited for her to deplane and they walked toward the rental counter.

"I need coffee. There's a kiosk up ahead."

He grinned. "Did you stay awake all night studying, Sunshine?"

"Not exactly." She took a breath and prepared to defend herself. "I talked to Finlay for about an hour after I left you."

"What the hell? You didn't think to discuss that move with me first?" His scowl would have quelled any type of rebellion from his kids, but it only annoyed Otto.

"I didn't have the energy to argue with you about it twice."

"What kind of logic is that?"

She shook her head as she approached the java counter and ordered an extra-large black coffee. "What do you want? I'm buying."

"Three donuts and an espresso with cream and sugar," he replied.

She placed the order, collected his donuts, and paid the bill. They moved to the side to wait for the barista to do her thing.

"Finlay says General Simpson is trying to connect with Reacher. He's put a flag on Reacher's bank account. No luck so far."

Gaspar's eyebrows dipped all the way to the bridge of his nose.

They collected the coffee and resumed the trek to the rental vehicles.

Gaspar gave in about two dozen steps along the way. "What else did Finlay say?"

"That was the most interesting bit. Otherwise, it was stuff about long conversations with Rose Sanderson. Oh, and how hot Rose Sanderson and Jane Mackenzie are." She filled him in on the rest while they got settled into the sedan and hit the road.

Gaspar said, "I've been thinking about Mackenzie and Bramall."

"What about them?" Otto's lip curled of its own accord. "You think they've partnered up?"

"To do what?"

He shrugged. "They were quick to ditch you after you were attacked in that bathroom. One of them did it. The other one didn't seem to object overmuch."

"So it's a threesome? Reacher, Bramall, and Mackenzie?" she asked. "Seems kind of crowded for Reacher to team up like that, don't you think? He's usually a solo act."

"Maybe. But we know he was working with Jane and Bramall before. According to your Boy Detective, anyway." Gaspar gave her the side-eye and then returned his attention to driving.

Otto said nothing, but she mulled the idea for a while.

Forty minutes after the plane landed, they stood in a small office at Fort Sam Houston waiting for General Sean Simpson, on base temporarily for briefings by the joint chiefs. Or so he'd said when Gaspar called to set up the appointment. Sounded like a boondoggle to get out of the Upstate New York winter weather to Otto.

Simpson was currently serving as the Superintendent at West Point, the big boss, what other colleges might call the president. He had held the position for a while. When he'd brought her up to speed, Gaspar said Simpson was smart, accomplished, and definitely no pushover.

Everything about the base, including this room, was probably under surveillance, she figured. Which meant they would discuss nothing of consequence in Simpson's absence, and probably not when he arrived, either.

After fifteen minutes the door opened, and a relatively fit, moderately young general entered the room. The kind of man who was a good role model for soldiers. He could have starred in a recruitment video encouraging young Americans to be all they could be. Which he probably had.

"I'm sorry to have kept you waiting," Simpson said, extending his hand to shake with both of them. Like most generals, he was polite and personable, too. Officers didn't rise that far up the ranks if they were obnoxious idiots.

He indicated with his palm. "Please sit."

When they were settled, he moved to the chair and leaned forward across the desk with a sincere look on his face. "How can I be of service to the FBI today?"

Gaspar took the lead. "As I mentioned on the phone, General, we're interested in two West Point graduates. Major Jack Reacher and Major Serena Rose Sanderson."

Simpson did not flinch. "I've never met either officer. I'm not sure how much help I can be to you."

Otto replied frankly, as was her habit. "Phone records show that Reacher called your office several times and spoke with you directly. Were those conversations off the record?"

"Off the record? Calls that come into a government-owned and operated facility?" His tone remained friendly. "You're sitting here asking me about the substance of the calls. How far off the record could they have possibly been?"

Not exactly an answer.

"We know you don't have much time," she nodded firmly. "Let's not play cat and mouse here. Records show Major Reacher called your office about Major Sanderson several times. The first time from a pay phone in rural Wisconsin."

"You know he called. But you don't have access to the contents of our conversations, is that it?" Simpson asked.

Otto ignored the question because the answer was obvious. If they had recorded calls, they wouldn't need to ask Simpson about the contents. "What did Reacher want to know? And what did you tell him?"

Simpson seemed to consider his options briefly. Perhaps he concluded he had no dog in the fight because he replied just as frankly. "Reacher said he'd found a West Point class ring. He knew the significance of the ring. He wanted to return it. He asked me for help with that. Mostly, he wanted background to locate the owner to return the ring."

Otto pursed her lips and nodded. The tale seemed unlike Reacher. But it also seemed to fit with Noble's story about meeting Reacher out west. She wasn't sure what to think.

"Supplying personal details about current or former military personnel is strictly prohibited about a dozen different ways, sir," Gaspar said. "The only possible chance it could happen would be a personal favor. Did you owe Reacher a personal favor, General?"

Simpson cocked his head and narrowed his eyes as if he could peer straight into Gaspar's heart and judge his intentions. "You served with us, didn't you Gaspar? Military police, right? Same as Reacher."

Gaspar nodded. His Army background was no secret. It was one of the things that made him valuable to Otto and got him assigned to the Reacher case.

She considered Gaspar her secret weapon precisely because his background was so similar to Reacher's. He thought like Reacher, which she did not. Of course, Simpson had pulled Gaspar's file. She'd have done the same.

"I won't take offense, Gaspar. As a favor to you," Simpson said. "You know how we operate and you know I didn't owe Reacher anything. But, one West Point grad to another, sure, I felt some loyalty to the man. Sanderson, too. The same with you."

Gaspar nodded. "Same here, General."

Otto nodded. She understood. Exactly the kind of oak-paneled bullshit military brass everywhere had engaged in since the beginning of time.

She folded her hands in her lap. "We're not trying to bust anybody's chops here. As we said when we called, our assignment is to complete a background check on Reacher for the Special Personnel Task Force. You are one of the most reliable witnesses to have talked to him in a while. We're interested in your impressions and evaluations."

"About what?"

"Reacher's fitness for duty," Otto said. "The assignment he's being considered for is classified above our clearance levels, so we can't tell you any more about that. But we're looking for his overall mental, emotional, physical, and financial readiness. Anything you can offer could make a difference when the big brass makes their decisions."

"Hard to hit the target in the dark, Otto," Simpson said wryly. He leaned back in his chair and folded his hands over a flat midsection. He probably had six-pack abs inside that shirt. The guy had it all. He was just about the best physical specimen for his age group that she'd ever seen.

"Don't I know it. Unfortunately, that's the job." She nodded. "Let's take it one thing at a time, then. Did Reacher need money?"

"He didn't ask for money."

"Was he sick, infirm, disabled?"

"If he was, he didn't say so. Remember, I didn't meet him in person."

"How was his mental status?"

"Mental status evaluation requires a visual inspection. I wasn't able to observe him at all. I can't say how he was dressed or groomed or anything like that. We talked on the phone. That's it."

Otto nodded. "Voice communications are better than visuals for assessing emotions, as you know. What was his emotional state?"

"Exactly what we'd all expect. He was professional and appropriately detached, as an army major should be," Simpson replied, with professional detachment of his own.

"How about his orientation to time and place?" Otto asked.

"He was as well oriented as you are. His attention span was good. When he didn't get what he wanted the first time, he called several times to follow up. His long-term and short-term memory were solid."

"You'd say he demonstrated good judgment, I suppose," Otto said.

"He demonstrated the ability to solve problems and make acceptable decisions given the facts on the ground, yes," Simpson replied.

Gaspar asked, "How did Reacher demonstrate problem-solving to you?"

"He answered my questions about his service and the reason for his interest in Major Sanderson to my satisfaction," Simpson said. "I asked him why he moves around so much, doesn't have a proper home."

"What did he say?"

"He said he gets uneasy. Can't stay in one place. He said he fought for freedom and his behavior is what freedom looks like." Simpson offered a steady gaze as if Otto should understand his point.

She spied his wedding ring glinting in the sunlight streaming through the window.

She nodded. "Reacher's nomadic behavior didn't seem normal to you, did it?"

"Not at all. Humans are nesters by nature. We like home and hearth and family and a beer after work and sports on weekends. All of that," Simpson replied.

"But?" Gaspar prodded.

"But he wasn't asking my opinion. He gave me reasonable, rational answers to my questions. Plainly. And in a straightforward way, as I expected." Simpson took a breath. "He didn't seem like an off-his-rocker wacko. Which is what you're really asking me, isn't it?"

"What did you give him in return, General?" Otto asked the tricky question and put him in a tough spot.

If Simpson told Reacher anything at all, he'd violated the rules, and he knew it, and she knew he knew it.

If he lied about Reacher now, in response to direct questions from the FBI, he was guilty of conduct unbecoming. Not to mention at least one federal crime, and probably a few more, if she took the time to list the possible charges.

Simpson had to know all of that. And he didn't seem the least perturbed by her impertinent question. "Have you read Sanderson's file?"

"We have," Gaspar said.

"You know she led her soldiers well. She was a credit to West Point and to the Army. She was wounded on active duty, for which she was awarded a Bronze Star and a Purple Heart. She is a war hero. No two ways about it. We owe her. Simple as that." Simpson paused and looked pointedly at Gaspar. "You know how it is."

Gaspar replied, "I do."

"Reacher had found her West Point class ring and wanted to return it. You know what those rings mean to our graduates, too." Simpson quietly knocked his gold class ring against the table. He nodded toward Gaspar's right hand, where a matching weighty gold West Point class ring with an onyx stone rested on his third finger.

"Yes, sir." Gaspar nodded in return. "The ring was hard won, General. Worn with pride. I'm not likely to lose it. You ever lost yours?"

Simpson frowned and shook his head. "Which was Reacher's point. He didn't believe Sanderson lost the ring. He thought she might be in trouble. He thought he might be able to help."

"What did Reacher say to persuade you, when you knew sharing personal information about Sanderson was inappropriate as well as illegal?" Otto pushed him. Maybe harder than she should have.

"He'd found the ring in a Wisconsin pawn shop, which wasn't a likely scenario. He figured Sanderson would want it back and he wanted to return it. Pretty simple, honorable behavior, don't you think?" Simpson arched his eyebrows. "If he'd needed money, he wouldn't have bought the ring from the pawn shop. But he did. He also went to a lot of trouble to find the ring's owner. Sounds like the guy is fit for duty to me."

Otto looked him squarely in the eyes. "But would you choose him for a highly classified assignment on your team, General? Today? Knowing what you know about him now?"

He said nothing. Which was all she needed.

A hard rap on the office door was followed by a uniformed soldier. "Sir, you're wanted in the conference room."

"Thank you, Hayes." The young man turned and left. Simpson stood. "Can't keep the chairman of the joint chiefs waiting, I'm afraid."

"You haven't heard from Reacher again, I assume," Otto said, as they walked toward the door. "Haven't made any attempts to reach him?"

He stopped, and his voice became quiet. "Not directly, no. But I heard from Sanderson a few weeks later. Her ring had been returned, and she was grateful. She was getting the medical care she needed."

"Was she treated at a veterans hospital?"

"Initially, she was. But after she moved in with her sister, she transitioned to private care."

"Were her injuries severe?" Otto asked.

He nodded. "Severe and disfiguring. She'd acquired an intractable infection, too. She needed quite a bit of medical attention. She said she had a long way to go, but she said Reacher was responsible for saving her life."

"I see," Gaspar said as if the news troubled him somehow. "Did she mean that literally?"

Simpson's gaze met Gaspar's, and he nodded once. "Yes."

He turned to Otto. "You've read Reacher's file. His career with us was…unusual. He was a star. But he also cut corners, brutally. He got away with it too many times. His methods became his way of life. Ingrained now. Habit. Instinct, really. You must already know you can't expect him to follow the rules."

"We do," Otto replied.

"You asked me for my impressions and evaluations of Reacher. Frankly, his Army file is unorthodox and potentially threatening." He paused as if he might not say more. Until he added, "My brief interactions with him gave me no reason to question the file's contents."

Gaspar nodded without comment.

"How so?" Otto asked.

"Reacher left the Army of his own volition. But he was only half a step ahead of a court-martial. I'd say his adjustment to a normal civilian life is unlikely, no matter how long he's been out there." Simpson looked at Gaspar and back to Otto a moment longer before he gave a curt nod.

"Which is why you're trying to reach him, right?" Otto asked. "To tell him Sanderson needs his help again?"

His eyes widened, but he said nothing. He turned to leave.

Otto called him back with another question, "We know you've been in touch with Sanderson the past few weeks, General. Lots of long chats on the phone. What's going on? What were you talking about?"

"Medical care, mostly. The kind of care she needed was expensive. She wanted advice about that," he said.

"What kind of advice?"

"She wanted private care. She wanted the Army to pay for it. I tried to help, but…" he shrugged. "She was free of her infection, but she needed expert, expensive plastic surgery. We're not set up to handle injuries like hers. Last time she called, she thanked me and said she'd find a place she could afford."

Gaspar said, "Did she mention her sister?"

"Only that her sister's husband was a philandering asshole. Her words," Simpson said.

Gaspar asked, "Sounds like Sanderson wasn't too pleased with her sister's choice."

"That's putting it mildly," Simpson nodded.

"I've met the husband. He's unstable. Maybe violent," Otto said. "We need to find her. She's in trouble. And we're not the only ones who are looking."

"Be careful what you wish for, Agent Otto." Simpson's last words were a warning. "Reacher won't care that you're FBI. He went to a lot of trouble to find Sanderson and save her life once. He'll be doubly protective of her this time, should he learn that *anyone* is trying to harm her again."

"Rex Mackenzie is the one who should be careful," Gaspar replied. "Neither Sanderson nor her sister have anything to fear from us. We're the good guys."

Simpson left, but his warning lingered in the cool air until Otto noticed that she was shivering. "Let's go. It's freezing in here."

CHAPTER THIRTY-THREE

Saturday, February 12
11:15 a.m.
San Antonio, Texas

THE SUNSHINE ON HER shoulders felt heavenly, even if the temperature was still a little cool at only sixty-nine degrees. The forecast called for low seventies later in the day. Given the sub-zero February she'd be returning to in Detroit, Otto planned to bask in the Texas warmth as long as she could.

Gaspar strolled along beside her until they reached the rental sedan and ducked inside. He took his position in the driver's seat.

Gaspar was number two on this assignment. Number two was always the driver, he'd insisted from the very first day they'd worked together. Arguing with him was useless; she'd given up long ago. He started the engine.

She settled into the passenger seat and retrieved an alligator clamp from her pocket. She fastened the lap belt, pulled the shoulder harness loose, and positioned the clamp at the retractor to give herself some wiggle room.

From behind his aviator sunglasses, Gaspar grinned and asked, "Where to now Dragon Boss Lady?"

"Let's find out." She reached for the Boss's phone and made the call.

He picked up, which was a bit surprising. Since he hadn't made the first move, she'd figured he was involved in other matters. She put the speaker phone on so Gaspar could hear the conversation, and she wouldn't need to repeat it later.

"Have you found Mackenzie and Bramall yet?" she asked before he could ask anything.

"You'd have been the first to know if I had," he replied. "They landed in Las Vegas. They checked into the Bellagio, just like Mackenzie said on the plane. The two women are not at that hotel, and Vegas is a big place. So they're trying to figure out what to do next."

"Do you have any video or anything else that's helpful?"

"Still checking," he said. "I take it you haven't heard from Noble?"

"Should I have?"

"He's making some progress. Still no ID on the dead woman. But he's made the connection to the U Store Stuff facility in St. Louis. He's headed there."

"What does he expect to find?"

"He's pieced together a few things about Mackenzie."

Gaspar said, "Like what?"

"He suspects Mackenzie has been laundering money for Bavolsky's crime syndicate for a number of years. He's probably right about that." He paused. "Chicago PD speculation is that Mackenzie was forced to participate early on, got in deeper, and now wants to get out. Bavolsky is not keen on the idea."

"So the operating theory is that Bavolsky killed Mackenzie's wife just for fun?" Otto asked.

"It's hard to say with specificity before they identify the woman's body. But they think Mackenzie has something on Bavolsky and is using it for leverage. Wants Bavolsky to let him go, free and clear. Which, of course, is not how gangs work. The murder in Mackenzie's mansion might be a reply to Mackenzie's efforts to shake himself loose."

"Not a warning. He's sending a message," Gaspar said, swiping a hand through his hair. He fidgeted in the driver's seat, trying to get comfortable. "Bavolsky is saying not only no, but hell no. Mackenzie serves at Bavolsky's pleasure, or he dies."

The Boss replied, "That's what Chicago PD thinks. Noble says it makes sense and fits with all the facts."

Otto glanced at Gaspar. "Which means you didn't tell Noble about those two dead Bavolsky soldiers?"

"He'll figure it out soon enough. As long as he's occupied with all of that, we don't have to worry about him interfering with your mission," the Boss said.

"Did you find the two dead thugs?" Gaspar asked.

A long pause followed.

"Not exactly," he said.

Otto closed her eyes and shook her head. Finlay wasn't the only one who always had a hidden agenda. The Boss was ten times worse, and he was supposed to be on her team. This work was never straightforward or obvious.

Gaspar picked up the thread. "Meaning what?"

"Meaning we know where the bodies are, but we don't have public confirmation. Noble will probably get that in a few hours if he stays on task," the Boss explained. "If he doesn't get distracted."

Gaspar said, "Do we have recorded or transcribed contents of General Simpson's conversations with Rose Sanderson?"

The Boss was quiet for a long time.

"So what do we do now?" Otto asked, assuming he didn't have the audio. Or if he did have it, he wasn't sharing right now.

"You could ask Finlay," he snapped. "Otherwise, you're smart. Surprise me."

Gaspar punched the button to disconnect. "He took that well, didn't he?"

Otto shrugged. The tension between Finlay and the Boss had become a way of life. She was sick of dealing with it. Let them figure it out.

Gaspar grinned. "Where to, Suzy Wong?"

She considered the question. "Do you like baseball, Cheech?"

"Yeah, I guess. Sure," Gaspar replied, both eyebrows arched.

"My dad is a big Tigers fan. Baseball is almost a religion in my family. All my brothers played. Anyway, Dad also loves to read. One of his favorite books is a memoir by Doris Kearns Goodwin about growing up in New York with her family and the Brooklyn Dodgers. Dad read her book to us when we were kids." She paused and smiled at the quizzical expression on Gaspar's face. "Anyway, Dad always says you can't tell the players without a scorecard."

"Which means...." Gaspar said.

"Scorecards were sold at the stadiums back in the day. Probably before baseball uniforms had names and numbers. Definitely before public address systems and broadcasting. They're an elegant way to keep track of the players and the game. The art of scorekeeping, Doris Kearns Goodwin called it."

Gaspar shook his head. "Sorry, but you've lost me, Sunshine."

"That's precisely the point. We're lost. We need a scorecard. We've got too many players, and we don't know where they are on the field. We've got big gaps in our intel, too." She paused and found her personal phone. "First thing we need is a place to work. Let's find a hotel."

San Antonio had many to choose from, but she located a hotel on the Riverwalk downtown. She reserved a small suite with a conference room and requested a whiteboard with markers and an urn full of coffee. She also requested an atlas. The car's GPS provided directions, the valet parked the sedan, and they were ready to work within the hour.

"Where do you plan to start?" Gaspar had stretched out on one of the chairs with an unobstructed view of her whiteboard.

"Everything seemed to be running smoothly for Sanderson. Until it wasn't. The big question is what triggered all this," She wrote the word *triggers* at the top of the whiteboard followed by five question marks.

"Why did she disappear, you mean?" Gaspar asked.

"Noble said we have five missing persons. Let's start with them." She listed the names on the whiteboard as she spoke. "Rex Mackenzie, Jane Mackenzie, Rose Sanderson, Terry Bramall, and Jack Reacher."

"We've added more names since then, though," Gaspar said. "The real estate agent. What's her name?"

"Brooke Malone," Otto said, writing the name on the board. "We also have two unidentified men who arrived at the Mackenzie mansion and again at Mackenzie's dry cleaner business."

"Noble said neither one was Bramall nor Mackenzie. They might have been Jimmy Two and Little Hugh, but we don't know. So let's call them X and Y for now," Gaspar suggested.

Otto wrote the names on the board. "For completeness, let's add Big Mike Bavolsky, too. And General Simpson."

"Why?"

"He's been talking to Sanderson about something. He's put a message out to Reacher. He knows more than what he told us," she replied.

Gaspar nodded.

"We need to assume that X and Y could be neither Jimmy Two nor Little Hugh, though. So let's list all four," Otto said, writing it all on the board. "We can always combine them later if they turn out to be the same people."

She stood back and looked at the list. "We have at least eleven players and maybe twelve. Enough to field a baseball team and some spares."

She drew a diagonal line through Jimmy Two and Little Hugh. "We know both of these guys are dead."

Gaspar said, "One of the three women is dead, too."

"Right. But until we know which one, we can't do much with that." She looked at the list again and shook her head. "Okay, let's add locations."

CHAPTER THIRTY-FOUR

Saturday, February 12
1:05 p.m.
San Antonio, Texas

GASPAR SAID, "EASY TO cross off the two thugs. Since they're dead, we probably don't care where they are exactly."

"He didn't say so, but I suspect the Boss knows Jimmy Two and Little Hugh are cooling fast in one of those storage units in St. Louis," Otto said, making a note to that effect on the board. She took a swig of water and stood back to look at the board.

"Anyone else we can nail down?" Gaspar asked.

Otto thought about it and finally shook her head. She made notes on the board next to the names as she said, "Mackenzie and Bramall are in Las Vegas. At least one of the three women is still in the morgue in Chicago. Bavolsky could still be in Chicago, too."

"That doesn't seem like a safe assumption to me," Gaspar replied.

Otto put a question mark after Bavolsky's location. She stood back again to look at the list and cocked her head. "Is that it?"

"For now," Gaspar agreed.

She tapped her knuckle on her lips, staring at the whiteboard. After a few moments, she turned to him. "Let's look at that flash drive now. I've got some ideas."

While Gaspar opened the laptop and set up the secure hot spot, she refilled her coffee and paced the room to think. When he'd located the data, she took a seat next to him to look at the screen.

Otto selected a couple of dates at random and compared the spreadsheets to the bank records. She chose another set and then a third.

"We need a good forensic analysis of these documents," Gaspar said.

"It looks like three things are happening." She leaned back.

"Break it down for me."

She moved to the whiteboard. She wrote the number one followed by *collections*. "One set of spreadsheets is a record of collections from many customers. The amounts vary. The dates are semi-regular, I guess."

"Collection of what?"

"Given the amounts, the frequency, and who's involved? I'd say these are records of either gambling debts or protection payments, most likely," she replied.

"Drug sales, maybe?"

She shook her head. "I doubt it's drug sales because that would create a paper trail even a congested bloodhound could follow."

Gaspar grinned.

She wrote the number two on the whiteboard followed by *laundered.* "The collections are transformed by the magic of money laundering. The second set of spreadsheets are a duplicate of the first, same dates, same names. But the amounts are larger."

"How much larger?" he asked.

"Again, it varies, but by a factor of about ten, I would say. Sometimes more. Rarely less."

He nodded. "What about the bank records?"

"Like you said, lots of zeros. There's several million dollars here in offshore accounts." She wrote the number three on the whiteboard followed by the word *theft.* "Putting it all together, my best guess is these are records of illegal activity, money laundering, and a hefty slice of skimming off the top of the laundered cash."

"The owners of Polish Brothers Limited would kill to protect that kind of revenue," Gaspar said.

"You bet. In a cold Chicago second." She refilled her coffee.

Gaspar asked, "How does any of this help us?"

"I'm not sure yet. But it feels like we're getting somewhere."

He arched his eyebrows and said nothing.

"Pull up the sitemap for U Store Stuff's facility. That place is huge. But Bramall must have had a plan for those drugs when he arrived," she said.

"Bramall might have high-tailed it out of there right after you did. Could be someone else cleaned up." Gaspar clicked a few keys and pulled up a satellite view.

She leaned over his shoulder to view the screen. The U Store Stuff lot had to be at least a couple of acres. She scanned the brick buildings.

She pointed to the building housing Unit D-6. "Jimmy Two and Little Hugh's bodies were right here. Where are they now?

We need better video. He circumvented the CCTV, but what about the satellites?"

"Good question."

"Yes, it is." She nodded. "That place is near a sizeable airport. Since nine-eleven, every commercial airport in the country is watched constantly. There should be satellite coverage all over the place."

"If a video like that existed, don't you think the Boss and your Boy Detective would have found it already?" He clicked a few keys. "Here's what we've got. Nothing. According to this, you were never even there. Nor were Bramall or the two dead goons. In fact, Unit D-6 looks quiet and undisturbed for the entire night and straight into the morning."

She folded her arms and leaned back on one foot. "Except we have my body cam and my phone video, so we know what really happened. And when I went back there later in the day, Unit D-6 was empty and under repairs."

"Right."

Slowly, she pondered, "When I left, Bramall was there, and two dead guys were on the floor. The drugs and the money were still there. So where is all that stuff now?"

Gaspar stretched his legs out in front of him and folded his hands over his stomach. "Bramall wasn't murdered or kidnapped, because you were with him on that jet a few hours later."

"The Boss says Bramall had an accomplice. He thinks the accomplice was Reacher." She paused. "Because they worked together before. On Noble's case."

"He told me."

"Do you think that's possible?"

"Anything's possible," Gaspar replied. "But is it likely? I'd say no."

"Why?"

Gaspar shrugged. "Doesn't feel right to me."

She grinned. "You hate it when I say that."

"True. Okay, look at the logic." He took a deep breath. "Bramall had at least one helper. He simply couldn't have pulled everything off in the time allotted on his own."

"How'd they do it?"

Gaspar said, "They moved the bodies into the SUV, and the helper drove it to another unit. Bramall followed in his sedan. The helper opened the door and pulled the vehicle inside. Then he closed the door and locked it. He got into Bramall's sedan, and they drove back to D-6."

She nodded. His scenario was the same as she'd assumed. "After that?"

"They put the drugs and the shoeboxes into Bramall's sedan and drove them out of the lot," he replied.

"Not enough time." She shook her head. "That sedan didn't have enough cargo space to hold everything. They'd have had to make two trips. Or picked up a rented truck somewhere."

He clacked a few keys. "Sunrise in St. Louis on Friday was...6:56 a.m. But daybreak was about ninety minutes earlier. The workday had started for a lot of folks. People would have been coming and going. And the auctions started early, too."

She nodded, thinking. "Which means it's more likely that Bramall stashed the drugs in a third storage unit, intending to collect them later."

"He had more time before you saw him again, though. The drugs could have been on that Gulfstream 100. There's room for a fair amount of cargo on that jet if memory serves." He pulled up the specs with another few keystrokes. "Yep. It's got sixty-four cubic feet of baggage space. Depends on the configuration, but the drugs and money should have easily fit."

"One of them drove Bramall's sedan to the airport and left it there, don't forget." She turned her attention to something else. "Have we traced the serial numbers on those opioids to the manufacturer yet?"

"Still working on it. And before you ask, still working on the cash as well. We know it came from the Chicago Federal Reserve Bank. But we don't know the identity of the person who received it."

She nodded. "So, after all that logic, Chico, who was Bramall's accomplice?"

"My logic says it's gotta be Rex Mackenzie. I've got fifty bucks. I'm willing to bet," he replied.

"My gut says the same thing. Which makes me wonder why the Boss thinks it was Reacher."

"*If* he believes Reacher was the guy." Gaspar shook his head and tisked. "Come on, Suzie Wong. After everything he's put us through, surely you're over your Charles Cooper hero worship by now."

She shrugged. Gaspar was partially right. She had worshiped Cooper once. But more than that, she owed him. Her debt had not been repaid yet, and perhaps it never would be. Not that she'd be spilling her guts on that score to Gaspar. He had his secrets, and she had hers. She planned to keep it that way.

She stood up and stretched. Then she took off her jacket and her shoes to get comfortable. She drained her coffee and poured another cup.

She tapped the top of the whiteboard where she'd written the word *Triggers?????* She looked at the word as if it might identify the triggers by magic.

Which didn't happen. Not exactly. But something Simpson

had said teased her brain like a kitten peeking around the corner.

"Where did they put that road atlas I ordered," she said, searching the room until she found it.

It was a weighty spiral bound book, eleven by fourteen inches, three hundred pages, containing roadmaps for every state in the union, along with portions of Canada and Mexico. She opened the book to the two center pages displaying the full map of North America.

She ripped the two pages out of the book. Then she affixed the map to the whiteboard and stood back to study it.

"What the hell are you looking for, exactly?" Gaspar asked, squinting to see the tiny lines on the map.

"You heard the Boss. We're smart. We can figure this out," she replied with a smirk. "Unless you want me to just ask Finlay. Which would be a lot faster."

Gaspar scowled like he'd swallowed a whole lemon, which made her laugh. How could she possibly do this job without him? She didn't want to think about it.

Her phone vibrated on the table. The caller ID said Noble.

She turned on the speaker so Gaspar could hear and picked up. "Otto and Gaspar here."

Without wasting time, the Boy Detective said, "We found two dead bodies, a stash of opioids, and six hundred thousand dollars in cash at the U Store Stuff facility in St. Louis."

Otto shot a warning look toward Gaspar. Noble didn't know Otto had been there, and she wanted to keep it that way. The Boss would make sure Noble found out everything he needed to know.

"Congratulations," he said as if he didn't know anything about the cash or the drugs or the dead bodies.

Otto nodded.

Noble said, "The bodies were in one unit, while the drugs and cash were in another unit."

"And you think they're related somehow?" Otto asked.

"Possibly. We're looking at the ownership of this place. It could be tied to the mob. If it is, we'll apply for warrants. We may find more evidence of criminal activity in these units," Noble explained.

"Sounds like a long project," Gaspar replied. "We had a case like that in Miami a few years ago. Once we got into those storage units, we found all kinds of contraband."

Otto shot him a quizzical look, and he shrugged.

Noble said, "The dead woman in the Mackenzie mansion has been identified. Her name was Brooke Malone. The name has been released to the press."

"I see," Otto replied. "Was that the real estate agent?"

"Yes. But she used her maiden name only for professional reasons. She was married," he said.

Gaspar shrugged. "Who isn't?"

"Yeah, well, her husband has been notified. Turns out he's a local mobster named Big Mike Bavolsky. He'll be in custody by the end of the month, assuming we can find him."

"What do you mean?" Otto asked, widening her eyes.

"We've had Bavolsky and his crew under surveillance since his brother was arrested last year. Right at the moment, we can't find him." Noble said wearily. "Here's the punch line. Bavolsky's wife had been having a hot and heavy affair with Rex Mackenzie for the past couple of years."

Gaspar's eyes widened.

Otto drew a quick breath, pointed to her whiteboard where she'd written *Triggers?????* and said, "What do you make of that? You think Mackenzie killed her?"

"Hard to say. We didn't have a warrant for her business phones, so we had to get the recordings from the phone companies. We're checking them for more intel now." He muted the phone and talked briefly to someone else before he came back with a final sign off and then hung up.

After he hung up, Otto found the burner cell she'd been using with Finlay and pressed the redial.

"Can you run some passport checks for me?" she asked.

He replied, "Should I?"

"I've got twelve names. We need to know whether any of them have left the country in the past twelve months," she paused. "And if they've crossed a border, where and when. Got a pen?"

She read the names off the whiteboard, giving him time to write them down.

"Got it," Finlay said. "Anything else?"

"Any kind of video of the U Store Stuff lot in St. Louis. Forty-eight hours before and forty-eight after I intercepted Bramall at Unit D-6 should be enough to start. Can you send us that?"

"Yep," Finlay said. "I'll call you back within the hour."

After she disconnected, Gaspar said, "How about you fill me in."

"This whole thing is looking less and less random, isn't it? We know now that our twelve missing persons are all connected. What we don't know is why they shot out in all directions," she replied.

"Agreed."

She nodded, paced, sipped, and stared at the whiteboard. "Something happened. Something set this whole thing in motion about two weeks ago. Why did the sisters bug out? That has to be the key to all this."

She turned to the laptop and pulled up the surveillance video of the Mackenzie mansion and the dry cleaners. She pointed to the two men.

"One big hulking guy. One scrawny dude barely able to navigate with a cane," she said. "Who are they? They've got to have something to do with all this."

Gaspar said, "Our assignment is to find Reacher. You figure the Boss is right? You think that big guy is Reacher? That he's somehow the trigger in all this?"

"I suppose it's possible." She shrugged.

"But you don't like it," Gaspar replied.

She said, "I don't know. It feels like something is missing here. I'm not sure what it is."

CHAPTER THIRTY-FIVE

Saturday, February 12
2:25 p.m.
San Antonio, Texas

SCORPIO WAS EXHAUSTED, BUT he remained alert. He couldn't afford mistakes. Not now. Not when he was so close to Mexico. So close to success.

Hours ago, Thorn had pulled into a hotel parking lot near Rolla, Missouri, and they'd changed drivers. Scorpio had climbed into the SUV's driver's seat. He had full use of his right side. He could drive short distances when he needed to.

Thorn put the Oklahoma license plate he'd removed from a dirty truck at a fast food joint on an older white panel van and drove it out of the lot while its owner was sleeping.

The theft consumed less than five minutes on the clock.

Scorpio drove a dozen miles along the expressway and pulled off at the rest stop. Instead of following the turn into the comfort station parking lot, he took the entrance down an incline to a deserted maintenance building.

He pulled around to the back of the building and turned off the lights. Thorn arrived with the panel van and pulled up alongside.

Thorn transferred the drugs from the SUV to the panel van while Scorpio held Mackenzie's pistol ready and watched for approaching vehicles.

He hadn't expected any security or maintenance workers to arrive at that time of the morning, but he could have taken care of the problem if they had. Mackenzie's pistol would've done the job.

When Thorn removed all the SUV's cargo, including their personal possessions, Scorpio drove the SUV along a deserted side road to the high bridge. Thorn pulled in behind him.

Scorpio put the SUV's transmission in park, moved to the panel van, and climbed into the driver's seat while Thorn lowered the SUV's windows, revved its engine, and sent the SUV into the water below.

From his vantage point inside the panel van, Scorpio watched the black SUV until it sank below the water line.

Someone would find the SUV eventually. Scorpio would be long gone by the time it happened.

With Thorn behind the wheel again, they returned to the expressway and continued South.

The panel van had tight suspension and rode like a wild bronco. Long before they'd passed through Austin, Texas, Scorpio felt like the bronco had danced its hooves all over his body. He squirmed in the seat, attempting to find a comfortable position.

Thorn said, "We're about forty miles from the Universal Self Storage lot. How do you want to do this?"

The question was more important than it seemed.

He had chosen San Antonio because it was close enough to Mexico but not too close to be obvious. The population of San Antonio was greater than the population of Dallas. Scorpio figured it would be much easier to remain anonymous and undetected among San Antonio's one point five million people.

San Antonio was also a military town, which meant soldiers and their families were regularly moving in and out. Many lived off base and used storage facilities for their belongings.

A sizable Latino population lived in San Antonio, and about half of them were of Mexican descent. Which meant that travel between the US and Mexico was common and expected. The last thing Scorpio wanted was to stand out as he traveled across the border.

He chose Universal Self Storage because it was one of the largest of three dozen options and the online reviews complained about terrible customer service from the staff. Perfect.

He hoped to blend in, not stand out. To that end, he preferred chaos to calm, crowds to solitude, and untrained minimum wage workers to sophisticated high-tech surveillance.

Scorpio replied, "Let's go directly there. It's in a well-populated area. We'll have options."

"Let me pull over and change out this license plate." Thorn pulled into a busy shopping center. He backed the panel van into an empty parking space and left the van running with the weak air conditioner full blast.

Thorn had stolen several plates along the way. Each time they'd stopped, he'd located another white panel van and switched plates. They had picked up the last one in Dallas. An old van with a Texas plate pulling into the storage facility should draw less attention.

After he installed the plate, he returned to the driver's seat, fastened his seat belt, and pulled into the early afternoon traffic.

Universal Self Storage had a line of vehicles headed in and out. The gate was open, and the employee seated in the guard shack was talking on the phone as trucks, vans, and SUVs moved past at a steady pace.

Scorpio rented the unit online. He had completed the application and paid the rent for three years.

"Turn right when we get through the gate and turn left down to row twenty-two," Scorpio said.

"Ten-four, boss," Thorn replied.

He turned left as instructed and traveled almost a city block before Scorpio said, "This is it. 2213. Let me get out here because there'll be no room to open the passenger door inside."

Thorn waited until Scorpio had landed upright on the pavement. He maneuvered the panel van and reversed into the long, narrow garage. He removed the rear license plate from the van and parked within inches of the back wall.

Scorpio stood on the concrete enjoying the sunshine while Thorn hid the plate inside the van where it could not be seen through the windows.

He snugged the tarp they'd bought in Oklahoma to cover the drugs. He grabbed the bags, the heavy-duty padlock, and locked the doors.

Outside, he said, "What shall I do with the keys to the van?"

Scorpio held out his right hand. "I'll hold on to those. Secure the padlock and bring me that key as well."

"Will do," Thorn replied as he completed the tasks.

Scorpio stood back and examined everything. When he was satisfied that the situation was as secure as possible under the circumstances, he turned to walk toward the exit.

Thorn lumbered alongside, carrying the bags. Cars continued in and out. Other pedestrians were walking between the storage units. The place resembled a bustling airport.

They made slow progress but eventually reached the front gate and walked through to the sidewalk. A bus stop bench was located about half a block down. Scorpio walked toward it, and Thorn followed.

As they approached the bench, a bus headed to a hotel on San Antonio's Riverwalk arrived. They climbed aboard. Thorn paid the fair from change in his pockets, and they found a seat near the front.

They had not spoken to a soul, which was exactly what Scorpio had hoped for when he'd chosen USS to hold his property. So far, so good.

The ride into downtown was slow but uneventful. When the bus stopped in front of the hotel, Scorpio and Thorn disembarked with the other passengers. Thorn manned the bags.

"Let's get a room. Grab some sleep. Figure out how we'll get to Mexico," Thorn suggested.

Scorpio nodded, but his attention was focused on a small knot of tourists. They were gathered around a woman holding a sign above her head. The sign was printed with the words *Latino Tours – Mexico* in six-inch black letters. A motor coach pulled up to the curb, and she led a crowd of fifty or so to board.

"Problem solved," he muttered under his breath.

CHAPTER THIRTY-SIX

Saturday, February 12
4:45 p.m.
San Antonio, Texas

WHILE THORN SLEPT IN the other room, Scorpio checked the Chicago area news sites. He didn't have to search long. The murder at Mackenzie's mansion in Lake Forest was the lead story on all stations.

He cocked his head and narrowed his eyes. Something wasn't right. The volume of media coverage for one murder seemed extreme, particularly in a city where the homicide rate was among the highest in the country.

He zeroed in on one particular broadcast and turned up the audio.

Three head shots were displayed on the screen over the anchor's left shoulder. Two men and one woman. All three photos were publicity shots from a professional photographer. Scorpio recognized two of the three.

Rex Mackenzie and Babbling Brooke Malone.

The third photo was a beefy, balding Slavic man, identified as her husband, Michael Bavolsky. Like many women, Babbling Brooke didn't use her husband's name professionally. But even if she had, Bavolsky's name meant nothing to Scorpio.

Next was a short video clip of Babbling Brooke walking by her husband's side, leaving a courthouse in downtown Chicago. Watching her on the screen was different from meeting her back at the mansion. For one thing, she wasn't talking, which was the good news. The way she carried herself was totally different, too.

Everything that followed was bad news. Sweat broke out on Scorpio's forehead. He wiped it away with his sleeve.

The anchorman read his prepared text from the prompter. Big Mike Bavolsky was a businessman, rumored to be the head of a local crime family and the subject of multiple police investigations.

Mrs. Bavolsky had been an actress before they married. She'd become a successful real estate agent two years ago.

An actress? Scorpio's heart began to pound harder in his chest. She wasn't an actress. She was a porn star. He rewound the video and watched again to be sure. No doubt. None at all.

He'd watched her performance in *The Senator, The Waitress, and Her Friends*. She was the senator's dinner date. The only woman in the film who had survived.

Scorpio's armpits were sweating now. He pulled his jacket off and loosened his collar.

Next, the newscaster described the murder briefly. "Mrs. Bavolsky was shot and killed in an apparent home invasion in Lake Forest, police say. The murder occurred Friday afternoon. Mrs. Bavolsky was working alone during an open house at the home of Rex Mackenzie, a business associate of her husband's.

Neither Mr. Bavolsky nor Mr. Mackenzie could be reached for comment."

Scorpio turned up the volume and replayed the end of the report three times to be sure he'd heard correctly.

As the anchorman talked, a short video clip of three men rolled across the screen. Scorpio recognized two of them. Thorn had shown him the photos of the bodies inside that black SUV at the U Store Stuff lot.

"Big Mike Bavolsky's brother, Walter Bavolsky, and two others were convicted last year on multiple counts of money laundering and drug trafficking. The convictions were related to sales of controlled pharmaceuticals, including oxycodone and other opioids. Walter Bavolsky remains incarcerated at Statesville prison in Joliette."

Scorpio closed the video and sat back to think. A few things were now crystal clear in his mind, and all of them were potentially lethal. He ticked each one off on his fingers.

Mackenzie was connected to organized crime, just as he'd surmised.

The porn on that flash drive was produced by Polish Brothers Limited, probably owned by Big Mike and Walter Bavolsky.

The drugs Scorpio had taken from the U Store Stuff unit in St. Louis might not be the same drugs that Reacher stole from him. They might belong to Bavolsky.

The porn on that flash drive definitely belonged to Bavolsky.

The gemstones were probably Bavolsky's, too.

All that could be fixed. There was nothing, anywhere, that connected him to Bavolsky's property. At least, not yet.

Bavolsky could be arrested for drug trafficking any minute, too. If that happened, Scorpio would have time to sell the drugs before Bavolsky's crew came after him.

He hadn't set up the porn business on the dark web yet. He could alter the videos. And the dark web was a place where he could operate anonymously for years. Bavolsky would never know who stole them.

A fence for loose gemstones should be fairly easy to find in any major city.

All of which meant he had breathing room.

Scorpio admitted the most serious item last.

He'd killed a mobster's wife.

That could not be undone. If Bavolsky found him, he'd kill him for that alone.

A few hours' rest was out of the question. He could sleep in Mexico.

He opened his laptop again. He searched and found *Latino Tours*. A tour to Monterrey, Mexico, through Laredo, Texas, was scheduled to leave the hotel within the hour.

They would leave the bus once it crossed into Mexico at Nuevo Laredo on the Mexican side of the Rio Grande. The tour guide might be alarmed, but she wouldn't delay the entire bus to look for two missing passengers. Even if she did, she wouldn't find them.

He located a charter jet service departing from Quetzalcoatl International Airport for the flight to Guadalajara.

He made reservations using the counterfeit Swiss passports for the bus tour and Irish passports to book the jet. For the Guadalajara hotel, he used the Luxembourg passports and guaranteed the room with a credit card tied to a Luxembourg bank account held in the same name.

Maybe that would be enough layers of protection for now. Mexico was a place people could go to disappear. And Bavolsky didn't look like a genius on those news clips. Mackenzie wasn't a criminal mastermind, and he'd managed to rip the guy off. How smart could Bavolsky be?

He was feeling better when he closed the laptop, awakened Thorn, and stumbled toward the shower.

They were on their way to meet the tour bus outside the hotel with plenty of time to spare.

CHAPTER THIRTY-SEVEN

Saturday, February 12
5:25 p.m.
San Antonio, Texas

"I THINK JANE IS at the center of this. Jane went looking for
Rose. Jane is the one who rescued her sister, with Reacher's
help. Jane brought her sister to Lake Forest. It's Jane's husband
who's laundering money for Bavolsky and sleeping with his
wife. Jane's husband hired Bramall. It's all about Jane.
Everything." She shook her head and tapped the whiteboard.
"The trigger is something to do with Jane."

Gaspar nodded. "Okay. So the Boy Detective was right. This
whole thing is some kind of Thelma and Louise deal?"

"In the sense that the two sisters are on the road together for
some reason, I think so." She found the Boss's cell phone and
placed the call. Again, she put the call on speakerphone so
Gaspar could participate.

When the Boss picked up, she said, "Where is Bramall?"

"Funny you should ask."

"Meaning?"

"Meaning we don't know. He and Mackenzie reboarded the Gulfstream 100 about an hour ago. They didn't file a flight plan."

"You don't have eyes on the jet?" She controlled her anger. Barely. There were at least a dozen ways to find aircraft in flight. He could have that intel in an hour. Maybe less. So why didn't he?

"There's a lot of needles in that haystack," he replied tersely. "Most importantly for our purposes is another large-scale investigation by the Organized Crime Drug Enforcement Task Force. Which, as you know, is a multi-agency task force that includes federal and state agencies. This investigation is concentrated in Chicago. Indictments are due next week."

"Is Noble working on this?" Gaspar asked.

"Noble was not involved originally, but he has joined the effort. When the locals arrested Walt Bavolsky two years ago, they didn't know about the larger investigation. Now they do."

Gaspar asked, "Prescription opioids?"

"Heroin and fentanyl primarily. Smuggled from Mexico. Based in Mexico City, they think," the Boss replied.

"Mexico City? That's pretty unusual for heroin trafficking," Gaspar said.

"They're getting more brazen. The kingpins don't want to live in squalor anymore. They've got the money and they want to spend it," the Boss replied.

"Who's on the indictment list?" Otto said, with a sinking feeling.

"There were originally forty-six indictments charging various offenses. Big Mike Bavolsky and those two dead thugs, Jimmy Two and Little Hugh, were on the list." He paused. "Four additional names were added a few days ago."

Otto held her breath. She knew what was coming.

"Rex Mackenzie, Jane Mackenzie, Rose Sanderson, and Terrence Bramall."

Gaspar whistled. "What are the allegations against them?"

"On the first forty-six, charges range from drug trafficking to money laundering and a few firearms offenses," the Boss said.

"And what about the four latecomers?" Otto asked, and her stomach flipped.

"Aiding and abetting Bavolsky's crew in various ways," he took a breath. "The alleged facts are very specific. Times, dates, places, amounts. Sounds like they had an informant."

"You're thinking Rex Mackenzie had turned on Bavolsky while he was still sleeping with Bavolsky's wife? Trying to get Big Mike out of the way?"

The Boss replied, "We're still chasing that down. But it wouldn't have been the dumbest thing Mackenzie has done so far."

Otto replied, "The informants could have been Rose and Jane. Maybe Mackenzie found out. Maybe that's why he's chasing them."

"Possibly," the Boss said. "The indictments are on your server. The details suggest wiretaps and phone records, among other things. You can read them for yourself."

Otto said nothing. Gaspar waited, too.

The Boss said, "I checked those passports you asked Finlay about. Only three names on the list traveled outside the US in the past year."

"Let me guess," Otto said. "Jane Mackenzie, Rose Sanderson, and Jack Reacher."

CHAPTER THIRTY-EIGHT

Saturday, February 12
5:45 p.m.
San Antonio, Texas

GASPAR STARED AT HER as if she'd grown another head.

The Boss said, "I've sent you the dates and locations. You're going to Mexico City tonight. Gaspar, too. We intercepted communications. They're already on the way. We don't know why Bramall and Mackenzie are headed there, but we'll know before you arrive."

Otto said, "Do you expect Reacher to be in Mexico City waiting for them?"

The Boss paused briefly and then ignored the question. "Your flight departs in two hours. A car will pick you up in front of your hotel in twenty minutes."

As they were packing up, Gaspar said, "I have no idea how you think, Suzie Wong. You know that, right?"

She smiled. "No offense, Cheech, but I have no idea how you think, either. That's why you've been so helpful to me."

"What do you mean?"

"You think like Reacher. I don't."

His eyebrows shot up. "How did you know that those three passports would pop like that?"

She shook her head. "I didn't know. Not for sure. But it makes sense, doesn't it?"

He shook his head. "Not even remotely."

She pulled her bag to the door and stood to the side to hold it open. He limped through into the corridor and walked toward the elevator. He pushed the call button. The elevator doors opened immediately. They entered the elevator car and pushed the button for the lobby.

On the way down, she said, "We're not dealing with runaway teens without ID or the wherewithal to stay missing for two weeks. It's a reasonable assumption that at least one of the twelve adults used a passport and left the country within the last year. Checking passports should have been one of Noble's first moves. If he did a passport check, he didn't tell us."

"The Boss didn't mention the passports until after you asked Finlay, either." Gaspar nodded.

"But the Boss already knew those three had traveled outside the country, whether he told us or not." She paused. "If any of the others had used passports for international travel, he would have mentioned it because the others are not relevant to his desire to find Reacher."

"Why keep the intel about Rose, Jane, and Reacher from us, though?" Gaspar shook his head. "Some kind of test?"

"His motives are indecipherable." Otto shrugged.

Gaspar had another issue. "And the details in those last four indictments. You figure those came from one of the four who are being indicted."

Otto nodded. "But the question is, which one? What kind of pressure is being applied here? By whom? And to what end?"

The elevator stopped on the first floor, and they walked through the lobby toward the valet entrance. A *Latino Tours* bus bound for Monterrey, Mexico, blocked traffic at the valet stand. Passengers were boarding slowly.

The last few tourists were lined up behind a scrawny guy who walked with a cane. His left hand rested in his pocket. His gait was labored and twisty. The man standing behind him was huge. Probably at least two-hundred-fifty pounds and built like a linebacker.

Otto cocked her head and watched as the scrawny guy struggled to mount the steps into the big coach. The big guy waited patiently, although the tourists behind him were fidgety. The scrawny guy finally climbed into the coach, and the tourist line began moving again.

Gaspar cleared his throat. "Earth to Suzie Wong."

She turned her attention to him. "Did that guy look familiar to you?"

"What guy?" He stretched his neck to look at the line of tourists, but the scrawny man was already inside, and the tinted windows blocked the interior of the coach.

"The big guy," she shook her head as if to clear it of clutter. She didn't want to say he reminded her of Reacher, but he did. Reacher was a guy who often took the bus, too. It could have been him.

"I didn't see him," Gaspar replied with a shrug. "When we get the new files from the Boss, I've got fifty bucks that says we'll find Jane, Rose, and Reacher making trips to Mexico City within the past year."

"You're on," Otto replied, still preoccupied. She looked until she saw the car the Boss ordered parked a few spaces from the door and moved in that direction.

Gaspar followed. He tossed the bags into the trunk and joined her inside the cabin on the back seat.

He asked, "Why are you betting against Mexico City? Given that we're on the way there, under orders, it seems the obvious answer."

"Nothing about this case has been obvious from the first minute. Why start now?" She shrugged, still preoccupied. The driver pulled into the flow of traffic and headed toward the airport.

Gaspar asked, "What do you think we'll find in the passport data?"

"The Boss said Jane, Rose, and Reacher had left the country. He didn't say they'd traveled together, or what mode of transportation they used, or even when or where they came and went," she replied. Traffic was lighter now than it had been earlier. She glanced at her watch. They were making good time.

"Relax, Sunshine. It's a private jet. The pilot won't leave without us," Gaspar grinned.

Otto barely heard him. She was still preoccupied with the tourists in line at the coach. The big guy stuck out in her mind. Most of the men she'd seen in San Antonio were average height, average weight. He was the first oversized guy she'd noticed since they'd arrived.

Their driver pulled into the private airport and stopped on the tarmac near the waiting jet the Boss ordered. Gaspar climbed out of the back seat on the passenger side and met the driver at the trunk.

Otto followed, slowly. Her imagination was working overtime.

Not only had the big guy boarding that motor coach seemed familiar, but the scrawny guy did, too. Or maybe it was the pair of men together that had tapped her subconscious? She closed her eyes briefly to recall the way the scrawny guy twisted and struggled to walk and climb the steps into the motor coach. She'd seen that before. Twice before.

"Yes. That's it," she murmured as she gathered her bags and followed Gaspar to the jet stairs.

"What's what?" Gaspar asked.

"Maybe I'm crazy. We need to catch that *Latino Tours* coach."

"What are you talking about?"

"At first, I thought the big guy could have been Reacher."

Gaspar stared at her.

"But now, I think those guys are the same two guys we saw on the videotapes. At Mackenzie's mansion and at his dry cleaners," she said.

Gaspar shook his head. "Come on. How likely is that? We came here to interview General Simpson and then spur of the moment, checked into that hotel to work. Not likely that Reacher or anyone else connected with this case was getting on that bus, is it?"

She shrugged. "Which is why it didn't register in my mind at first. But the more I think about the way the skinny guy moved...."

"We need to go. Besides, they're on the bus, and it's already on the move. We probably couldn't catch it now even if we tried." Gaspar shook his head. "The Boss can chase it down. Tour buses crossing the border are required to have a manifest and collect passports and all that. Records will exist. If those guys are on that tour, they'll be easy enough to find. Tour buses have a defined itinerary. Those two guys don't move very fast. You don't have to carry the whole load on everything, Sunshine. Let the Boss do something for a change."

"You're right. Go on inside. Download the new files. I'll make the call." She found the Boss's cell and pressed the redial button. He didn't answer after ten rings. She left him a voicemail message with the details about the *Latino Tours* coach and the two men inside. He'd have plenty of time to sort out the intel before this flight landed in Mexico City.

She hurried up the jet stairs.

CHAPTER THIRTY-NINE

Saturday, February 12
6:25 p.m.
In flight to Mexico City

OTTO STEPPED INTO THE Gulfstream 500, one of the newest
private jets on the market. She quickly recalled the plane's
features. Depending on the configuration, the G-500 could seat
up to nineteen passengers.

The good news was that the G-500 could fly high, fast, and
far. The bad news was that it needed about a mile of runway for
takeoff. Which meant a limited number of airports could
accommodate it.

Two pilots were required. Assuming these two were
competent and the machine well maintained, the four-hour flight
to Mexico City should be uneventful.

Otto glanced around the cabin. "Wow."

"Not bad at all, is it?" Gaspar looked up from his laptop
and grinned. He was the only other passenger. He was seated at
a desk next to a big screen television. "Stow your bags in the

back and look around. I'm almost done downloading this stuff."

She figured the plane must have been seized from a wealthy oil baron or the head of a successful drug cartel. The interior was definitely customized to suit luxurious tastes.

For starters, there was more room inside the cabin than some Manhattan apartments. The décor was contemporary, shiny black everything and buttercream leather upholstery with burnt orange throw pillows. Plush seats resembled those in a private screening room any Hollywood mogul would find acceptable.

The galley was nicer than her apartment, featuring granite countertops and a modern sink and appliances. The lavatories were likely the same.

In the back of the plane were two couches on opposite sides of the cabin, which probably converted to exceptionally comfortable beds. She stashed her bag in the roomy closet next to Gaspar's.

She returned to the front of the cabin and sat across the aisle from him. The door had been closed, and the engines were rumbling. "I've been on a lot of private planes. When I was working for the consulting firm, quite a few clients owned Gulfstreams. This is definitely the most impressively appointed G-500 I've ever seen. How about you?"

"Scarlett's clients have some fancy jets. But this one can compete, for sure." He shrugged and kept working while the jet taxied to the runway for takeoff.

After they were in the air and reached cruising altitude, Gaspar unbuckled his seat belt and stood to stretch. He handed over his laptop.

"Take a look at the files. I'll be right back." He walked toward the lavatory.

Gaspar had downloaded encrypted files from the secure servers and opened them. The Boss had sent reports as well as still photos and videos. She started with the passport data.

Three folders were labeled J. Reacher, T.J. Mackenzie, S.R. Sanderson. Each folder contained files.

She opened the Reacher files first.

Reacher's passport had been used only once. He'd returned to the United States on a bus from Canada last summer, crossing the border through the tunnel from Windsor to Detroit.

Which didn't make her uneasy at all. He probably wasn't in Detroit because of her. Not back then, anyway. She'd never heard of Reacher until November, which was long after he'd crossed from Canada.

She watched the short video recorded at the customs agent desk at the checkpoint. Reacher was dressed in work clothes. Jeans and a blue chambray shirt with cuffs rolled to mid-forearms. The shirt made his eyes seem blue as cornflowers, even in the bad video.

He stood at the counter and looked directly at the agent like a man with nothing to hide. She couldn't see his feet, but she guessed he was wearing brown work boots. He usually did.

He squared his shoulders in front of the customs agent, handed over the passport. The agent asked a couple of routine questions.

There was no audio recording of the exchange, but Reacher's answers must have been satisfactory. The agent nodded and returned the passport.

Reacher stuffed it into his pocket and walked through, carrying nothing. No luggage, no duffel.

She played the video a couple more times. The scene unfolded precisely as she expected. Nothing out of the ordinary at all.

Also in the folder was a copy of Reacher's passport. It was a ten-year passport, issued six years before. Old, but still valid.

She turned next to the folders for both sisters. The first thing she noticed was the volume. Each sister's folder contained several files. She ran through them quickly. None reflected trips to or from Canada, which allowed her to breathe a bit easier.

Americans could travel into the US from Canada without a passport if they showed other acceptable forms of official ID. But surely if the sisters had done so, the Boss would have included those records for completeness, if for no other reason.

Looked like Jane and Rose had been traveling together quite a bit, though. Several times in the past year, they had traveled to exotic places like India, Brazil, Malaysia, Singapore, and Costa Rica. They took a two-week Mexican Riviera cruise just last month, departing from San Francisco and visiting several ports.

Rex Mackenzie said Rose and Jane had booked a trip to Thailand two weeks ago, but never showed up for departure. These passport records confirmed that. No travel to or from Thailand was listed.

Gaspar returned to his seat bearing hot coffee in travel mugs.

"Nectar of the gods," Otto said, accepting the mug with a pleasurable whiff of the best aroma on earth.

"I found some snacks, but I couldn't carry everything. Hang on." He set his mug down and walked back to the galley. He returned with a tray of cheese, crackers, nuts, and fruit.

"Found this in the fridge," he said, handing her a black and white china plate along with a burnt orange linen napkin.

"You could get a job as a flight attendant if your new gig with Scarlett doesn't work out," she teased.

"You're welcome," he replied equably, resettling into his

seat with a plate of snacks. "Find anything interesting in those files?"

"Several interesting things." She nodded, swallowed the cracker she'd nibbled, and sipped the hot coffee. She held up an index finger. "One. Even in the bad videos, Jane Mackenzie is astonishingly beautiful."

"Yeah, I saw that from the passport photos. Who looks good in those things?" He grinned.

She held up a second finger. "Two. Rose is the same height as her twin sister, and that's where the similarities stop. They are definitely not duplicate copies."

He raised one eyebrow. "No?"

"Not even close. Here, look at this video." Otto found the one she wanted and pulled it up on the screen. She turned the laptop so Gaspar could see.

"In every one of these videos, Jane looks directly into the cameras. She smiles and flirts with the customs agents like a movie star," Otto said as she finished the cracker. "You've got a bunch of daughters, Chico. You know how women behave. Look at Jane's appearance, her behavior."

Even in these poor-quality videos, Jane appeared beautiful, relaxed, and pampered. Her blonde mane was expensively tousled. Makeup minimalist but not minimal. Sophisticated preppy style clothes were chic and pricey and fit her perfectly. The casual handbag she tossed across her body was Chanel. Her body looked toned and trim. Flexible and agile. She moved like a woman who owned the world.

Gaspar, on the other hand, chewed like he'd been starved for a week. He grinned appreciatively. "She's something, all right."

"Now pay attention." Otto clicked a couple of keys and pulled up another file and turned the laptop toward him. "This is

Rose. Her video was recorded only a few seconds after Jane's. Same trip. Same time. Same customs agent."

Rose barely glanced at the customs officer. Her hair was covered by a hood that concealed her features. She'd been asked to push the hood back, which she did quickly. Messy gray-blonde hair tumbled out around her shoulders for a couple of moments, until she raised the hood and poked it back inside. Her ill-fitting wardrobe consisted of jeans, sneakers, and a hoodie in every video. She didn't wear any kind of handbag. Everything she carried with her was stuffed into her pockets.

"Play the videos again," Gaspar said. He nodded slowly as he watched the second time. "I see what you mean."

She said, "Every one of these video files shows the same thing. Jane looks beautiful and perfect. Rose? Not so much."

"Amazing Jane. And, what? Defiant Rose?" he replied thoughtfully.

Otto cocked her head. "I don't know if I'd call Rose defiant, exactly. It's hard to categorize her. Jane's easier."

Gaspar watched the videos again. "In what way?"

"Jane's posture is confident, self-assured, and I guess I'd say flirty. Rose's posture is…not the same. Confident and self-assured, but also no-nonsense. Like she can take care of herself, and she's willing to prove it."

"I can buy that. She's a West Point grad. An infantry officer. She survived five tours in Iraq and Afghanistan. She can definitely handle conflict. It's instinctive after all that training and experience." Gaspar polished off the last of the food on the tray.

"The other odd thing about these passport files is how many there are. Twelve trips, most of them recent," Otto said. "These two have been traveling the world. They could be on another vacation now, actually."

"Vacation? I thought they were missing?" Gaspar arched his eyebrows and widened his eyes. "Didn't Noble and Bramall both say that? Didn't Rex Mackenzie hire Bramall to find them?"

"There's no missing persons report filed, though. How do we know they're missing? All we have is Rex Mackenzie's word on that, right?" Otto nodded. "And he certainly seems to be at the center of whatever's going on here."

Gaspar said, "You're just saying that because the guy's a scumbag."

She grinned. "Well, there's that."

"Tell me what else you found out in those video files. We've got another couple of hours of flight time to kill." Gaspar stood up with the empty tray and his cup and limped toward the galley. "Be right back. Talk loud. I can hear you."

She watched him closely, which she didn't often have the opportunity to do. His gait was off. He held his forearm close to his right side. About every third step, he paused slightly to reposition himself. Perhaps when he thought she wouldn't notice, he slipped his hand into his pocket for another Tylenol.

Gaspar had been seriously injured long before she'd met him. He'd had similar combat training to Reacher's and to Rose Sanderson, for that matter. He'd survived his Army career. It was his FBI experience that had disabled him and almost cost him his life.

He loved his wife and kids like crazy. He'd do anything for them. But it was sheer grit and determination and family that kept him going. Simple as that.

What was it that General Simpson had said about Rose's injuries? *Severe and disfiguring. She needed expert, expensive plastic surgery. We're not set up to handle injuries like hers. Last time she called, she said she'd find a place she could afford.*

Otto pulled up the list of trips reflected on Rose Sanderson's passport. She connected to the internet, typed in the list of destinations as a group, and pushed the button to search.

In less than half a second, a list of hits was returned.

The top hit was *Medical Tourism Market*.

She leaned in, clicked on the article, and read through quickly.

"Okay. No shouting on airplanes. I get it. Tell me what you know," he said when he returned to his seat. "I'm ready."

"Do you know what medical tourism is?"

He grinned. "You mean like take a vacation in Brazil where you can get a cheap and quick Brazilian butt-lift?"

"I was thinking more like India for a heart bypass, but yeah, sure, that's the idea." Otto nodded.

"It's kind of a thing in Miami, my wife tells me," he said. "Several women she knows have been to Brazil, only to return looking more toned and terrific than they'd get from a nice month on the beach."

"In countries that have socialized medicine, long waits for care are common, even if the patient has the means to pay for the procedures," Otto read from the website. "Medical tourism is a means to get faster treatment. Basically, for Americans, it's about quality medical care abroad at lower cost. I think that's what Rose has been doing."

Gaspar frowned. "Rose Sanderson was injured in to service her country. She's entitled to health care at Veterans Administration hospitals. She isn't required to pay for her medical treatment. And the US has the best medical care in the world."

"Sure, but remember that Simpson said she wanted plastic surgery that the VA couldn't handle?" Otto clacked keys on the laptop. She checked each of the destinations on their passports again. "She'd be a private pay patient for that. She was concerned about affordability, too."

His frown deepened. "You think that's what this is all about? That the two sisters aren't missing at all? They left the country to get plastic surgery for Rose?"

"Maybe. Or maybe it's both." Otto fell back in her seat to think. She recalled Rex Mackenzie's behavior on the flight from St. Louis. "Rex Mackenzie doesn't know where Jane and Rose are. I'd bet money on that."

Gaspar nodded. "And Noble and Bramall believe they're missing, but that information came from Rex."

"Let me check something." Otto completed two more quick searches on Gaspar's laptop. "That's what I thought. Some of the top destinations for medical tourism require visas and waiting periods. Others are accessible without a visa if the tourist has a US passport. And Mexico is similar in that regard to Canada for US citizens. Mexico doesn't require either a visa or a passport."

"Yeah, US citizens can live in Mexico indefinitely with very little paperwork," Gaspar said. "My in-laws retired to Mexico because it's a lot cheaper and they can come back to visit the kids and grandkids."

"Did they move to Mexico City?" she asked.

He shook his head. "Guadalajara. It's more upscale but still affordable and safe. Good services. He can drive his BMW and not worry about bulletproofing. Guadalajara is more like what they're used to in Miami, but cheaper."

Otto checked the web. "Chico, you're a genius."

He grinned. "I've been telling you that for weeks."

"The cruise Rose and Jane took last month to the Mexican Riviera stopped in Puerto Vallarta. Which is a short flight from

Guadalajara." She clicked a few more keys. "Guadalajara is booming in medical tourism. Including one of the best cosmetic surgery facilities in the world. Celebrities get their work done at this place. The before and after photos show amazing results."

"So you think Rose and Jane left the cruise ship in Puerto Vallarta and moved on to Guadalajara for Rose?" Gaspar asked.

"It's feasible, isn't it?" Otto said.

"The timing's not right." Gaspar cocked his head. "If they didn't come home from that cruise like he claims, he'd at least have known to look for them in Mexico. Why would he go looking in Vegas? Doesn't make sense, does it?"

"Next time I see him, I'll ask before I shoot the bastard," she snarled. "But if I'm right, we're more likely to find them at this clinic in Guadalajara than Mexico City."

Gaspar nodded, picked up the phone, and called the pilot. "We've received new orders. Change course for Miguel Hidalgo y Costilla Guadalajara International Airport."

When he hung up, he said, "The pilot says the change shortened our travel time. We'll be landing sooner than expected."

She nodded. "Tell me everything you know about Guadalajara."

"For starters, it's a huge place. My father-in-law says the metro area has about seven million people." He shrugged.

"Which means we need to find Rose and Jane before we land."

"Just how do you propose to do that?"

"With a little help from our friends," she replied.

CHAPTER FORTY

Saturday, February 12
9:15 p.m.
Guadalajara, Mexico

THE BOSS HAD PROVIDED a car and driver familiar with the area. He'd delivered them directly and quickly to their destination. Even so, they'd arrived at El Mejor Cosmetic Surgery Clinic well after sunset. The Clinic was closed, which allowed Otto and Gaspar to stare from the back seat without attracting attention.

To maintain its reputation and appeal as the medical tourist's nirvana, no expense had been spared. The place was stunning.

The clinic was located on the top floor of a modern skyscraper near downtown. The views from up there had to be spectacular. Otto had located a few photographs showing the offices with windowed curtain walls which provided an expansive view of the city and beyond. The surgeons lived in penthouses above the clinic's medical facilities.

Medical care here might be affordable, but it was also extremely profitable.

El Megor Clinic was an outpatient facility. Those who required inpatient surgery were treated at a hospital instead.

After surgery, a patient's recovery period could last from weeks to months, depending on the procedures they'd endured. The clinic facility did not provide aftercare. Instead, patients returned to the even more stunning Segovia Alcazar Hotel next door.

The Segovia Alcazar Hotel, a dedicated aftercare facility, resembled the famous Spanish castle. Online photos showed rooms similar to luxury hotel suites but provided hospital-like amenities.

Segovia Alcazar was attached to the clinic by a system of underground tunnels. Patients checked into the hotel before the surgical procedures and were wheeled through the tunnels to their suites afterward.

Patients stayed at least a week and then returned to their homes where private home health care was provided for as long as necessary.

In Beverly Hills or New York City, such aftercare would cost $2,000 a night, or more. Here, the cost was less than $500, including meals. Which meant the prices were steep, but the care experience was stellar, the testimonials Otto had found all claimed.

"We don't know Rose's suite number. We'd never get in the door in a US hospital unless we got really lucky or found a clueless guard," Gaspar said. "So your plan is to sit around the lobby and watch until Jane or Rose show up? Sounds like a colossal waste of time doesn't it?"

"I'm feeling lucky," she said.

He scowled and said nothing.

"My plan is to get her suite number and knock on the door. I'm related to plenty of blonde beauties, believe it or not. I'm here to visit my cousin, Rose. I was supposed to be here with her when she had her surgery, and I got delayed." Otto said with a nod. "It'll work. I'm not worried."

Gaspar ran splayed fingers through his hair. "Hell, we don't even know if she's using her own name. Rex Mackenzie is looking for her, and she probably knows that. She's using an alias, don't you think?"

"Both Jane and Rose seem at least that smart to me. Definitely. But surgery needs to be scheduled and medical records provided in advance," Otto said.

"So Rose may have registered under an alias, but her medical records would reflect her real identity," Gaspar said.

"Exactly. Finlay and the Boss are searching the files for the alias and Rose's suite number. Until they find it, we can wait. Or we can try something more creative," Otto replied.

He arched both eyebrows. "We don't even know what kind of surgery Rose had. Because we have so few details, anyone working the reception desk is likely to be suspicious. She might not even be here anymore. We don't know when she had the surgery. She could have checked out by now."

"If we can't get what we need, we'll come back in the morning. But we're more likely to get in tonight. I want to try since we're here. You can wait in the car if you want," Otto said with a frown.

He shook his head and sighed. "You're going in, I'm going in."

"Just follow my lead. It'll work out. Or it won't. We'll do the best we can." Otto opened the door to leave the car. She told the driver, "We'll be inside for a while. We'll call you when we need you to pick us up."

She headed toward the front entrance of the hotel and Gaspar followed, shaking his head. The driver pulled away from the curb.

Gaspar hurried to catch up, limping on his right leg as he often did when he'd been inactive for several hours. "Just be prepared to knock on every door in the place. And hope we find her before they call security."

"The thing we really need to hope is that Reacher is sitting there holding her hand when we find her."

He frowned. "Why would you want that?"

"Because I don't think he'll make a scene in a place like this," Otto said. "If he's here, we can have a reasonable conversation with him. Figure things out."

"What things?"

She shook her head. "Hell if I know. One thing at a time, Cheech. Let's find Rose and Jane first. We'll deal with everything else as it happens."

"You're the boss," he said equably. But he oozed disapproval.

The front entrance of the Segovia Alcazar Hotel was covered by a striking blue awning that ran from the curb. A uniformed doorman wearing white gloves opened the door to admit them to an expansive lobby decorated in Spanish marble.

Otto looked around the awe-inspiring lobby. Perhaps the building had been a thriving hotel at one time before the booming medical tourism business became more profitable. A long reception desk stood off to the right side.

"Wait here. I'll be right back." Otto said, placing a hand on his arm like a wife would do. He stopped to admire a six-foot floral display as if he found it fascinating.

Otto moved purposefully toward the reception desk where a young woman was working at a computer. Her brass name badge over her pocket identified her as Maria.

"May I help you?" Maria asked in accented English, with a large helping of concern in her voice that matched the sympathy in her large brown eyes.

"Oh, I hope so," Otto said, practically pleading. "I'm looking for my cousin. She had surgery, and I was supposed to be here with her. My little boy was sick, and then my plane was delayed, and I am so very late. I wasn't able to be there with her, and I'm just devastated. I need to find her right away, and I'm not even sure which room she's in."

Maria nodded her understanding. "I can find the room number for you. What is your cousin's name?"

Otto glanced furtively around the lobby. She lowered her voice. "Her real name is Rose Sanderson."

Maria's eyes widened and her nostrils tensed. Her internal battle between the desire to maintain Rose's privacy while providing the utmost in patient care required by her employer played across her sweet features.

"Let me see," Maria said, typing Rose Sanderson's name into the computer.

That search would turn up no results. Otto had already tried.

Maria shook her head slowly. "I'm not finding her in our system under that name. I'm sorry."

Otto nodded, glanced right and left to be sure no one could overhear, and lowered her voice. "She's not using her real name here. The surgery is a surprise for her husband. She doesn't want anyone to know."

"When did she check in? Maybe I can find it that way," Maria said.

Otto replied, "I'm not sure exactly. Within the past two weeks."

Maria gave her another soulful look and shook her head slowly. "I don't know how to help you. Our guests are registered by names and arrival dates...."

"Oh, dear," Otto wrung her hands as a distraught cousin would do. "Have you had a lot of patients checking in recently from the US?"

"I'm afraid so. At least half our guests are Americans," Maria replied.

"I see." Otto took a deep breath. "Her sister's with her. Jane Mackenzie. Do you have her registered, maybe?"

Maria typed the name into her system and came up empty again. She shook her head once more. "I'm so sorry."

When people chose fake names in situations like this, they often selected the name of a person they knew. Otto had scoured Rose's files and made a list of names. Until she had access to the computer files, she couldn't try them herself.

Maria had been helpful so far, but she'd become suspicious and give up soon. Otto thought Maria might try one more name. Maybe two more. But that was probably her limit before one of Maria's supervisors came to stop her.

If Otto knew Rose at all, she might have been able to make an educated guess. As it was, she knew she'd be taking a shot in the dark.

One name had come up in Rose's VA hospital records. A soldier she'd been close to, according to the charts. They'd dated awhile after they were both discharged. He'd died around the same time Noble claimed Reacher appeared on the scene.

Her sister probably didn't know the guy. Maybe Rose had feelings for him back then. Perhaps she still did. It was worth a shot.

Otto leaned closer to Maria and lowered her voice even further. "She told me she might use the name of an old friend. Maybe that's what she did. Do you have her registered under the name of Porterfield?"

Maria took a deep breath and nodded. "I'll check."

She typed the name into her system. Almost instantly a big smile lit her face from lips to eyes. She was really a beautiful girl. Natural beauty not supplied by the surgeons at El Megor Clinic.

Maria pulled a small square of notepaper from a cubbyhole and wrote "S. R. Porterfield" and the suite number on it. Otto took the note and thanked her profusely. She didn't dare request a room key.

"I'm glad to help," Maria said because she truly was. She gave directions to the elevators, and Otto walked toward them, turning left at the first corner.

Gaspar joined her at the elevator. His hands hung in his pockets. "Where are we going?"

"Suite 706."

"Is she up there alone?" Gaspar asked.

Otto replied, "Let's find out."

CHAPTER FORTY-ONE

Saturday, February 12
9:45 p.m.
Guadalajara, Mexico

OTTO TAPPED HER FOOT as the elevator lifted ever so slowly to the seventh floor. The doors opened at a pace only a snail would love. They exited into a wide, tiled corridor leading left and right of the elevator.

Like any good hotel, the suite numbers were posted with arrows directing visitors. Suite 706 was on the left about halfway down the hallway.

They walked side-by-side. Gaspar unbuttoned his jacket.

"You think you're going to need your weapon?" she asked.

"Rose knows her way around a gun. Jane does, too, probably. They both grew up in Wyoming. If they're armed, we need to be prepared, even if Reacher's not in there with them," he replied. "Better safe than sorry."

Otto nodded and unbuttoned her jacket as well. When they reached Suite 706, Gaspar stood to one side. She pressed the doorbell and waited on the other side of the door.

After two full minutes, she raised her hand to push the bell again.

"Just a moment," a female voice said.

Otto heard the deadbolt slide. The handle turned, and the door opened.

Jane Mackenzie stood on the other side dressed in the same expensive casual style Otto had seen in all the customs videos. Even without makeup, she was startlingly beautiful.

She was maybe five-two and a hundred pounds, which made her slightly taller and heavier than Otto. Her long, thick hair was heaped and wild and tangled. The color would have been called strawberry blonde if she'd bought it at the drugstore, which Otto was fairly certain she didn't. Pale, perfect skin over delicate, superb bones, as if every minuscule imperfection had been airbrushed.

She might have been expecting a visitor, but she was surprised to see Otto and Gaspar standing across the threshold. Her eyes were startlingly green but guarded, even as her pupils dilated in surprise. Radiant but composed. And puzzled.

Otto pulled out her badge wallet and showed her ID. "I'm FBI Special Agent Otto, and this is my partner, Carlos Gaspar. May we come in, Mrs. Mackenzie?"

"What's this about?" she asked, still blocking the entrance.

Otto replied, "It's complicated. We need to talk with you and your sister."

"Rose? Why?"

"You really don't want to discuss this out here in the hallway, do you?" Gaspar said. "Let's go inside."

Jane finally decided to let them walk through. She closed the door behind them.

"Rose is sleeping. She had surgery ten days ago, and she's tired a lot," she said. She led the way to a small sitting room and gestured them into chairs while she perched on the loveseat across. "Tell me why you're here. Is it Rex? Has something happened?"

"You and your sister have been reported missing," Otto said. "Your husband doesn't know where you are."

"With any luck, we can keep it that way." A second voice, eerily the same tone, and timbre as Jane's, replied from the bedroom doorway. Rose walked into the room and joined her sister on the loveseat.

Other than her voice, nothing about Rose was identical to Jane. She was dressed in pajamas, a robe, and slippers. Her hair was pulled back into a low ponytail. Her green eyes were dull and listless. Her face looked like it had been scrubbed hard with an abrasive cleanser. Several layers of her skin had been debrided. Faint scars, probably from prior surgeries, were still visible.

"It's impolite to stare," she said.

"Yes, of course. I'm sorry," Otto replied. She cleared her throat. "I've met Rex Mackenzie. I can't say I blame you for leaving him."

"Rex Mackenzie's a son of a bitch," Rose replied. "He can live with his mistress in his mansion and leave us the hell alone."

Otto nodded.

Gaspar said, "You mean Brooke Bavolsky, I assume?"

"Yes." Jane shuddered. Her magnificent green eyes clouded. Her chin quivered as if she might cry.

Rose placed her hand over Jane's and squeezed reassuringly. Then she cleared her throat again.

Jane said, "I'll get you some water."

When she left the room, Rose took the chance to speak quietly. "Jane married Rex while I was deployed. She seemed happy with him initially and he was good to her at first. By the time I moved in there, he was far from the kind of man I wanted my sister to be married to."

"In what way?"

Rose took a breath. "You have no jurisdiction here. You can't arrest me or return me to the States. Is that what you've come for?"

"No," Otto said. Rose was right. There was nothing they could do without miles of red tape and clearing mountains of bureaucracy.

Rose nodded and said, "The same goes for Jane. There's nothing you can do to her, either."

Gaspar replied, "It would be a lot of work, but we could probably manage to get you back to the States if we wanted to. You explain your side of things and then we'll make a decision."

Rose looked pointedly at Gaspar's West Point ring. She said, "I have one of those."

He nodded. "I know."

She paused another few moments before she said, "You know I was seriously wounded in combat. When I came home, I was a mess. You've probably seen the files, so you know. Jane found me. She picked me up, dusted me off, and took care of me until I was almost as good as new."

"Almost?" Gaspar said.

"Everything functioned again. Doctors cleared up my infections. For a while, I was addicted to opioid painkillers, but I got clear of that, too." Rose paused for a steadying breath. "But I was horribly disfigured. From my injuries. And scars. I needed expensive, complicated plastic surgery on my face if I had any hope of living a normal life. I'll never be as beautiful as Jane again, but doctors promised I can look like a woman instead of a monster."

Otto began a gentle protest, but Rose held a palm flat out to stop her. "The VA couldn't do the job and I couldn't pay for those expensive Beverly Hills surgeons."

"So you came here," Otto said.

Rose nodded. "Eventually, after a lot of research, yes. By that point, Rex and Jane were barely speaking to each other. Jane was determined to help me pay for medical care and she didn't want to ask Rex for money."

"They were married. She'd be entitled to half their marital assets if they divorced. The money was hers," Otto said.

"That's what she decided. Over a period of months, she liquidated some assets and withdrew funds from accounts she thought he might not notice. And we searched for the right place to go," she said.

"Didn't Rex ask about all that traveling you two were doing?" Gaspar asked. "Wasn't he at least curious? Or even suspicious?"

Rose shrugged. "By that point, I don't think he cared where Jane went or why. He just wanted her out of the way. He had bigger problems."

"What kind of problems?" Otto asked.

She took a deep breath. "We don't know the full extent of it. We found out that Rex was involved with a Chicago crime ring. His girlfriend? Brooke? She's married to the head of the Polish mob. They call him Big Mike Bavolsky."

Gaspar nodded but said nothing.

Rose continued, angrily. "Turns out Rex had been laundering money for Bavolsky for years. He was skimming money, too.

That's how he could afford that mansion. It was only a matter of time until Big Mike found out. Rex was a walking dead man. I didn't want Jane caught in the middle of all that."

"Okay." Otto shook her head. "But something happened, didn't it?"

"What do you mean?"

"Why did you leave now? Why not last month or next year?" Otto asked.

Rose narrowed her eyes and gazed steadily at Otto for a full minute. "Rex is a mean bastard. He was acting like a cornered animal. He must have known Big Mike was coming after him."

"He had to have been expecting that?"

Rose took another deep breath and exhaled loudly. "I mentioned I had been addicted to opioids for a while, right? When I weaned off, I had a stockpile. Rex stole them. He must have thought he could barter with Bavolsky."

Gaspar said, "And that didn't work?"

She shook her head slowly. "You probably know there's a big investigation going on in Chicagoland. Somebody put a tap on Rex's phones. They must've heard him talking with Bavolsky about the drugs. He must have told Bavolsky the drugs were mine."

Otto said, "Which means your name is now a part of the investigation."

"I've got friends. I was told that both Jane and I were going to be indicted. They hoped to pressure us into testifying against Rex. They want to use Rex to put Big Mike and his crew away forever." She paused and looked directly from Otto to Gaspar. "Jane didn't deserve any of that. All she did was marry a scumbag and help her sister. I couldn't let her go to prison, could I? No way."

"So you packed up and slipped away when Rex couldn't stop you."

"Not that he'd have wanted to stop us. He stole my drugs. That should get him out of the hole with Bavolsky. He doesn't want Jane, either. He's a fool. He can live happily ever after with little Miss Brooke," she sneered.

"Except he won't be able to do that," Gaspar said.

"Why not? Jane's out of his way, and she's never going back there." Rose jutted her chin defiantly.

"Because Brooke Bavolsky was murdered on Friday afternoon," Gaspar replied. "In Rex Mackenzie's house. Which I'm guessing Big Mike isn't going to be all that happy about."

Jane came in from the kitchenette. If she heard any of their conversation, she gave no indication.

Otto looked up. "You've been gone a long time. Was someone else back there with you?"

Rose shook her head. "We had a visitor earlier. He left about half an hour ago."

"Why?" Gaspar asked.

Jane said, "He gets uneasy. He likes to move around."

Otto asked, "Was your visitor Jack Reacher?"

Jane said, "You know Reacher?"

"Where did he go?" Gaspar asked.

In the haughtiest of tones, Rose replied, "What possible business of yours could that be?"

CHAPTER FORTY-TWO

Saturday, February 12
10:30 p.m.
Guadalajara, Mexico

THE JET SCORPIO HIRED touched down at the airport in Guadalajara without incident, after a long and grueling day of travel. The moment he set foot on the tarmac at the base of the jet stairs, the weight and pressures were left behind. He was both exhausted and energized. He felt like slapping Thorn a high five, but he settled for a big grin instead.

The warm night breeze bathed his skin comfortably. He had managed to sleep a couple of hours. He needed a shower and a meal. After that, he'd be ready to face the future. He took a deep breath of free air, perhaps the first freedom he'd breathed in many years.

He already felt more comfortable here than in Rapid City, and he'd lived there for a decade. Guadalajara was going to be his home for the rest of his life. Perfect.

Thorn collected the bags and they walked into the terminal, which was busier than he had expected so late in the evening. Guadalajara had a significant population and quite a bit of tourism. Everything in the airport was open and crowded.

"Do you want to eat here or wait until we arrive at the hotel?" Thorn asked, standing near a busy restaurant entrance.

Diners lined up at the door. All the tables were full, both inside and outside. Others were crowded around the bar waiting.

"If we leave now, we'll reach the hotel in about twenty minutes. We can get room service, or find a restaurant nearby," Scorpio replied.

"Ten-four, boss. Ground transportation is this way." Thorn inclined his head toward the exit. He waited for Scorpio to walk in front.

Scorpio moved slowly under the best of circumstances, but he quickened his pace. As they stepped onto the escalator to ride down to the ground floor, two men caught his attention. He squeezed his eyes shut for a moment and opened them again for a better look.

He wasn't mistaken. He recognized them both.

He'd met with the first one back in Rapid City months ago. A private investigator. He was looking for Rose Sanderson back then. He'd said her sister hired him. Scorpio had not seen him since. What was his name? Bramall. That's right. Terrence Bramall. From Chicago.

He recognized the second man right away, although Scorpio had never spoken to him. Rex Mackenzie. In living color.

"Well, well, well," Scorpio said quietly.

Mackenzie's flash drive rested in Scorpio's pocket, where his damaged left hand touched it often, like a talisman. Maybe that had worked better than a lucky rabbit's foot. After all,

Mackenzie was not fifteen feet ahead of him on the escalator in a country where they might both disappear forever.

Scorpio kept his eye on Bramall and Mackenzie as they reached the bottom and walked off toward the ground transportation exit.

To Thorn, he said, "See those two guys straight ahead?"

"I do. That looks like Mackenzie. Who's the guy with him?"

"Guy's name is Bramall. Retired FBI. Last time I saw him, he was with Reacher."

Thorn's eyebrows popped up. "That so? You figure they're here to meet Reacher now?"

"Only one way to find out," Scorpio said. "Get us a car and driver. And keep your eye on them. Whatever they're doing here, this is my chance to take care of Mackenzie."

"Ten-four, boss. I'll meet you outside," Thorn replied. He moved ahead, closing the distance Bramall and Mackenzie had gained.

By the time Scorpio reached the curb, Thorn had secured a car and driver. He had stowed the bags in the trunk of the sedan. He'd also bribed the driver to pursue the other vehicle. Given the city's reputation for inexpensive services, Thorn appeared slightly shocked by the high cost of the bribe. Supply and demand, he figured.

Scorpio stepped into the sedan and the driver pulled away from the airport, speeding up to catch Mackenzie's car.

Both vehicles blended into traffic and headed toward the city.

Scorpio had never been to Guadalajara. The modern buildings and good roads pleased him. Businesses along the roadside were recognizable US franchises. Burger joints and other fast food emporiums were the same as those he had seen on the drive from Chicago. Retail businesses were familiar American and European discounters, shops, and brands.

Traffic was congested. American cars, trucks, and SUVs mingled with luxury vehicles from Germany, Japan, France, and Great Britain.

When they entered a part of the city where the nightclubs and restaurants were plentiful, the women were dressed in expensive couture, and the men were equally well attired. The streets were clean, the sidewalks wide, and all were brightly lit. Rooftop bars and restaurants perched atop the buildings.

Scorpio smiled. Rapid City had never been as vibrant late at night. Not on Saturdays or any other day of the week. He was going to love living here. He knew it. He felt at home already.

In a quieter section of the city, the driver slowed, pointed through the windshield, and said, "The car has stopped at Segovia Alcazar Hotel."

Thorn told the driver, "Wait back here. Let's see what happens."

The driver snugged closer to the curb on the opposite side of the street, half a block behind Mackenzie's car. There was a scattering of pedestrians on the sidewalks, and the traffic had thinned a few blocks back.

Scorpio lowered his window. Warm air wafted into the car and kissed his face. From a rooftop across a narrow side street by the hotel, strains of live jazz floated on the breeze.

The black sedan had pulled up in front of a hotel that resembled a Spanish castle. A royal blue awning arched over the royal blue carpet that led to the front entrance. Mackenzie stepped out of the back seat, and a few moments later, Bramall followed.

They walked to the front entrance where a liveried doorman opened the door, and they went inside.

"What is this place?" Scorpio asked.

"Segovia Alcazar Hotel," the driver said again as if the answer was obvious. He pointed to the high-rise next door. "That's El Megor Cosmetic Surgery Clinic. Tourists come to the clinic for facelifts, boob jobs. Then they stay at Segovia Alcazar Hotel until they get better and go home."

How civilized, Scorpio thought. But why would Mackenzie and Bramall come here? Was Reacher recovering from surgery?

Not likely.

But Mackenzie's wife seemed like the type to get herself nipped and tucked. Scorpio had never met Jane Mackenzie, but he knew the type. A beautiful woman like that thrived on one thing only. Beauty. Which didn't last forever.

Thorn said, "Seen enough, boss? Our hotel is a couple of miles away."

Scorpio considered the situation for a couple of minutes. He was tired. He'd like to rest before he confronted Mackenzie. His stomach growled. The nuts and dried fruit he'd eaten on the plane were a distant memory.

But if he lost sight of Bramall and Mackenzie, could he find them again? They might be flying out tonight. If he came back tomorrow, they could be in the wind again.

It was a risk he was loath to take.

"Pull up to the door," he said. "We'll get out here."

When they were standing on the sidewalk, Thorn still handling the bags, Scorpio said, "Get inside before they disappear. Find out where they're going. But be discreet about it."

Thorn shoved the bags in a corner near the entrance and strode inside.

Scorpio fumbled along behind until he reached a comfortable sofa in the lobby. He didn't see Thorn anywhere, so he sat on the sofa to wait.

He didn't wait long. The elevator doors opened, and Thorn emerged. He nodded.

Scorpio used his cane to leverage off the sofa's plush seat and made his way to the elevator.

Thorn pushed the call button. "Mackenzie and Bramall entered Suite 706."

Scorpio nodded. He entered the elevator car, and Thorn punched the button for the seventh floor.

CHAPTER FORTY-THREE

Saturday, February 12
11:25 p.m.
Guadalajara, Mexico

THE DOORBELL RANG. ROSE cast a meaningful glance at her sister. No one moved.

The bell chimed again. And again.

"Want me to get that?" Gaspar asked. It was a reasonable question. He was seated in the chair closest to the door.

When neither sister answered, and the bell rang a fourth time, he went to the door. "You're expecting Reacher to return, I take it? You don't want him to know we're here. Is that it?"

Gaspar opened the door just as the bell was ringing once more. "May I help you, gentlemen?"

From her vantage point in the sitting room, Otto couldn't see the visitors. But she recognized the voices when they said almost simultaneously, "Who the hell are you?"

The sisters must have recognized Bramall and Mackenzie, too. Everybody stood up. Otto unbuttoned her jacket. The last time she'd seen Bramall and Mackenzie, someone almost choked her to death. She still had bruises on her neck. They wouldn't catch her by surprise again.

Rose was the first to find her voice. "You're not welcome here, Rex. Bramall, get him out of here."

"Brave words for a woman wearing pajamas," Rex replied. He gave the door a hard shove, catching Gaspar unaware, and strode into the room.

Bramall followed. The sitting room was not large enough to accommodate six. Everyone remained standing.

"Don't get your panties in a wad. We're not staying long." Rex's gaze swept across his wife. He saw Otto last. His face reddened, and his nostrils flared. "Why are you dogging me? What the hell do you want?"

"Take it down a notch, Rex." Bramall laid an arm across Rex's chest, which did nothing to subdue his heavy breathing.

"This is Rex Mackenzie. I'm Terry Bramall," he said. "You're Otto's partner, Carlos Gaspar, right?"

"The one and only," Gaspar quipped. "The ladies don't seem to want your friend here. It's late. You should go."

"We'll go when we get what I came for," Rex snarled. "Hand it over, Jane."

Jane's eyes widened. She put her right hand to her throat. "Hand what over? I don't have anything that belongs to you."

"That's bullshit, and you know it," Rex raised his voice to a level the entire seventh floor could hear. "Give me my flash drive and I'll go. You can keep the money. There's plenty more where that came from."

"I have no idea what you're talking about!" Jane shouted.

Rex shoved Bramall's arm aside and pushed closer to Jane. "You took it. You took the flash drive. Give it to me."

"Get out! Go back to Chicago and your precious Brooke. She's a mobster's wife. You know that, right? When Big Mike Bavolsky finds out you're screwing her, you'll be the one who gets screwed, Rex. You can count on that."

He seemed to deflate on the spot. His shoulders slumped. He dropped his gaze and lowered his voice. "You're a fool, Jane. You've always been a fool. You actually think my little dry-cleaning business was supporting our lifestyle? Where do you think all the money came from, huh?"

Jane gasped. Rose stepped in front of her sister.

"She didn't take your flash drive, Rex. I was there. I'd have seen her do it," Rose said as if she was talking a man down off a bridge.

Rex snapped. He reached into his pocket and pulled out a nine-millimeter pistol. He pointed it at Jane. "Give me the flash drive, Jane. That's all I need. Right now. I'll kill you to get it back. That should tell you how serious I am."

Jane shook her head. "I don't know what you're talking about. I don't have your flash drive."

"Liar! You stole the flash drive from my safe. You stole my money. And you killed Brooke. I'm not screwing around, Jane. Give me that drive."

Her eyes opened wide. She gasped and slapped a palm over her mouth. She whispered, "Brooke is dead?"

He sneered. "Like you didn't notice when you shot her in the face."

"*Me?* I didn't kill anyone!" Jane shook her head and plopped down on the loveseat. "I can't believe you'd accuse me of murder. I took the money. That's all. I figured I was entitled. I've put up with you for ten years, Rex. Doesn't that entitle me to something?"

He kept the gun steady, aimed in her direction, but he seemed unsure for the first time since he'd burst into the room.

Now was Otto's chance to disarm him. She spoke up. "I found a flash drive in that storage unit in St. Louis. I didn't know it was yours. You can have it back."

He glanced toward her. She saw that he wanted the flash drive more than he wanted his wife back. He must have been terrified of Big Mike Bavolsky. Based on what Otto knew of the man, Rex was smart to be afraid.

"The flash drive is in my pocket. Let me get it, okay?" She reached into her pocket and Rex went wild.

"You're trying to trick me!" he yelled.

"I'm not. I swear. Let me get it."

He aimed the gun directly at Otto's head. He nodded. "Slowly. You pull a gun out of there, and I'll shoot you without a second's hesitation."

"My gun's in my holster, Rex." She pulled her jacket aside to show him the shoulder holster snugged against her body.

Then she pulled the flash drive from her pocket and held it out to him in her palm.

"You bitch! That's not my flash drive! Where's the real one?" He waved the gun.

Jane screamed. "Rex, stop! Stop!"

Otto had been watching for a chance to disarm or disable him. He'd taken a physical position that made the task impossible. The room was too small and the risk of harm to others too great. Rex wasn't rational. He'd kill at least one of the sisters fast, no matter what she did. Even a big, tough, man like Reacher would've been stymied. For now.

She had to wait. Hope to talk him through until the play changed.

Before she had the chance, Rose changed everything.

She jumped up and rushed toward Rex.

"Rose!" Jane screamed.

The effort proved foolhardy.

He drew his gun back and delivered one swift, hard blow to her temple.

Rose staggered.

Mackenzie grabbed her and put the barrel of the gun directly to her head. She slumped against him, stunned by the blow.

He became strangely calm again. "You know what, Jane? I believe you. Rose is the one. She did it all."

Jane was crying now. "She didn't. She hasn't done anything, Rex, I swear."

"You don't have the guts, do you, Jane? You never did." He shook his head. "Of course, it was Rose. She's a decorated war hero. A trained killer. We know that. One of the best West Point could produce. She's a thief and an addict, too. It had to be Rose."

"Rex," Bramall said calmly. "This isn't helping. Let her go. We'll find your flash drive. It's here somewhere."

Rose's eyes were unfocused. Her head wobbled. She tried to bite Rex's forearm. She didn't get a good grip. Nor did she do much damage, but the bite was hard enough to make him angrier.

He gripped her harder and shoved the gun barrel against her head, pushing her head down against her shoulder.

"You bitch! I'll kill you!"

"Yeah, well, go ahead. Do it, Rex. Do it now. Then these FBI agents will kill you. You'll never get your precious flash drive. You'll never get anything else. Ever."

He grabbed her tighter. "Give it back!"

Otto watched for an opening. She could drop Rex with one shot, but Rose was in the way.

Rose's speech was slurred, but firm. "Listen to me, you moron. I took your money. You know why? Because you took my drugs. You sold them to Bavolsky. I know because you're about to be indicted. The feds came to me. Told me your days are numbered. Even if you get out of here, you're a walking dead man."

He squeezed her throat with his forearm until her raw face turned faintly purple.

Then he loosened his hold. "Where. Is. My. Flash. Drive."

That was the moment when Rose changed her tactics. Her body went slack. She stopped fighting. She nodded.

"Okay. I took the flash drive. I hid it."

He squeezed her throat and then released it again. "Where?"

"Next door. The clinic. On the roof outside my doctor's penthouse."

The answer infuriated him. "Why did you hide it there?"

Her voice was raw. Barely a whisper. "Because no one would find it."

Rex bent closer to hear.

Before Otto had a chance, Bramall used the momentary distraction as his chance to move.

Rex caught the movement in his peripheral vision.

He swept the gun toward Bramall and fired. Bramall went down. Blood bloomed on his torso.

Jane screamed. She bent to help Bramall.

Otto kept her eyes on Rex, waiting for her chance, but Rose made a very effective human shield.

CHAPTER FORTY-FOUR

Sunday, February 13
12:05 a.m.
Guadalajara, Mexico

INSIDE THE ELEVATOR, THORN and Scorpio stood apart, eyes straight ahead. The elevator was mirrored. They made eye contact only with their reflections.

"What happened downstairs?" Scorpio asked.

"When I came into the lobby, Mackenzie and Bramall were at the reception desk. They weren't getting very far with the desk clerk, and Mackenzie was annoyed. Impatient. Bramall stepped in, calmed things down," Thorn said.

"Did you hear the conversation?"

Thorn shook his head. "Only a few phrases. Mackenzie said something about his wife. The words surgery and recovery were mentioned a couple of times."

"What was your impression? Was he inquiring about surgery for his wife?"

"It seemed like he thought she was registered here and the desk clerk wouldn't confirm it," Thorn replied.

Scorpio nodded. He guarded his own privacy. He approved of closemouthed desk clerks.

"Somehow, Bramall got the suite number. When they took the elevator, I slipped in with them. They pushed the button for the seventh floor, so I pushed eight. They got out on seven. I got out on eight and ran back down the stairs to seven just in time to see them going into 706."

Scorpio nodded again. "Did you see who was in the suite?"

"No. But whoever it was, Mackenzie seemed surprised. He barreled inside and Bramall went after him. They closed the door, and I came down to find you." Thorn finished just as the elevator stopped on the seventh floor.

Scorpio stepped out and Thorn followed. They walked down the wide hallway to 706. Scorpio heard raised voices inside. He listened outside the door.

He heard men and women talking but couldn't make out the words. He didn't recognize the voices. He'd never talked to Rex or Jane Mackenzie. But he'd had a couple of conversations with Bramall and Rose Sanderson.

He gestured to Thorn. "Can you tell how many people are in there?"

Thorn stood close to the door for a couple of minutes. He shrugged. "At least four. Two men and two women. Maybe more."

"Is one of them Reacher?" Scorpio asked.

"I've never talked to him. But maybe. There seems to be a third male voice. It could be Reacher, I guess," Thorn replied.

"Who are the others?"

"I can try to get that from the desk clerk, but I'm more likely to get escorted out the door by security." Thorn pointed to the button by the door handle. "Or we could ring the bell and go inside. We keep hanging around, we're likely to get reported by one of the other guests."

"I don't want to be cooped up in that hotel room with six people. Especially if they're armed," Scorpio replied. "Let's get them out here. Where we have room to move."

"How do you want to make that happen, boss?"

"Easiest way is to pull the fire alarm. Some people will stay in their rooms and wait for assistance. If we're lucky, some will panic. They'll rush into the hallway and head toward the stairs."

"The elevators will probably shut down automatically. They don't want people in elevators during a fire," Thorn said.

"Right. I'll wait here to see who comes out of 706," Scorpio said. "You wait at the staircase at the end of the corridor. Anybody from 706 tries to escape down those stairs, follow. Stay with them. I'll catch up."

Thorn had already moved a couple of paces toward the stairs when Scorpio said, "Unless it's Reacher. If he comes out, subdue him. But don't kill him. I want to do that myself."

"Ten-four, boss," Thorn said.

Scorpio scrambled back to the elevator lobby. He glanced down the long corridor. Thorn was in place.

He located the fire alarm and pulled the square red lever straight down.

Before he could do anything more, an ear-piercing siren wailed. The wailing continued without interruption. The sound was loud enough to cause permanent damage to human hearing.

Several doors opened on the corridor. People came out, milled around, asked questions.

The siren did not abate.

The door to Suite 706 remained closed for three full seconds.

Scorpio put both palms over his ears and waited. His patience was rewarded.

The door opened. Rex Mackenzie stepped across the threshold, dragging a woman along. He had a hard grip on her arm. Her body was covered in full pajamas and a bathrobe. She wore slippers on her feet. Her face looked like a burn victim's.

More guests left their rooms and came into the hallway, which quickly became overcrowded with semi-panicked patients and caregivers wearing night clothes. A few were tethered to IV poles, drains, catheters, and portable oxygen tanks.

Mackenzie tightened his hold on the woman's arm and dragged her along toward the stairway at the end of the hall, where Thorn was waiting.

Scorpio's forward movement was slowed because of the congestion. He walked toward Suite 706. Before he reached the doorway, a petite Asian woman and a Latino man emerged. Neither was Reacher.

The Latino man looked up and down the crowded corridor. He saw the exit sign above the door to the stairway, gestured toward the Asian woman, and both headed in that direction.

Scorpio finally made it to the open doorway of Suite 706. He looked inside. He saw Bramall on the floor, his left torso covered by a bloody towel. His face was pale, ashen, and his breathing shallow. Jane Mackenzie was with him, administering first aid.

Reacher was not in the room.

Scorpio kept moving down the hall.

CHAPTER FORTY-FIVE

Sunday, February 13
12:30 a.m.
Guadalajara, Mexico

GASPAR LED THE WAY, breaking a trail between the milling and panicking people in the hotel corridor. Otto followed closely behind, like a salmon swimming upstream. She saw Rex Mackenzie ahead, moving faster because he was bigger and had a head start. She had to assume he was dragging Rose along with him, although she couldn't see Rose.

Mackenzie reached the stairway at the end of the corridor. Otto saw the top of the door as it opened and then closed behind him.

He was headed toward the tunnels that would lead him to the penthouses at the top of the clinic building next door. Rose said that's where he'd find his flash drive. Otto briefly wondered what data could possibly be so important that Mackenzie was willing to kill to get it back.

But he'd left no doubt that he would kill anyone who got in

his way. Which probably meant he'd keep Rose alive until he found the flash drive.

When Mackenzie and Rose reached the stairwell, they'd move faster. They'd run through the tunnels to the clinic, and then take the elevator up to the penthouse.

Gaspar and Otto continued through the bodies, making progress like swimming in molasses. Finally, they reached the stairs. Gaspar pulled the door open and slipped into the stairwell. Otto followed half a minute later.

When the stairway door closed, she heard footsteps heading down. Gaspar's footsteps were uneven and slow. Heavy footfalls in leather soles slapping the treads belonged to two men. The third was a woman's soft slippers brushing the concrete. The order was man, woman, man, Gaspar.

Who was the man chasing Rex Mackenzie? Whoever he was, he was moving fast. Much faster than Gaspar could.

Otto picked up her speed. She held onto the handrail and fairly flew down eight flights of stairs, passing Gaspar along the way.

When she reached the bottom, she flung open the double door to the tunnel.

The tunnel walls were covered with green subway tiles. The floor tile was a slightly darker color. Bright fluorescent lights in the ceiling reflected everywhere off the shiny tiles, blindingly.

The tunnel was twenty feet wide. Plenty of room for moving hospital beds with patients in them, and all their post-surgical paraphernalia. Medical equipment was stored along the outside walls. Wheelchairs, beds, even oxygen tanks on wheels.

Up ahead, Rex Mackenzie pulled Rose swiftly along. A big man followed behind, trying to catch up.

"Mackenzie! Stop!" Otto yelled.

He turned his head to look back over his shoulder. He saw the big man coming up fast behind him. He stopped a moment to unhook a chain holding a group of oxygen tanks resembling a fat bundle of steel cigars. He gave the tanks a huge shove, and they clanged to the floor and rolled in all directions, blocking the man's progress.

Mackenzie yanked Rose's arm and pushed her through the next set of double doors.

Otto kept running. She heard footsteps behind her. She turned to see Gaspar coming up as fast as he could, struggling with every step. He waved and she kept going.

The big man ran through the oxygen cylinder obstacles and made it to the double doors. He pushed hard in the middle where the two doors met and they opened wide. He ran through.

Otto was a dozen yards behind him, running all out. She pushed through the doors and found herself standing in an empty elevator lobby with a staircase to one side. She heard more heavy footfalls on the stairs.

The elevator was on its way up.

She took the stairs.

After two flights, she couldn't hear the big man's footsteps up ahead. When she came to the landing on the second floor, she opened the door. It led to another elevator lobby. This one held four elevators. Two were already on their way up to the penthouse level.

She pressed the call button on the third car. It was waiting behind the doors. When they parted smoothly, she pushed the button for the penthouse and pulled out her phone.

She sent two texts.

One to Gaspar: "Meet me on the roof."

The second to the Boss: "Reacher's here. Extraction required."

She grabbed her gun from her holster and tapped her foot as the elevator slowly ascended. The ride gave her a chance to catch her breath.

What seemed like a century later, the elevator stopped at the penthouse level. The door to the roof was open. Cautiously, she approached the open door. She crept forward as quietly as possible, weapon ready.

A cool breeze blew through from outside. Music from a nearby rooftop jazz bar floated on the air. Voices were carried with it.

She heard Mackenzie first. "Give me my flash drive. That's all I want. I'll leave you here with Jane. Frankly, I don't give a damn what you do after that."

Rose's reply was quieter. Otto couldn't hear the words.

The elevator bell dinged behind her and the doors opened. Gaspar stepped out, weapon drawn. Cautiously, he approached her position.

"Where are they?"

"I'm not sure. There's another guy out there," she said.

"Reacher?"

She shook her head. "I don't think so. I'll go right. You go left."

He nodded.

CHAPTER FORTY-SIX

Sunday, February 13
12:45 a.m.
Guadalajara, Mexico

SHE STEPPED THROUGH THE door and flattened her back against the wall. The evening sky was cloudless and filled with so many stars that even the light pollution couldn't dim its enchantment. The music grew louder as she rounded the elevator's vertical shaft enclosure.

When she reached the corner of the wall, she stopped and took a cautious look. She was on the cross-street side of the building. The rooftop jazz bar seemed closer than it actually was. A trio was playing. A few couples were dancing. Patrons were scattered at small tables.

The roof's views of the city lights were spectacular. She knew none of the landmarks, but the lights alone were well worth the time required to admire the vista.

She heard Mackenzie talking to Rose, but she couldn't see them from this vantage point. Like many modern roofs, this one was flat. While there was plenty of flat space, it was interrupted by HVAC and other equipment that blocked her sight lines.

The good news was that if she couldn't see Mackenzie or the other man, they couldn't see her either. She took a chance and dashed from the cover of the elevator shaft to the smaller cover provided by an HVAC unit nearby.

Mackenzie's voice was louder here. The jazz club's noises were louder, too. She could no longer hear what he was saying.

She crouched lower and moved closer. From here, she could see Mackenzie. He still held Rose's arm in a bruising grip. They stood near the edge of the roof adjacent to the jazz bar. She thought she heard the elevator bell ding again. But it could have been the music.

She returned her attention to Mackenzie, watching for the right moment to intervene. He and Rose were close to the edge of the roof where the penthouse had glass doors opening onto a carpeted patio, furnished with comfortable seating and a gas fire pit.

The next few moments happened too quickly. When she sorted it all out later, she thought it went like this:

Gaspar knocked something over. It hit the roof with a loud clang.

The big man pivoted toward the sound and shot twice. Gaspar returned fire. All four shots missed.

A fifth shot whizzed across from the jazz bar on the adjacent roofs. This bullet was true. The big man's head exploded, and he crumpled to the roof.

Otto looked toward the jazz bar, but her view was obstructed. She couldn't see the shooter.

Another man had come out of the elevator lobby onto the roof just when the kill shot hit. The scrawny guy who walked with a cane. He dropped his cane to the ground, drew a weapon, and fired toward the shooter.

Otto didn't see where the shot landed.

She raised her gun and aimed. The movement was purely instinctive. Driven by muscle memory. Practiced a thousand times. Maybe two thousand.

She squeezed off two rounds.

The scrawny man's life was over. Just like that.

When the first shots were fired, Mackenzie grabbed Rose and held her in front of him.

Otto stepped into the light where he could see her off to his right.

"You shoot me, Otto, you'll hit Rose first!" he called out.

"You'll only get one of us, Mackenzie." Gaspar stepped out on Mackenzie's left side, weapon aimed and ready. "So make your shot count."

Mackenzie's eyes darted left and right like a cornered animal, sweeping his weapon from side to side. He took two steps back, Rose's body still pressed against him. "I'll throw her off the roof. I will. I swear!"

Otto heard the faint sound of a helicopter approaching from the direction of the airport. The jazz trio on the opposite roof had never missed a single beat. If the scrawny man had hit the shooter over there, the patrons were blasé about it.

"Let her go, Rex," Otto said. "She doesn't have your flash drive. She told you it was up here just to get you away from Jane."

Mackenzie's eyes darted to her. His nostrils flared. "I should have killed you when I had the chance."

"But since you didn't, you should put your gun down. Two men are already dead. You can live to fight another day."

"I'm walking out of here," he said. "Get outta my way. Or I'll throw Rose off this roof. I swear I will." He lifted her feet off the ground like a child lifting a rag doll, as if to prove that he could make good on his promise.

The helicopter was coming closer. The building had a helipad on the roof. Most medical facilities did. Perhaps the Boss had sent this one. But even if he hadn't, she said, "Hear that, Rex? It's a helicopter. I ordered it. Know why? To take you back to Chicago to stand trial. You've been indicted. You and your pal Big Mike Bavolsky."

"That's kidnapping. You can't do that."

"Watch me. You're going back, Rex. Count on it. Question is, do you want to go back on your own two feet? Or would you rather we put you in a pine coffin?"

Before he had a chance to reply, a loud noise clanged against the roof. Mackenzie whipped his head around toward the noise.

Otto rushed forward, weapon aimed. Rose saw what she planned to do. While Mackenzie was disoriented, Rose kicked him hard in the groin with her heel. He bellowed in pain and released her. She fell onto the roof and scrambled out of the line of fire.

Mackenzie's rage moved the barrel of his gun toward Otto. He shot once. A split second later, she shot back. His shot went wide.

Her shot pounded him center mass. He stumbled backward with the force of the blow.

One step. Two.

And he fell off the edge of the roof, but he was already dead before he hit the ground.

Rose crawled to the edge and looked over. Otto ran to pull her back.

The helicopter banked to the right about two hundred yards before it reached the rooftop and continued on.

Through it all, the jazz music never stopped.

CHAPTER FORTY-SEVEN

Sunday, February 13
4:00 a.m.
Guadalajara, Mexico

OTTO AND GASPAR SEARCHED the two bodies on the roof.
Rose identified the scrawny man, the one with the cane.

She said, "That's Arthur Scorpio."

"You knew him?" Gaspar asked.

Rose shook her head. "No. I just know who he was."

Otto knelt next to the body and patted him down. From
a deep jacket pocket, she extracted a hinged jewelry box
four inches wide, six inches long, and almost four inches
deep.

Rose stared, "That's Jane's. Our mother gave it to her. She
looked everywhere for it before we left. How did this piece of
scum get hold of it?"

Otto pushed the lever aside and used both hands to open the
tightly hinged lid.

The box was lined with purple satin and the interior was divided into three equal sections. The left and right sections contained loose gemstones.

"Are these Jane's, too?" Otto asked.

Rose replied, "They belonged to our mother. My father was not reliable with money. Mom didn't believe in banks, and she always worried she'd be left destitute one day. She gave the box and the stones to Jane before she died. She said they were her legacy to us because we could always sell them if we needed to."

The center of the box held a high capacity data traveler flash drive with a zinc alloy metal casing. Otto held it up. "This must be the flash drive Rex was so desperate for. Do you recognize it?"

Rose shook her head. "I've never seen that before."

Otto dropped the flash drive into her pocket. She closed the jewelry box and handed it to Rose.

The Boss's helicopter arrived for the extraction Otto had requested. A crew of six jumped out. Four of the men collected the two bodies from the roof. Two more men brought Mackenzie up from the street on a gurney and shoved him into the helo, too.

When the extraction team had all the bodies on the helo, the leader said, "Are you coming with us?"

Rose said simply, "No."

Otto replied, "I've got things to finish up here."

Gaspar said, "Looks like I'll be sticking around, too."

They watched the helo rise above the roof and fly north for a few minutes.

"Will you and Jane go back to Chicago now?" Gaspar asked.

Rose shook her head. "We left because Bramall told us about the indictments. He was working with the investigation. He's the one who supplied all the details for the indictments against us."

"Why did he do that?" Gaspar asked.

"Because I'd been drug addicted. I bought and sold. I had my reasons. Good ones. But the law doesn't care about excuses." She gave them a pointed look. "Bramall set it up. We'd get immunity and testify against Rex. That way, we'd be clear as far as all the various cops were concerned. We could live without the threat of criminal prosecution. This whole thing would be behind us, once and for all."

"What about Brooke Bavolsky? Who killed her?" Gaspar asked.

"I honestly don't know. She was alive when we left. We've been here the whole time all that was going on." She nodded toward Scorpio. "My money's on him, though. He's always been scum."

Otto said, "Was Reacher really here with you?"

Rose nodded. "Supe set it up."

"You mean General Simpson?"

She nodded again. "Reacher helped us get down here. We couldn't fly or take any other kind of transportation that would record where we were going. So we took buses and we hitchhiked. He's good at moving around without leaving a trail of breadcrumbs, you know."

Gaspar said, "Oh, we know."

"Where is he now?" Otto asked.

"I don't know. He said he can't stay in one place too long. He gets uneasy. He needed to move on." She shrugged.

By the time they made it back to Suite 706, order had been restored. Patients and guests had returned to their rooms. Bramall had been moved to a hospital, and Jane was alone. She had been crying, but she'd composed herself before Rose hugged her and handed over the brown jewelry box that was their mother's legacy. Which started the waterworks again.

Otto told Gaspar she'd meet him at the airport and left to check one last thing. She didn't expect to find Reacher across the street at the rooftop jazz bar. But she felt compelled to try.

CHAPTER FORTY-EIGHT

Monday, February 14
6:00 p.m.
Detroit, Michigan

AFTER THE ALL TOO brief time in the warmth of Mexico, Otto flew home to Detroit. The moment she stepped outside of the airport to catch a taxi, bone-chilling cold assaulted her senses. She was still too hyped up to sleep, and she had piles of paperwork to handle. She asked the taxi to drop her off at her office.

She completed the required reports, including just the bare facts. Rex Mackenzie was dead. Rose and Jane stayed in Guadalajara. When Rose's face healed, she'd be a beauty once more. Although the sisters would never be the same again, they were free to reinvent themselves now.

They were unlikely to return to Chicago where Big Mike Bavolsky, Noble said, had hired a contract killer to deal with them. Noble had a lead on Bavolsky's location. If Bavolsky was apprehended things could change for Rose and Jane. But Otto didn't think they'd change their minds about Chicago. Too many bad memories.

As Otto typed the words and they appeared on the screen, they seemed surreal. Overwhelming fatigue colored her recollection of everything that happened on the Guadalajara rooftop. She saw Rex Mackenzie go over the edge in a continuous loop in her head. Dutifully, she recorded each action leading to his death.

The Boss said they'd found a key to another storage unit in San Antonio in Scorpio's pocket. When the locals went into the unit, they found another stash of drugs.

Noble was getting warrants for both the St. Louis and San Antonio facilities. He expected to find more contraband and figure out how to trace it all to its source. The obvious answer was an inside man at the pharmaceutical company. She expected to read about another big drug bust one day soon. Noble was a rising star at DEA, for sure.

She left out all mention of Reacher. She'd never actually seen him. She'd run over to the jazz club as quickly as she could get there, but Reacher wasn't there.

She talked to the bartenders and a few of the patrons, who were all too drunk to recall a massively big man dressed in work clothes and heavy boots shooting a gun across the roof. If Scorpio's first shot had hit him, no one seemed to notice. Gunshots were not uncommon in Guadalajara, they'd said.

In the end, she gave up the search and left Guadalajara after Rose promised to tell Reacher to call her.

He'd called her before, so the possibility wasn't laughable. But she wouldn't hold her breath until he did so again. She had plenty of questions to ask him, and the Boss would be pleased if calls from Reacher could be traced.

Truth to tell, she wasn't altogether sure what she'd do if he called, anyway. Her feelings about Reacher had become more complicated, and she didn't have the mental clarity to sort them out tonight.

Wearily, she put the last period in place, sent the report, and closed up her desk.

Which was when she noticed the comforting quiet in the office. She was alone in the room where she felt safest in the world, surrounded by the best security on the planet.

She remembered it was Valentine's Day. Everyone else had already gone home to sweethearts and lovers.

On Valentine's Day, memories of her ex-husband surfaced with less bitterness. He'd been a stellar Valentine. In the beginning. But that was long ago, and she'd had no real sweetheart to celebrate with since the divorce.

At the moment she was just fine with that. She was too tired to go out, anyway. She closed her eyes and realized just how exhausted she really was.

There were beds in the building. She could sleep here. But she wanted to get home, plop into bed, and sleep for twenty-four hours straight.

She donned her coat and gloves and headed for the elevator to the underground parking garage. She leaned her back against the elevator's wall and closed her eyes for the short ride down.

The car stopped at the basement level with a jolt.

She stepped out of the elevator and headed toward her usual parking spot around the corner, on the back side of the elevator.

Her phone vibrated in her pocket with an incoming call. She fished it out and saw a couple of delayed text messages from the Boy Detective. Both said the same thing. "Call me. Urgent."

Her phone vibrated again. She dismissed the two texts and

checked the caller ID. A smile lifted her spirits when she saw it was John Lawton, her favorite Treasury agent.

She'd been trying to schedule a date with him for a few weeks now, but their schedules never meshed. He lived in New York City and she didn't. That was the first problem, but not the only one.

She answered as she always did. "Otto."

"Happy Valentine's Day," Lawton replied.

Her smile widened. "And right back atcha."

"Are you free for dinner?" he asked.

She blinked. "What?"

"Dinner. You know. Two people. Nice restaurant. Wine. Candlelight. Surely you've heard of it," he teased.

"Are you here? In Detroit?" She turned her head left and right, and then twisted her body around to look behind her.

Which was when she saw a bulky man in a black overcoat. He was approaching from a parked SUV two aisles over. She didn't recognize him, but she didn't know everyone who worked in the building.

He was more than six feet tall and the overcoat made him appear almost square from his shoulders to his hips. Both gloved hands rested at his sides. An old-fashioned fedora covered his hair and the wide brim shadowed his face.

Lawton said, "Kim, are you still there?"

Something about the bulky man alerted her internal radar. She shivered with an overwhelming sense of déjà vu.

He walked straight toward her from the shadows. The garage was badly lit by ceiling fluorescents. A few of the bulbs flickered and others were burned out.

"Yeah. Sorry, John. Let me call you right back." She ended the call and slid the phone into her pocket.

Perhaps she was overreacting after Guadalajara, but she was only a dozen steps from a concrete support pillar broad enough to cover a petite woman. She hurried across to put the column between her and the approaching threat. She drew her weapon and prepared to shoot.

If he walked on by, no problem. She didn't mind staying alive and feeling foolish later.

The man's pace never faltered. He was four yards away now. He moved directly toward the pillar.

Two yards away, he altered his path to pass on the pillar's left side. Otto kept her weapon ready and moved to keep the concrete column between them.

When he walked past, heading toward the elevator, she released her breath.

He approached the corner at the elevator hoistway.

Almost simultaneously, the Boy Detective's voice shouted from her right side. "Bavolsky! Stop!"

The big man whipped his head to the right, toward the voice. He saw her.

For the first time, she spied the pistol in his hand.

His right arm raised in one long, quick, gracious arc, like a ballet dancer.

He positioned the gun without even the briefest hesitation, prepared to shoot.

Half a moment before he squeezed the trigger, Otto fanned out from her position behind the pillar, aimed, squeezed off two shots, and ducked behind the concrete once again.

She heard another shot ring out from the Boy Detective's position.

The man's body jerked with the near-simultaneous impact of all three bullets.

His arm fell wide.

He fired a split second too late.

His shot hit the concrete pole near her shoulder and ricocheted across the garage.

Otto aimed again, but his lifeless body had already hit the ground.

She heard running footsteps fast approaching and spun her aim toward the threat.

"Otto! Don't shoot! It's me! Noble!"

She held her fire and peered into the shadows. He ran beneath a working fluorescent light ten feet away and paused to let her see. She lowered her weapon to her side.

He ran up to the body and checked the big man's neck for a pulse. She walked toward them. Noble looked up. He shook his head.

He stood and holstered his gun. "I tried to warn you."

She nodded, still breathless.

For the first time, she got a good look at the big man.

It was a face she recognized, although she'd never seen him in person before.

Fair hair. Icy blue eyes. A nose that had been busted a few times.

The visceral reaction came first.

A surge of adrenaline flooded her body. Her heart pounded hard and fast. Her stomach churned.

Dissociation followed almost instantly as if she was floating outside her body, watching from above.

"Jack Reacher!" she cried out.

The sound of her own voice jarred her awake. She raised her head, disoriented until she recognized her surroundings. She'd fallen asleep at her desk. She squeezed her eyes shut and opened them again, to be sure.

"Get a grip, Otto," she said aloud, sternly. The effects of adrenalin rush weakened but persisted. "Of course, that didn't happen. You dreamed the whole thing."

Her heart slowed, but her gut still churned. "Your car's not in the garage. You took a taxi here, remember?"

The disassociation settled. She was grounded in her chair once more. "Go home. Sleep. You're exhausted."

The experience was a message from her subconscious, she knew. But what was the message? Reacher had saved her life once. He wouldn't try to kill her. Would he?

Shaking her head and feeling foolish now, she collected her belongings and made her way to the elevator.

Her phone vibrated in her pocket. She checked the caller ID. A confused smile crossed her lips when she saw it really was John Lawton this time.

"Hi, John," she said, still a little shaky.

"Happy Valentine's Day," Lawton replied.

Her smile widened as she stepped into the elevator car and pushed the button for the lobby. "I was just dreaming about you."

"Well, that sounds promising," he said with pleasure in his voice. "Are you free for dinner?"

The other big news is Diane Capri—a friend of mine—wrote a book revisiting the events of KILLING FLOOR in Margrave, Georgia. She imagines an FBI team tasked to trace Reacher's current-day whereabouts. They begin by interviewing people who knew him—starting out with Roscoe and Finlay. Check out this review: "Oh heck yes! I am in love with this book. I'm a huge Jack Reacher fan. If you don't know Jack (pun intended!) then get thee to the bookstore/wherever you buy your fix and pick up one of the many Jack Reacher books by Lee Child. Heck, pick up all of them. In particular, read Killing Floor. Then come back and read Don't Know Jack. This story picks up the other from the point of view of Kim and Gaspar, FBI agents assigned to build a file on Jack Reacher. The problem is, as anyone who knows Reacher can attest, he lives completely off the grid. No cell phone, no house, no car…he's not tied down. A pretty daunting task, then, wouldn't you say?

First lines: "Just the facts. And not many of them, either. Jack Reacher's file was too stale and too thin to be credible. No human could be as invisible as Reacher appeared to be, whether he was currently above the ground or under it. Either the file had been sanitized, or Reacher was the most off-the-grid paranoid Kim Otto had ever heard of." Right away, I'm sensing who Kim Otto is and I'm delighted that I know something she doesn't. You see, I DO know Jack. And I know he's not paranoid. Not really. I know why he lives as he does, and I know what kind of man he is. I loved having that over Kim and Gaspar. If you haven't read any Reacher novels, then this will feel like a good, solid story in its own right. If you have…oh if you have, then you, too, will fee! like you have a one-up on the FBI. It's a fun feeling!

"Kim and Gaspar are sent to Margrave by a mysterious boss who reminds me of Charlie, in Charlie's Angels. You never see him…you hear him. He never gives them all the facts. So they are left with a big pile of nothing. They end up embroiled in a murder case that seems connected to Reacher somehow, but they can't see how. Suffice to say the efforts to find the murderer and Reacher, and not lose their own heads in the process, makes for an entertaining read.

"I love the way the author handled the entire story. The pacing is dead on (ok another pun intended), the story is full of twists and turns like a Reacher novel would be, but it's another viewpoint of a Reacher story. It's an outside-in approach to Reacher.

"You might be asking, do they find him? Do they finally meet the infamous Jack Reacher?

"Go…read…now…find out!"

Sounds great, right? Check out "Don't Know Jack," and let me know what you think.

So that's it for now…again, thanks for reading THE AFFAIR, and I hope you'll like A WANTED MAN just as much in September.

Lee Child

ABOUT THE AUTHOR

Diane Capri is an award-winning *New York Times, USA Today,* and worldwide bestselling author. She's a recovering lawyer and snowbird who divides her time between Florida and Michigan. An active member of Mystery Writers of America, Author's Guild, International Thriller Writers, Alliance of Independent Authors, and Sisters in Crime, she loves to hear from readers and is hard at work on her next novel.

Please connect with her online:

http://www.DianeCapri.com

Twitter: http://twitter.com/@DianeCapri

Facebook: http://www.facebook.com/Diane.Capri1

http://www.facebook.com/DianeCapriBooks